LAIRD OF SIGHS

HIS HIGHLAND HEART SERIES BOOK 6

WILLA BLAIR

PRAISE FOR WILLA BLAIR'S NOVELS

HIGHLAND TALENTS SERIES
HEART OF STONE

"...Fast paced and well written with passion, charismatic characters and romantic, thrilling storyline. Perfectly wicked and dangerous! Simply put, WOW!"

— MY BOOK ADDICTION AND MORE

"...you'll pick up to read again and again."

— READING BETWEEN THE WINES BOOK CLUB

"With a little highland magic, anything is possible. I loved this story. A must read and now amongst my favorites."

—TIMELESS LOVE AND ROMANCE

HIGHLAND HEALER

"This is a great novel. Lovers of Hannah Howell's highland novels will love this."

— ROMANCING THE BOOK

"This story is action-packed and full of twists and turns that will keep readers on their toes. It is fast-paced and has a sweet romance that will warm your heart. Well written and full of imagination, this story is a must read for historical romance fans!"

— THE ROMANCE REVIEWS

"...a rich, enjoyable read."

— SATIN SHEETS ROMANCE

THE HEALER'S GIFT

"A Highland romance with a truly great hero...the story is compelling..."

— IND'TALE MAGAZINE

"A story of mystery, regret, hope, danger and trust...The characters are endearing, the story is fulfilling, and the set up for the remainder of the series presents an open invitation to dive right in. THE HEALER'S GIFT is a highly recommended read."

— FRESH FICTION

HIGHLAND SEER

"...this is different enough from other Highland romances to stand out from the pack. Ms. Blair's writing style is natural and evocative..."

— ROMANTIC HISTORICAL REVIEWS

"16th-century intrigue, muscled men with claymores and a doomed romance — is it any wonder I was reluctant to leave the rich, riveting world of HIGHLAND SEER?"

— USATODAY HEA

WHEN HIGHLAND LIGHTNING STRIKES

"Ms. Blair is a consummate storyteller...Can't wait for more from this magical author."

— MY BOOK ADDICTION AND MORE

"Ms. Blair has an easy to read talent for bringing a story to life."

— LONG AND SHORT REVIEWS

HIGHLAND TROTH

"Scottish romance at its best!"

— IND'TALE MAGAZINE

"...an exciting, romantic, historical tale full of angst, action and searing hot passion...With plenty of adventure and the twist of an old murder, HIGHLAND TROTH by Willa Blair, kept me hooked from beginning to end. A wonderful Highland romance."

— FRESH FICTION

HIS HIGHLAND HEART SERIES
HIS HIGHLAND ROSE

"Masterfully and brilliantly written Scottish Romance...!"

— MY BOOK ADDICTION & MORE

HIS HIGHLAND HEART

"The plot was honestly a masterpiece. It was well thought out and orchestrated. Right out the gate I was hooked! The hero had immediate book boyfriend appeal."

— LONG AND SHORT REVIEWS

"Willa Blair knows how to make a story come to life and sweep you away on a beautiful journey into the Highlands...This is a Scottish adventure you won't want to miss!"

— BOOKS & BENCHES

HIS HIGHLAND LOVE

"Beautifully written and masterfully executed!"

— MY BOOK ADDICTION AND MORE!

"Fiery passion burns bright in HIS HIGHLAND LOVE! Readers who enjoy Highland romance should definitely try Willa Blair's books."

— BOOKS & BENCHES

"If you love romantic highland stories of warriors and danger, love and honor, you'll find this story intriguing as well as enjoyable."

— THE READING CAFE

HIS HIGHLAND BRIDE

"Ms. Blair has delivered a wonderful and captivating read in this book where the chemistry between this couple was strong; the romance hot..."

— BOOK MAGIC, UNDER A SPELL WITH
EVERY PAGE

"This is a very enjoyable and well-written book to satisfy any historical romance lover, especially one who enjoys forbidden love!"

— IND'TALEMAGAZINE

CONTEMPORARY ROMANCE
WAITING FOR THE LAIRD

"Willa Blair spins a beautiful romance set in the Scottish Highlands full of suspense, history and mystery... I highly suggests you pick it up and enjoy."

— NIGHT OWL ROMANCE

"About 3:00 am I finally had to force myself to stop...yes, it was that good. Give yourself a treat and grab this book..."

— THE READING CAFE

"A contemporary romantic tale with a touch of history—and ghosts...Waiting for the Laird by Willa Blair is a delightful romance and unexpected adventure set in Scotland."

— BOOKS AND BENCHES

WHEN YOU FIND LOVE

"When You Find Love is a beautiful romance filled with combative personalities, a family curse and a love that can't be quenched. Character-driven plot with supernatural undertones make this a must-read. The ending was so fantastic, I didn't want it to end. If you love fantasy romance, you'll be smitten with When You Find Love."

— N.N. LIGHT'S BOOK HEAVEN

SWEETIE PIE

"Willa Blair is known for her Scottish historical paranormal romance. She changes genres with a modern Scottish lass who escapes to the Big Island of Hawaii. SWEETIE PIE is a delicious pupu - Hawaiian word for appetizer. Blair delivers a sweet novella that captures the Aloha spirit of the island."

— K. LOWE

CHAPTER 1

SCOTTISH HIGHLANDS, SUMMER, 1413

"I've been looking all over for ye," Anders Sutherland told his twin Stellan when he found him in the stable tightening the girth around his horse.

"Tormund and I were going out for a wee hunt. If ye want to come with us, ye'd best hurry. He should be here any minute."

Anders shook his head. "Send him if ye want, but we canna go."

Stellan dropped his forehead onto his saddle and then straightened, frowning. "Dinna tell me. Da wants to see us."

Anders grinned. Their twin connection that let them sense what the other felt worked best at close proximity. "I dinna have to say a word. Ye ken he does."

Stellan sighed, unbuckled the girth, and lifted the saddle from his mount's back. "Do ye ken what Da wants?"

"Nay, but I saw a ghillie go into Da's solar and out again no' too long ago."

"So, news of some sort. Mayhap Domnhall is on the move again."

"Back to his island, I hope." After the bloody battle called Red Harlaw two years before, Domnhall of the Isles and the Duke of

Albany's man, the Earl of Mar, had continued their attempts to lay claim to the Ross territory south of Sutherland.

"An end to their dispute over Ross would be good news." Stellan finished stripping the blanket and tack from his mount in time for Tormund to arrive.

"Dinna tell me," he said and groaned.

"We willna," Anders and Stellan answered in unison.

Stellan shrugged. "I dinna ken how long this will take. Ye'd best go without me."

"Ye are going to waste this beautiful morning?" Tormund pursed his lips. "Ye ken where we were headed. Catch up if ye can. In the meantime, I'll see if any of the other lads want to go."

"Mariota might want to take Valkyrie out," Stellan suggested, knowing his wife liked nothing better than to watch her hawk on the hunt. "Dinna let her ride too far or too fast," he cautioned. She was carrying their second child.

"I'll see if she wants to go," Tormund promised and left them. Stellan hung his mount's tack on a peg and tossed the blanket over the stall's wall, then turned to Anders. "I'm ready."

They entered the laird's empty solar together, then doubled back out to the great hall.

"Where did he go?" Stellan's annoyance at being summoned to an empty solar was plain in his tone.

Anders shook his head and perched one haunch on a trestle table top, content to wait. "I dinna ken, but since he sent me after ye, he shouldna be gone long."

A few minutes later, their father walked up to them and gestured toward the solar with a rolled up vellum in his hand. Once behind his desk, he dropped into his seat. They settled into chairs opposite his desk while he unrolled the missive. "Seamus MacKay sends word that he needs our help."

"What kind of help?" Stellan punctuated his question with a frown.

Anders knew what he had to be thinking. Relations between

the two clans had improved dramatically when Stellan's new wife Mariota became the MacKay laird, and continued even after she abdicated in her friend Seamus' favor in order to marry Stellan and move to Sutherland. Seamus had been in power long enough to have rooted out any overt challenges to his leadership. But there had been trouble in MacKay before Seamus took over. If he was asking for help, discontent within the clan leftover from the time of Mariota's father's lairdship must have made its way out of the shadows. Or was it something else?

"Naught to do with Seamus," Sutherland said. "The MacKay healer needs a supply of herbs for a wee lad who canna breathe as well as he should. Their healer is nearly out of it. Their supply spoiled after someone left a window open in their herbal and a storm blew in. 'Tis out of season now. I showed Seamus' request to our healer. She tells me we have what they need in plenty. The sooner we get it to MacKay, the better for the bairn."

Anders exchanged a look with his twin. "So, 'tis urgent?"

"Aye. Stellan, ye have made the trip more times than most."

"It takes a good part of three days, but could be done faster if needed."

"What about sailing?" Anders couldn't think of anyone who'd timed the trip to MacKay by sea. "Surely 'twould be faster to sail up the coast than to make the trip on land."

"The sea route is too dangerous to depend on," Sutherland cautioned, lifting his chin. "Save in a time of great need."

"Do ye remember the question Mariota posed when she first came here?" Stellan asked Anders.

"Aye, and we didna have an answer for her. Then." He lifted an eyebrow at his twin.

At their father's questioning look, Stellan added, "Mariota once asked about the fastest way to get from Sutherland to MacKay. 'Twas never an issue, though we toyed with the idea of making a contest of it."

"We could do that. One of us rides, one takes a *birlinn* and a crew." Anders had every expectation his father would laugh him and Stellan out the door. It wasn't the first time they had brought their father an untried idea. Some had been innovative, some foolish. Anders braced himself for a refusal.

"I'd tell ye both to forget it," their father said, leaning forward and resting his elbows on top of his desk, his fingers interlinked, "but the MacKay healer's need is real."

After a great deal of discussion, the twins agreed that Stellan would ride northwest across Sutherland and MacKay territory to reach the MacKay stronghold on the Kyle of Tongue on Scotland's northern coast. Anders would sail a *birlinn* through the Pentland Firth between the northeastern tip of mainland Scotland and the Orkney isles. Despite excellent chances of being battered by the winds and strong currents in that passage, Anders was betting that sailing would be significantly faster—if the weather held and the tides ran in their favor—while his older twin believed they knew the overland route well enough that Anders couldn't possibly arrive at MacKay first.

Their father's gaze moved to Stellan. "Ye willna travel alone," he added with another frown. "Ye will take sufficient escort."

Stellan nodded.

Sutherland shifted his gaze to Anders. "Ye will round up a crew. Experienced sailors all. I am concerned about those waters between Sinclair and Orkney—as must ye be. The Pentland is no place for novices." The Sutherland *birlinns* varied in size, but most needed a crew of as many as a dozen men to row if the wind failed. A dozen experienced sailors would be a challenge to find.

"We've gotten through it twice before." Anders knew their father wouldn't take that as a boast. It wasn't. The seas in that area were known to be dangerous, and no one took that passage lightly. Many ships had been lost in those waters. "'Tisna easy, but if the weather holds, we can do it. I'll bring Tomas. He'll relish the chance to fight the Pentland again, and he can help pick the rest of the crew."

"Ye are no' to chance it unless conditions are favorable," Sutherland demanded as he stood. "Summer storms are unpredictable. I willna lose either of ye to this competition. The goal is to get the needed herbs to MacKay, no' to take daft risks. Stellan is likely to reach there first, and the supplies ye carry, while helpful until the next harvest, will no' be so urgently needed. If sea conditions threaten, ye will turn back."

"I could take that as a challenge." Anders crossed his arms over his chest as he took a deep breath, doing his best to tamp down on the excitement that was starting to bubble in his blood. His father would see it and call the whole thing off. MacKay would get the needed herbs, but neither twin would take them.

Sutherland snorted. "I kenned ye might. But dinna disobey me in this. That strait is dangerous."

Anders nodded. His father was right. One never knew until reaching the Pentland what one might face. It was deadly. But if conditions were favorable, it might also be the fastest way to reach the north shore of Scotland and MacKay.

A few hours later, Stellan and Mariota watched from a table across the great hall as Anders rounded up the men he planned to take with him from the crowd still gathered after the midday meal. The rumble of conversation and laughter made the air of excitement in the clan obvious. News of the upcoming contest had spread throughout the keep. The men wanted to go with him or with Anders. The women worried, but also seemed to be discussing who was most likely to win.

Tomas came in from the bailey with another man, saw them and nodded, then took a seat with the other men Anders had gathered.

Stellan was glad to see Anders still planned to include Tomas. No one else had his experience through the Pentland Firth. Anders had mentioned Tomas when they met with their father earlier, but since then, Anders might have decided on someone younger and stronger.

Mariota took a sip from her cup of cider, her gaze on the men with Anders. "Ye are no' really thinking of doing this?"

Stellan squeezed her free hand, pulling her gaze to him. "We must. Ye ken why."

Early in the morning, he and Anders would collect the herb that was the reason for their trip, then head out. The healer was busy packing it into small pouches intended to keep it dry. They would be dispersed among the different horsemen going with Stellan, and others packed even more carefully against getting wet to travel by boat with Anders. Stellan didn't like to upset Mariota, but in this case, the Laird deemed the risk worth taking. They would ready what they needed tonight and in the morning, they would go.

"Why no' both travel by land? Choose different routes and find the fastest way overland?"

"Because we ken Sutherland and we've been between the border and MacKay often enough to ken that ground, too."

A few minutes later, Anders finished speaking to his men and joined them.

Mariota repeated her objections.

"Of course we are doing this," Anders told her and flashed his irresistible grin.

Stellan could see that it failed to have Anders' desired effect.

"We've been thinking about this since ye asked whether 'twas faster by land or sea when ye first came here. We were riding along the firth," Stellan told her. "Do ye no' remember that?"

"I do, of course," she replied. "I dinna think ye'd be daft enough to actually test it, or that yer da would agree. Ye ken how long it takes to ride to MacKay. Taking herbs for the bairn willna change that. Why must ye make a race out of it?"

"We have never ridden to MacKay with the intent of making the best time possible. Nor have we sailed there from Dunrobin. And we must both go at the same time so the conditions are as close to the same as possible for both of us," Anders explained, his tone unexpectedly the voice of reason.

Mariota didn't look convinced.

"There is naught reasonable about this daft idea of yers," she complained. "'Tis unnecessary and puts both of ye at risk for nay reason. What if ye get hurt or yer *birlinn* sinks or—"

"That willna happen," Stellan told her and put an arm around her. "Ye dinna need to *fash*. We ken what we're doing." Mariota was never this fearful. He would expect her to demand to go with them, not hear the ring of panic in her voice. The bairn she was carrying, their second, due near midwinter, must be making her anxious.

"And I ken ye are both daft. I've married into a clan of *eejits*!"

"She's worried about ye, Brother," Anders assured Stellan.

"She should be worried about ye. Ye are the one who will be sailing."

Anders shrugged and held out his hands, palms up. "'Tis what I prefer."

"And I am happier on dry land," Stellan said and chucked Mariota under her chin, lifting her gaze to his. "So, ye see, I'll be well."

"Ye had better be." Her lips compressed into a thin line. "The last time ye came home from MacKay, ye were full of holes."

"The man who put them there is dead, Love, as well ye ken."

Alber MacKay had harassed and assaulted Mariota and her hawk, Valkyrie, into running from MacKay into Sutherland territory. There, she happened upon a Sutherland hunting party led by Stellan. She never would have done such a risky thing had her father, the MacKay laird, believed her when she complained of

Alber's treatment and the peril he threatened. But her father had taken in Alber as a young lad after his father was killed. He didn't believe the man Alber had grown into capable of such behavior, or that she had successfully defended herself against him. After Alber got his hands around Mariota's throat and she fought him off, she knew she was out of time and out of alternatives. She snuck out of MacKay in the middle of the night, a decision that changed her life and MacKay—and one that eventually pitted Stellan against Alber in a vicious fight that led to Alber's death and almost to Stellan's. He knew reminders of those days would only upset her, and so did Anders.

Anders raised a hand. "Do ye nay care what might happen to me?"

"Captured by Viking raiders?" Mariota replied. "Shipwrecked in enemy territory? Lost at sea in a storm? How many ways can a *birlinn* come to grief?" Mariota ticked the alternatives on her fingers.

Anders faked a shudder. "I think those are quite enough," he told her.

"At least ye'll have a crew with ye," Stellan said. "Ye canna row a ship that size alone."

"Ye'll have an escort. I told ye Da wouldna agree to ye making such a trip by yerself, even if ye do have the fastest horse in Sutherland."

"Nor would I," Mariota chimed in. "But I ken ye are wiser than to risk that. There are too many places and too many ways to come to grief. I'll be thinking about every one of them while ye are gone."

AFTER THE EVENING MEAL, Stellan and Mariota returned to their chamber. He could see she was still unhappy about his upcoming trip. Normally, she was the one soothing his frustrations, but tonight, he would have to care for her. It was something he enjoyed doing and something he would miss while they were separated. But that separation would make homecoming and their reunion all the sweeter.

While Stellan filled his travel pack, she paced around their chamber, moving things from one place to another and back again, and rubbing her rounding belly. Her favorite cat, Carlie, watched with narrowed amber eyes from her perch on Mariota's pillow. "I'll go up to the nursery and make sure Beathan is settled for the night," she finally said and moved toward the door.

Stellan intercepted her and wrapped her in his arms. "He is fine. Laire is well used to caring for him, and she will fetch us if he needs us."

"I ken she will. I—"

"Our son's nurse is nay the issue. Ye are *fashed*. Love, ye dinna need to be. I will be well. But I will miss ye and Beathan, and this wee one, as well," he added, putting a hand on her warm, round belly.

"What if aught happens and ye canna return before the birth?"

"'Tis months away, Love. I'll be back in a sennight or a wee more." He bent and traced his lips over hers. "I'll think of ye every moment I am gone."

"I'll think of ye, as well, Husband. And miss ye in my bed."

"I'm nay gone yet," Stellan told her and pulled her closer. He stroked her spine and down over her firm arse. "We still have hours together. I ken how I would like to spend them. Do ye?"

"Ach, Stellan, ye ken I do."

"Then let me help ye," he said and turned her so he could unlace her kirtle. He slipped it from her shoulders and let it drop to the floor around her, leaving her in her shift. He picked her up and placed her on the edge of the bed, then dropped to his knees to remove her boots.

"Yer turn," she told him, her gaze warm and soft as she studied him.

He stood and kicked off his boots, then stripped out of everything else.

"Ye are the handsomest man in all of Scotland," Mariota told him. "Nay other can compare to ye."

"Nay even my twin?"

"He isna ye. Ye ken fine I can tell the difference between ye. Did I no' prove that to ye while we were still at MacKay?"

"Aye, Love, ye did, and I am forever grateful."

"As ye should be."

"And how may I show my lady my gratitude this e'en?"

"That, ye ken fine as well," she said and gave him the smile he'd been hoping for.

Stellan stroked the bottom of her foot, making her laugh, and scaring Carlie into abandoning her warm perch on the pillow for a cushioned chair by the hearth. Then he bent to the joyful task of seducing his wife. Packing could wait.

CHAPTER 2

The next morning, Mariota stood outside Dunrobin's keep with hands clasped tightly at her rapidly disappearing waist and watched her husband and his twin brother prepare to set off in opposite directions. Stellan stood just inside the gate, dressed for several days' ride in heavy woolen trews and plaid with a long sword slung in its scabbard on his back, boots, and a wool bonnet. He carried more blades on his person, tucked out of sight but reachable, plus a dirk at his belt and *sgian dubh* tucked in his boot. He was talking to his father and his twin, but his gaze kept lifting to her. He'd visited the nursery first thing this morning to see their son, and had already kissed her goodbye, but still, she wanted to run after him and hold him one more time. That she could not do, not in front of the entire clan. Instead, she kept her chin up, held back her tears, and gave him smiles full of love and pride for the mission he undertook.

Stellan's men were dressed and armed similarly. Each carried packets of the herbs the MacKay healer had requested under their clothes to help them stay dry. If anything happened to any one or several of the men, at least some of the herbs would get through. The men waited for Stellan outside the gate with his horse, ready to ride to the northwest across Sutherland into MacKay territory. She could see the cross-guard and pommel of another longsword rolled up in his spare plaids and topped by packages of food and skins of water and wine Cook had provided.

To Mariota, their preparations seemed excessive. After all, she'd ventured out into the same territory from MacKay with little more than a broken-down horse and a hawk. But Stellan wanted to ensure no trouble found them that could not be dealt with before it grew worse. Even though it was still late summer, the Highland weather could change hour by hour, bringing rain or even sleet and snow on the higher hills. They were wise to prepare for anything.

Laird Sutherland finished speaking to his sons, came and stood beside her, outwardly calm and watchful, but she had come to know him well enough to see the tension in his shoulders and in the fine lines around his eyes. His head turned and his gaze shifted from Stellan to Anders as the twins hugged each other, and then separated, ready to go their own ways.

Anders sketched a bow toward her and the throng milling around the bailey to watch the beginning of the race. That raised a cheer, and he grinned, waved, and signaled to the men going with him to follow him across the open ground outside the gate to the cliff stairs.

Below, on the North Sea's shore, the Sutherland *birlinn* waited for them to board and venture north then west across the top of Scotland. He and his men would sail past a narrow strip of Clan Gunn territory and a wider swath of Clan Oliphant before they passed Clan Sinclair territory, a rival of long-standing with Sutherland.

With good weather, Anders would likely reach MacKay first. But that was not guaranteed. If they ran into trouble on the Pentland Firth, Sinclair or a small Keith holding would be their only opportunities to come ashore before reaching MacKay territory and her former home, castle Varrich, deep in the Kyle of Tongue. Anders had chosen the more perilous journey. His ship could face deadly dangers, a quest he would never return from. But despite what she'd said to him earlier, she couldn't imagine anything happening to him. He was irrepressible. Good natured, yet as competent—and confident—as his minutes-older twin. She told herself not to borrow trouble. She cared for him as a brother, and wished him well.

Her gaze shifted back to Stellan as he swung onto his horse to more cheers and well-wishes shouted by their people. In addition to riding Sutherland's borders, Stellan had made the trip from Dunrobin to MacKay several times. Barring accident or attack by man or beast, he and his men could have the safer of the two trips, but no one had ever made it in such haste. Mariota couldn't help her concern for him, though surely everyone at MacKay knew that Sutherland was sending help. She'd never found out if her tormentor at MacKay had left behind followers who might still cause problems along the route. She consoled herself that Seamus would have mentioned any trouble within the clan caused by former friends of Alber's and would be prepared to defend against them if need be.

Sutherland muttered, "They'll keep safe," surprising her. Was he speaking to dispel her fears, or his own? Her husband, father of her son and another bairn on the way, was also making a trip that could prove dangerous. Even deadly.

She glanced aside at him, reluctant to take her gaze from the retreating figure of her husband, but needing to determine if his father's attention had truly strayed from his sons to reassuring her.

His gaze followed Anders, shifting briefly to Stellan before he disappeared around the corner of the Dunrobin tower, headed inland. He looked at Anders again as he disappeared little by little down the cliff steps. So he'd spoken to put his own mind at rest. She didn't like the sense of disquiet that radiated from him.

"Aye, they will keep safe," Mariota assured her father-in-law just as softly, hoping to ease both their fears. If Laird Sutherland heard her, he'd know she'd heard his words. She hoped he would accept her encouragement as much as she longed to accept his. She had to believe he spoke truly. But she didn't like the concern in his tone.

Was this leave-taking so different from when the clan went to war? For many years, the Sutherland laird had lived with the reality that many men lost their lives in such battles. Did he ever come to accept it? She didn't know how to ask him, and while watching both his twins leaving, this was certainly not the time.

Mariota dreaded the day she watched Stellan ride into battle. She loved him, and loved her life at Sutherland. She couldn't imagine going on without him, raising their wee son without him, or the bairn she had yet to give him. The very thought of losing him made cold chills run down her spine. She crossed her arms and hugged her middle. Nay, she would not think that way. Stellan would return home, and so would Anders and all their men. Mission accomplished, medicinal herbs delivered to MacKay's healer, fastest route determined for once and for all. No other possibility was acceptable. Or imaginable.

A FEW HOURS LATER, Anders took a deep breath and let it out slowly, enjoying the tang of salt in the fresh breeze, the warmth of the midday sun on his skin, the surge of the tiller against his hand and the slap of oars as the men rowed through calm seas. Summer was moving past its height. Though the longest days of the year were waning, they'd made him eager for new horizons and new adventures. Fair weather always tempted him to travel. The call from MacKay and the way Sutherland chose to answer it had come at a perfect time.

He'd been too long at home. Posturing by Domnhall and Mar

over Ross territory had abated to the point that Sutherland had not felt the need recently to send him traveling around the Highlands to see what news he could carry home. Or what trouble they needed to prepare for, including whether Islemen or Royalist troops were on the move again.

Instead, he'd watched Stellan settle into blissful married life with Mariota, the birth of his heir Beathan and their anticipation of a brother or sister for him. Anders had played the conversation he'd had with his twin at Stellan's wedding over and over in his mind, including the vow he'd made never to settle and to find a bride he could love as Stellan loved Mariota and she loved him. A bride he could bring home so that he and Stellan could rule Sutherland together when the time came, as they'd vowed to each other when they were nine years old and about to be fostered away from Sutherland and away from each other for the next seven years.

The frustration of sitting at home, tempted by the same lasses he'd known all his life, but knowing none of them were his Mariota, made him eager for any change. Stellan had found a bride at MacKay. Perhaps he would, too.

At the very least, this quest got him away from home, away from the all-too-familiar aspects of his life, and fed his need for new horizons. He expected the run across the Pentland Firth would be as much adventure as any man on this *birlinn* needed. Beyond that, he would take what came and hope for the best.

Which was why he was on this *birlinn*, sailing north, testing the more hazardous route while his twin rode hard to the northwest, trying to beat him to MacKay. The sun glinted on the ripples that disturbed the smoothness of the North Sea. This near the coast, he could see the shore break, white with foam, at the foot of cliffs interspersed with rolling hills that sloped gently down to the sea.

"We need more wind if we're to win yer wager," Tomas

commented from Anders' side at the stern. "We canna match the speed of a good blow by rowing."

"Aye, 'tis a long way to row," Anders agreed. "We didna bring enough men to row the whole route. But I'll wager once we get up the coast a wee, we'll have all the wind ye want. And more than ye want once we get to the Pentland. Have a care what ye wish for."

"Aye, and I ken it." Tomas scanned the sky in all directions. "'Tis calm now, but 'twill change soon."

Anders frowned at the sky, looking for what elicited Tomas' prediction. "What do ye see that I dinna?"

Tomas shook his head. "Naught now, lad. But I feel it in me bones. Mayhap tomorrow? Nay. We'll ken by this night. For now, 'tis time to row. Before long, we'll put up the sails." He slapped Anders on the back and stepped away to take the place of one of the other men at an oar.

Anders followed and did the same after another man came to relieve him at the tiller. He enjoyed the pull and tug on his muscles of the oar in his hands, but Tomas' words concerned him. Tomas was the most experienced sailor Sutherland had. He'd crossed the Moray Firth countless times, sailed the Scottish coast south nearly as often, and braved the Pentland Firth successfully three times. If Tomas was wary of a change in the weather, Anders knew to pay attention to him. How much time did they have before their fair weather changed to threaten them? Tomas said they'd know by this night.

Their men were strong, and their *birlinn*, though not the largest in Sutherland's small fleet, was seaworthy. They could face almost anything the sea threw at them. But to be sure, they stayed just in sight of the coast. Any closer and they might run aground on a sandbar or drowned sea stack. Further out to sea with a cloud-covered sky and no stars to guide them, they could lose their way. They would put into shore if things got too wild. Anders understood why Stellan preferred the hazards of dry land over being at the mercy of wind and waves. He would not risk his men or Sutherland's *birlinn*.

❦

A SUDDEN RISE and drop followed by a spray of cold water in his face woke Anders from a deep sleep, sleep he'd earned taking his turns at the oars during the hours when the wind fell off. They'd had a good following wind later in the afternoon, but it had died with the sunset, leaving them again to row in shifts.

He looked up, but the stars were hidden behind clouds. Tomas had been right. The weather was going to turn against them. How soon? He rolled to his feet and made his unsteady way aft to the tiller. The sea swell had increased, so had the rise and fall and side-to-side sway of the *birlinn*. If that kept up, some of the men would be hanging over the side soon, emptying their bellies. Tomas stood at the tiller, eyeing the sky. "'Tis like to blow," he announced. "If we're smart, we'll put ashore and let it pass over us."

"And let Stellan reach MacKay first?" Anders kept his tone light. He'd known this was a possibility. "Where are we?"

"By my reckoning, before we lost the sky, I'd say we're close to Sinclair Bay."

"Bloody hell. In view of Girnigoe castle is no' someplace I would choose to go aground. Can we make it past Sinclair territory to Oliphant or Keith?"

"Oliphant is behind us. A wee Keith seafront faces into the Pentland. We're along Sinclair land until after we turn into that strait."

"Damn." Fate was favoring Stellan even in the race.

"If it comes to that or drowning, I'll take me chances with Sinclair," Tomas said. "Wouldna ye?"

Anders nodded. "Aye. But let's no' do that yet. We've been in rougher seas than these. Take us closer to shore for now."

Before long, the seas got much rougher. First the wind picked up, then the rain hit in sheets, blowing sideways. Squalls intensified the heavy seas. Tomas and he traded a look. The *birlinn* was no match for these conditions. Anders nodded and Tomas turned the tiller, aiming their pointed bow toward the shore now hidden in the dark behind sheeting rain and wave peaks. Lightning flashes provided the only glimpses of the coastline. Anders went forward to scan for a safe landing place. At first, the brief lightning flashes only showed cliffs, but Anders knew the rough seas between them and those cliffs would hide what lay at their feet. One with a small, sandy beach would let them wait out the storm protected from Sinclair patrols, but they would risk the *birlinn* being battered to pieces against cliff walls if the tide rose too high before they could escape. He wouldn't endanger his men that way if he could help it. A gentler slope that led upward out of the range of the storm tide would be safer. Anders hoped to find one of those. Any Sinclair with any sense would not venture out in this weather tonight.

Eventually Anders spotted a small beach without steep cliffs behind it, just a gentle rise to the upper meadows and rolling hills beyond them. They rowed hard for it. He stayed forward, on the lookout for submerged rocks that could wreck the *birlinn* and leave them stranded—or worse. He turned to wave a course correction to Tomas when a wave hit them broadside, not quite tipping over the *birlinn*. The only one of the men not anchored by the oar they held or the tiller, he groped for a handhold and missed. Anders had only a moment to see crates of their supplies spilling over the side as he pitched overboard and sank. Stunned by the sudden fall and the shocking cold of the water, he kicked to the surface. A flash of lightning showed him the beach they were headed for, but he'd lost sight of the ship in the dark and the wave peaks dancing higher than his head.

Damning his luck, he swam, knowing the exertion would help keep him warm in the freezing water. He was tempted to kick off his boots, but he'd need them on the beach, so he worked against the drag of his clothes and boots. Before long, the effort and the cold took their toll. When a crate bobbed by, he grabbed it and hung on, praying the wind and tide would push it to shore. And praying it didn't contain the herbs the MacKay bairn needed. With those, even if Anders didn't make it, the *birlinn* could continue and complete their mission.

Still, he knew the crew would abandon that mission to search for him. He should hear them calling for him, but over the roar of the waves and the bellow of thunder, he didn't hear any voices. They were probably bailing sea and rain water as fast as they could to keep their ship afloat, torn between that, trying to find him, and making it to the same beach he was fighting to reach. He called out whenever he could, but got slapped with a mouthful of sea water with each attempt. He kicked and kept an eye on his goal, that strip of lighter sand barely visible now and again as the choppy waves ebbed and rose. His muscles began to cramp and he knew if he didn't make shore very soon, he would drown. He redoubled his efforts, but the crate seemed to have become more of an impediment than a help.

In the next lightning flash, his desperate attempt to pierce the rain and sea spray for the *birlinn* only showed him an oar floating nearby. Despite dreading what a loose oar might mean for his ship, he reached for it. It would be easier to grip, and it would move more cleanly through the water. It was also too far away. He let go of the crate and swam for it. A wave spun it out of his reach and he cursed his luck. Why had he let go of the crate?

Something cracked into the back of his head and drove his face into the water. He came up sputtering and seeing stars for the moment it took the oar to swing closer. He grabbed it and hung on, wincing at the sudden dizziness and pain inside his head. How hard had he been hit? By the crate? With this cold numbing every part of him, his injury could be worse than it seemed. But he was determined to survive. Stellan wouldn't know what to do without him, he told himself. And their father would be furious he'd pushed the crew to go on when they knew the weather would turn against them. He had no choice but to make it to shore.

But the chill of the water was turning his skin to ice and his muscles stiff and unyielding. He wasn't sure he could hang on. He kicked, groaning at the cramped muscles that protested his insistence on movement. Somehow, he made it to the beach, his feet finding unsteady footing in the relentless pull and tug of the pounding surf. He staggered and fell onto jagged rocks, skinning his palms, shoved himself again to his feet using the oar's handle as a crutch, fell again and barked his shins on submerged rocks. Eventually, he pulled himself out of the water and a few feet up the beach. There, the head wound and the cold water took their toll. The black night crowded in and covered him until he knew nothing more.

CHAPTER 3

The route from Sutherland to MacKay was as familiar to Stellan as the area around Dunrobin, but he couldn't help the shiver that ran down his spine as they crossed a burn not far from the Sutherland keep to the far side where more than a year ago Alber MacKay had ambushed him. If it hadn't been for Stellan's link with his twin, he might not have survived the day. He'd managed to kill Alber, eliminating his threat to Mariota forever, but Alber's arrows in Stellan's shoulder and arm, along with the blood he lost in the battle they fought, had nearly finished him, too. In the midst of the fight, thinking he might actually lose his life, he'd made a heartfelt appeal to his twin to take care of Mariota if he didn't survive, and the emotion in that plea had been enough for Anders to sense something was very wrong. Stellan still thought it miraculous that Anders found him as quickly as he did. Despite the difficulties that link had caused at times during their lives, he would be forever grateful for it.

Enough time had passed since the day he fought Alber and nearly died for the blood that had soaked the ground to have washed away. Undergrowth had spread and thickened. Even the trees were a wee bit taller where they overhung the burn. But

Stellan would know this spot till the day he died. Alber had almost succeeded in taking his life, the future he and Mariota had been about to embark upon, their son, the next Sutherland heir, and the bairn she carried now.

He hoped the bairn would be a lass with spirit like her mother's, but he'd be overjoyed either way. Their wee family was growing, and God willing, that would continue. He hoped for the same for Anders. One day, his twin would find a lass who made him feel what Stellan felt for Mariota. Anders had sworn at Stellan's wedding he would not settle for anything less. Stellan hoped he got the chance. He couldn't bear the thought of losing his twin. What must Anders have thought when he came upon Stellan lying near the burn, bloodied and half dead? Neither of them needed to go through anything like that again.

His friend Tormund gave him an assessing look, but didn't comment as Stellan kicked his mount into a gallop. Tormund pulled up next to him and nodded. His friend understood. The sooner they got away from here, the better. His men followed, alert to any trouble.

Later that day, a sudden storm blew up and slowed their progress. The route between the hills could be easily traveled in fine weather, but this rain came down in sheets, making the track slippery and hiding details of the path ahead. They kept going, slowly and carefully, with spare plaids over their heads and tenting around them to keep them dry and warm. There was no shelter, so it made no sense to stop. Fortunately, the storm blew over after a few hours. They picked up their pace until the gloaming, then found a place to spend the night, though they couldn't find enough dry wood to build a decent fire and dry some of their clothes. Exhausted, they slept without posting a guard. No one with any sense would be out in these hills after that storm.

Stellan woke with a start during the night. He lay awake,

listening, wondering what had disturbed him, but heard nothing. None of the other men stirred. Relieved, he went back to sleep.

They were up and traveling early the next morning, but before long, Stellan called a halt and groaned at the view spread out before him and his companions. The pass that provided a shortcut through the mountains on the west side of Sutherland territory was blocked by a huge mudslide, still wet and glistening from the previous night's storm. Fallen trees crisscrossed the path and continued to drip. Mud filled in between them, covered in some places by drifting leaves and remnants of broken and uprooted shrubs. "That storm we went through yesterday must've been even more fierce through these hills," he muttered, more to himself than to the others. But Tormund heard him.

"I'd say so. That pass has never been closed in my lifetime, save in the depth of a cold winter."

"We daren't try it," Gregor added. "We'd risk losing the horses in that muck. They'll break legs for certain."

Stellan nodded. "I ken it. We'll go around. It'll add a day to the trip and likely means Anders will beat us to MacKay, but we've nay choice."

"Ye dinna think the storm affected the seas to the north?"

Stellan shook his head, though the Pentland Firth's reputation for sinking ships was never far from his mind. "'Tis too far to ken." But he'd had no strong sense of danger from his twin, so he had no reason to think Anders would be delayed. But at the same time, he felt that something wasn't right. He hoped it was a problem Anders could solve without delay and not a problem in the Pentland Firth that would put his twin, their men, and the *birlinn* at risk.

A memory of waking during the night came back to him, but he dismissed it. Likely an owl hooting had disturbed his slumber. He hadn't sensed anything then and wasn't certain what he felt now.

He pressed his lips into a thin line and concentrated on

reaching out to his twin. *Where are ye, Brother?* Pain lanced through his head and he squinted against it. His reward for trying so hard, he presumed. The link they had was too unreliable to depend on. Though it had helped save his life after Alber attacked him, the man who wanted Mariota for his own—or dead, it wasn't helping him now. The vague, formless sense of something he could not even put a name to disquieted him, but he didn't sense imminent danger facing his twin. Not yet.

ANDERS CAME to with the slap of a wave in his face, still clinging to the oar with cramped fingers. He managed to loose his hold and dragged himself further up onto the pebble-strewn sand of the beach, where he collapsed onto his back. How had he managed to get himself as far out of the water as he had? How long had he been out? Stars gleamed overhead, providing enough of a glow to confirm he'd reached shore, and not some distant sandbar. The sand further up the beach transitioned to a thin strip of pebbles that softly glowed in the reflected starlight. Beyond it, the ground was covered with grasses, low and high. Shrubs and trees made a wall that marked the limits of his vision, at least until the sun came up.

His head hurt like he'd indulged in the worst drunk he'd ever inflicted on himself, pounding with every heartbeat. As painful as it was, it was also reassuring. Even after his swim, his pulse was strong and steady.

What was he doing in the cold ocean in the middle of the night? The question haunted him. Was he close to home? Where was home? That thought led to a terrifying realization. He didn't know. Nor did he know who he was. His couldn't recall his name. Damn his aching head. How long had he been in the water? Long enough, it seemed, to freeze every thought, every memory he'd ever had.

He heaved himself up onto hands and knees. If he could stand, he would see further, and might be able to tell where he was. That might tell him who he was. But as soon as he tried to push up onto his feet, one leg gave out and he collapsed back onto the sand. He lay there, panting, unable to move for the searing pain behind his eyes, the sudden nausea that brought salty brine up from the depths of his belly. Determined not to drown on dry land, he rolled to his side and spit up as much as he could before his strength gave out completely and shivers began to rack his body.

He needed to find some shelter, somewhere he could get dry and warm or he'd die where he lay. He knew that, but could he act on it? He collapsed onto his back, dispirited.

The sky out over the water had taken on the pearly luminescence of the hour just before dawn. So that was east. He was somewhere on Scotland's eastern coast. But where? Off to the north, the sky remained dark. Storm clouds? He needed to find shelter, and soon.

He took his head in his trembling hands and turned it first one way, then the other, pressing down as he did so, trying to hold the pain at bay and keep his belly from rebelling against the movement. It didn't work, but he did see the thing that might save his life—or be the end of it.

The curve in the beach to his north told him he was on a bay. A castle stood high on a bluff above it, torches blazing at the corners of its walls. If he could find a way up to it, Highland hospitality would oblige the inhabitants to help him. If they subscribed to that notion. If he was in the Highlands. If he could get to the castle. So many unknowns. He had to try. Making the effort was better than lying here, waiting for cold and the agony in his head to kill him.

He rolled again to his side, then forced himself up. His belly rebelled at the movement, bending him double while he fought to expel more seawater, all the while trying to keep his head from bursting. When the spasms passed, he straightened and looked around, hoping to see a path, or a route up to the castle. It was still too dark to make out anything at ground level.

He took a careful step, praying that his leg would support his weight. Pain shot from his shin to his hip, but he stayed upright. Not broken, but injured. Was he bleeding? He was too wet and cold to be able to tell. Determined, he limped forward until he reached the border of shrubs and trees. There, he found a broken branch long enough to use as a walking stick. Hadn't he had an oar? How could he have left it behind?

From that point on, he was able to move more easily and with a little less pain. But the climb to the castle was almost more than he could manage. The ground was damp and slippery in places, making his footing as uncertain as his head. Wet leaves and grasses added to the moisture in his clothes. Had it rained, too? He thought he was soaked through by the sea, but perhaps it had been rain all along. Nay, he'd cast up salty water. He'd been in the ocean.

He stopped several times, bent double to calm his racing heart and suck in lungfuls of air. As the morning light increased, he took stock of his injuries. His leg was gashed, his breeches torn, his hands scraped raw in places where he had either fought to avoid submerged rocks, or abused them dragging himself up onto the beach. His head still pounded, but his belly had emptied itself to the point that it calmed. Small mercies.

The low, thin trees around him provided something he could hold onto and helped him stay on his feet and keep moving. By the time the sun was fully above the eastern horizon, he was on the approach to the castle gate, but he'd used his last reserves of strength. His head was still pounding, and he was dizzy and so weak, even the smallest step took as much effort as fighting a battle.

He reached the studded oaken gate and pounded on it with a

closed fist. With his strength ebbing with each blow, he feared no one would hear him.

Eventually, voices above him told him someone had heard or seen him coming. He stepped back from the door and looked up, grimacing as the pain spiked in his head. Two guards looked down at him, distrust written in their raised eyebrows.

"Who are ye? What do ye want?"

"I'm injured. I need help," he managed to croak out, surprised that he had any voice at all.

"Go away," one of the guards demanded, but the other pulled his fellow back and spoke sharply to him. The first guard disappeared.

"Let me in. I canna harm any of ye. Look at me." His torn clothes had yet to dry, blood streaked the leg of his trews, and when he realized whatever still dripped onto the side of his face was warm, he discovered the site of the wound making his head pound and the morning sunlight feel like daggers plunging into his eyes.

He put a hand on the gate to hold himself up while he waited for them to decide what to do. He hoped they'd hurry.

He thought he must be imagining hearing a woman's voice on the wall walk, but in minutes he caught a glimpse of a lass peering over the wall at him. She ducked back out of sight.

Why was she up there?

He heard her voice again and looked up. She was back. The first thing he noticed before he squeezed his eyes shut against the light was her hair, hanging in a thick braid over one shoulder. Not blonde, not red, something in between. She was nearly as tall as the guards flanking her. And her face—how to describe an angel? Would she be an angel, take pity on him, and make the guards open the gate to him? He prayed so.

AILSA SINCLAIR CURSED her father as she looked down on the bedraggled man leaning heavily on the oaken door below her. She added a softer curse for her mother, too. Why had they gone to Orkney without her? Couldn't one of them have stayed at home? And why had her brother Boden chosen today to go hunting? Though he was three years younger than Ailsa, he was the heir, which meant he was responsible for Sinclair. If he was here, she would not be faced with this conundrum. She wouldn't be in charge. She wouldn't be the one to risk Sinclair castle. If this went wrong, if anything happened to anyone within its walls, she would be blamed for the decision she made.

She could always deny the man entry. But he seemed exhausted. He was injured and likely unable to leave Sinclair land under his own power. There was no stray horse in view. He was wet. Had it rained overnight? Aye, it had. A storm. She recalled the noise and the bright flashes of lightning that penetrated between the slats of the shutters over her window. So, he'd been out in the storm, and now that she looked more closely, perhaps he'd slipped and fallen on wet ground. Several times. She could see blood on his face and clothes.

Or had he fought someone? Was he dangerous?

Silly question. All men were dangerous.

But the more she studied him, the more she wondered. He stood with his back to the door now, resting his head against the wood, eyes closed. Despite his battered condition, he was the most handsome man she'd ever seen. Tall, muscular, broad-shouldered and long of leg, his dark hair was plastered to his head by rain or blood, exhaustion making his lips thin and pale. But his jaw was strong, his nose straight, and his hands wide and powerful.

A shiver of—what?—ran down her ribs. Fear? Nay. Desire? Surely not.

He didn't seem threatening. But her mother had told her

again and again that all men were dangerous. And this was most definitely a man.

"Have ye looked yer fill, lass?"

How dare he! How did he know? His eyes were closed. Besides, it was her job to look. To weigh what she saw and decide. Did he want her to deny him entry?

"Why are ye here?"

"I dinna ken where else to go." He lifted his head from the door, opened his eyes, winced, and looked up at her.

"Who are ye?"

"I dinna ken that, either." He lifted a hand to his head and shrugged. "Sorry. I'm bereft of answers at the moment. If I could come in, get dry, have yer healer tend to me, perhaps some answers might come back to me."

Was he deliberately refusing to answer her questions? Bargaining for entry and for care? And taunting her, too? She opened her mouth to tell him to go away, but hesitated. What if that was not what he meant? He looked, well, gorgeous, but also exhausted and beaten. How far could he go on his own? Sinclairs were not inhospitable. Her mother was one of the kindest people she knew. Her mother would let him in. She would argue with the laird, Ailsa's father, if need be.

What would the laird do?

So many questions and conditions ran through her mind, she feared she'd been staring at the man far longer than was proper, especially when he stared back.

"I dinna think I've ever seen hair the color of yers," he said suddenly, "and I ken many lasses. 'Tis beautiful."

He looked ready to collapse, and yet he complimented her hair?

He was trying to flatter her into letting him inside Sinclair's gates. That decided her. "Ye'd best be on yer way," she told him with a frown.

On her clan's bible, she would have sworn she saw tears glint as his expression fell to hopelessness. Then his eyes rolled back in his head and he dropped to the ground, loose-limbed. He'd made no effort to catch himself. He must have passed out. Or had he? Dear God, what if he'd just died? "Go get him and take him to the healer," she commanded the nearby watchmen.

"But Lady Ailsa—"

"Dinna argue. Fetch him to the healer. Now!" What if her indecision had killed him? Her heart broke, guilt swamping her. Dear God, had she killed the man? Her mother would never forgive her. Depending on who he was, or where he came from, her father might not, either. Surely someone would come looking for him.

She picked up her skirts and made her way to the stair down to the bailey in time to see the stranger carried in under the iron spikes of the portcullis. It took four of her men to move him. They continued toward the keep as she ran down the steps, then followed them inside to the Sinclair herbal.

CHAPTER 4

*A*ilsa got around the guards and their burden in the great hall and hurried into the herbal ahead of them. The Sinclair healer, Maighread, was working there when she arrived. "We've got an injured man," Ailsa told her.

Maighread looked up at the sound of her voice, saw the men following her, and gestured for Ailsa to help her clear off one of her long trestle tables. "Who is he?"

"We dinna ken," Ailsa told her as the men set him down on the tabletop. His lower legs and feet hung off one end. Maighread had them shove another table under them. "He showed up at the gate, then collapsed." Ailsa swallowed. "Is he dead?"

Maighread bent to watch his chest and put a hand on his throat, feeling for a pulse. "He's alive." She waved away the guards who'd carried him in and lifted an eyebrow at Ailsa as she walked around the table, studying the man as she went. "Look at him," she said once the other men left. "Banged up a wee, for certain. He took a nasty crack on his head. But he's a bonnie lad. He didna say anything? Who he is? Where he's from?"

"Nay. 'Twas odd, he didna seem to ken. Said he was bereft of answers."

"Hmmm." Maighread continued her inspection down his body, turned and moved back up to his face and head. She tutted over the blood, then said, "Coulda lost some or all of his memory with that head wound," she muttered. "It could come back. Eventually."

Ailsa crossed her arms and rubbed them, trying to soothe away her fear for what this man might have to go through. "Eventually?"

"Aye, or never. Hard to say. Naught on him but his léine, trews, and water-stained boots. Nay clan insignia. Nay plaid. Naught. Ye are a mystery, my lad."

"Can ye help him?"

"Heal his hurts? Aye. Retrieve his memories? Nay. He'll have to do that himself."

Ailsa moved up from the man's feet to join her, studying their mystery guest as she went. He was not only big, he was tall.

"Those muscles were honed in training and in battle," Maighread said, pointing to the width of his shoulders and arms, the depth of his chest. "By the lines around his eyes, I'd say he's in his early twenties. About the right age for a lass like ye, aye?"

Ailsa ignored Maighread's comment. What else could she do? Admit that even in his present condition, he interested her? To Ailsa, the lines around his eyes spoke of fierce concentration, but more bracketing his mouth were evidence of frequent laughter. Would he be as charming as those laugh lines hinted? Or was his laughter cruel and given at the expense of someone else?

"Aye, he's a bonnie lad, he is," the healer remarked again. "Imagine what he'll be like when he's back on his feet."

Ailsa's pulse spiked. "When will that be?" He'd be formidable. Had she brought a danger to her people inside their walls? That worry would be with her until her father returned from the north. Her brother Boden would insist on moving this man to the dungeon, but she couldn't allow that, not while he needed Maighread's help.

"A few days, mayhap more," Maighread told her as she began to pull the man's léine from his trews. "Help me shift him. He may have injuries I canna see under these clothes."

"I'll call for the guards to come back," Ailsa said, suddenly reluctant to approach their visitor.

"Nay," the healer answered as she tried to roll the man to his side. "Well, aye, ye'd better. He's a heavy one."

Relieved, Ailsa left the healer and sent the first two men she encountered in the great hall back to help her.

Ailsa's friend Siobhan waved her over to her table. "Have ye broken yer fast?"

"Nay, there wasna time. The guards summoned me—"

"I heard they carried in a man. Who is he?"

While they ate, Ailsa told her the little they'd learned while he was still awake and talking. "'Twas strange. He's injured. His clothes were still wet from the storm last night, and he canna recall his name."

"Or he says he canna."

Ailsa heaved out a breath, relieved to hear her friend give voice to her suspicion. "Or that. But Maighread looked him over and said his head wound might have affected his ability to remember anything, so I guess 'tis possible."

"Is he handsome?" Siobhan flirted with many of the lads in the clan, but to Ailsa's knowledge, she'd never lain with one.

"Aye, even though he doesna look his best this day." Maighread's words came back to her in a rush. What would he be like when he was back on his feet? What if he was a good person who'd had some bad luck? Mayhap he was even a laird or heir from one of the clans to the south. She let herself dwell on that for a few moments while she finished her porritch, thankful that while she chewed, Siobhan wouldn't expect her to divulge any more. It was more fun to suppose he could be someone special than a danger to the clan. Could he become special to her? Her father had been hinting at making a match for her. At twenty summers, she would soon be past prime marriageable age. Her mother kept telling him not to rush her, to let her choose her own mate, but they were surrounded by unfriendly clans, and she rarely saw any men she hadn't grown up with. She couldn't imagine marrying a Sinclair, and even years ago on a rare family trip to Kirkwall in Orkney, no one had caught her eye. How she was expected to find a suitable man was beyond her. Unless one just walked up and knocked on her gate.

ANDERS WOKE up with a throbbing head and sucked in a breath between clenched teeth. The urge to sneeze reassured him. He was where he could be cared for. He'd know a herbal anywhere by the smells of drying herbs, and from poultices and tisanes a healer prepared and used.

The image of an angel with hair that gleamed like a Highland sunrise filled his mind. Had he dreamt her?

He pressed his hands over his eyes and swore at the pain in his head and the sting in his palms. He'd hoped by the time he slept, some of his discomfort would have abated, but, wait. He stilled and let the sensations in his body come to the fore. It had. Somewhat. He kept his eyes closed as he took stock of a thirst that made his throat so dry, he thought it would choke the life from him. And pain in every other part of his body that revealed his injuries, but they seemed less troublesome than they had before he slept.

He opened his eyes, squinted against the dagger blade of brightness piercing them. "Damn," he muttered, but opened them again, this time slowly, squinting until they adjusted and he could see. A small square window was open, letting in light and a cool breeze. Shelves filled one wall. Drying herbs tied into bundles hung from the rafters, adding to the scents filling the chamber and confirming what he'd sensed when he first woke up. That was an improvement over his situation last night on the beach. Or was it longer ago than that? He must have been given something for pain, and possibly a sleeping draught. He could only guess how long he'd lain here, unconscious and defenseless. Could he have been lucky enough to stumble onto a friendly clan? It seemed so.

At least it seemed some of his memory had come back. He remembered pulling himself up onto the beach and part of the trek to the castle he'd spotted on the cliff. And a name. *Anders.* Was it his? What about the rest of his name? Did he have a clan, or at least a small family? Where were they? Where was he? Was this home?

Frustrated, he forced himself to sitting, surprised to note that he'd been stripped out of his clothing. All of it. By the healer? That didn't bother him. He was as proud of his body as any man. But his skin itched where salt dried on it. And he was cold. More than anything, he wanted answers. Next though, he wanted a hot bath and a pitcher of watered ale all his own to drink. Mayhap two. A lovely lass to bring it to him and to wash his back would not go amiss, either.

The linen sheeting covering him from toes to waist was itself covered by a thick plaid, and another pair, now crumpled on his lap, had kept his upper body warm. His palms were wrapped in a layer of linen that covered the scrapes he'd felt when he pressed them to his eyes. He flipped aside the lower cover and saw his leg wound had been bound up. Replacing that cover, he touched his head. The wound there was also covered with a bit of muslin and probably some concoction of the healer's to hold it in place. Someone had tried to take care of him. He appreciated that. But where were his clothes? He wrapped the upper linen and plaid over his shoulders and around his upper body, grabbed the lower set, and stood, swaying and fighting for equilibrium with one hand on the table he'd arisen from, and the other clutching his temporary cover in front of his lower body. After a few moments, his breathing steadied and his head ceased spinning. He wrapped himself in the lower plaid, tucked and tied it as best he could and prayed it would not fall off him at an inopportune time. Barefoot on the cold stone floor, he wished for his boots, but they, too, were missing. Had everything been taken to be cleaned and repaired? Clearly whoever cared for him did not expect him to revive this soon.

That gave him an opportunity to look around, if only out the herbal's door, to see what he could learn before someone arrived to question him.

He padded to the door and opened it far enough to peer out, but all he could see was a wall on the opposite side of the corridor. There was no sound in reaction to the door moving, and no sign of a guard. The healer must have expected him to sleep longer. So he opened it wider.

Most keeps would have the herbal near the kitchen, and this one, judging by the scents wafting by that made his belly growl with hunger, was no exception. The kitchen lay in *that* direction, which meant the great hall lay in the other, but he couldn't see it for the turn in the corridor. Which seemed wrong. It should be straight. Why did he think that?

He looked the other way. The kitchen would have at least one door to the outside, probably into a kitchen garden, and possibly near a postern gate to allow the cook's helpers to get outside the castle's walls to search for herbs as well as other things the healer needed, too. Just like at home.

But where was home? Not here. Of that he was certain. He struggled to recall, but the effort only made his head hurt worse. He had a sense of familiarity with the herbal, the kitchen, and where the great hall should be. It wasn't much, but it was a start. If he needed a way out, the kitchen might provide an avenue of escape. But not without his clothes and boots, or something more substantial than the linen and woolen wrappings currently covering him. He gave an involuntary shiver and closed the door.

He couldn't explore further until he was dressed, even to beg something to eat from the kitchen.

He turned and spotted a small pot hanging from a hook, it's metal bottom polished and bright. He moved to it, curious. Could he see his reflection in it? He could! He stared at the face before him, dark haired, with dark stubble, a straight nose, wide mouth, and strong chin. His eyes looked bruised and tired, but given what he'd been through, he wasn't surprised. On the whole, his image pleased him, making him snort. Somehow, he knew his appearance had always made him attractive to lasses. He was certain he'd enjoyed that. Would it help him here? Perhaps it already had.

Instead of continuing his inspection, he turned to the window to see what its view might tell him before the healer returned.

A FEW HOURS LATER, Ailsa finished the chores she'd taken on while her parents were away and found she couldn't delay any longer. Curiosity drove her to the herbal. The man lying there under the care of the Sinclair healer was a mystery. A stunningly handsome mystery. Was he as kind as he was handsome? He was built like a warrior who had fought many battles. Would that make him cruel? Dour? He hadn't seemed to be when she spoke with him at the gate, but there, he was injured and desperate. Being polite could have been a tactic to gain him the help he needed. One never knew.

She nodded to the man stationed outside the herbal by the head guard, Raghnall. "I want to check on our guest."

"Maighread just left to get something to eat. She said her patient is still asleep," he told her.

She opened the door slowly, and peeked in. Their visitor lay on one of the cots the healer kept for the sick or injured she had to care for through the night. So, he'd been awake enough at some point for Maighread to move him from her table. He lay on his back, sprawled as only a big man could do, one leg straight, one bent, one arm over his head and the other off the edge of the cot so that broad fingers trailed on the stone floor. Two plaids covered him, but where they gapped, she saw taut skin over muscle. He shifted as she watched, and kicked the lower plaid off one long leg. He rolled to his side and the plaids slid off his shoulder and down his upper torso, revealing his chest. The ridges of muscle made her mouth water, as did the smattering of dark hair helping to define them. Was it as soft as it looked, or crisp and crinkly? Her fingers flexed with the need to find out. To touch him. To wake him and ... do what?

She'd seen bare-chested men, lots of them, lots of times, on the practice field, during games that were part of the annual fair, even naked men coming out of the sea or standing from a bath in the stable after hours of working with horses. She knew what men were made of.

Why did this one entrance her? She'd barely spoken to him. She knew nothing about him. Sadly, he seemed to know nothing about himself. Perhaps it was because he was new to her. If he was a blank slate, she might enjoy writing on him.

Losing most of his covers to the cold room must have roused him. Suddenly, his eyes opened and he pushed up to sitting, dragging the lower plaid along with him so that nothing else was revealed.

She knocked softly on the door, pushed it open, ignoring the guard's quick, "Lass," in objection. To reassure him, she left the door open.

"Ah, ye are awake. Is the healer about?" She hoped her knock would convince him an earlier one had awakened him, not that the door had already been open to her curious gaze.

He wrapped the spare plaid around his shoulders and scrubbed his fingers over his face. Upright, his shoulders and chest looked even broader than when he lay sleeping, and the dusting of dark hair continued down his taut belly to be covered by the lower plaid.

Ailsa needed a distraction. "Does yer head still pain ye?"

"A wee, but 'tis better than before," he said, his voice stronger and deeper than it had been while he begged entrance to Sinclair's keep. He lifted his gaze and looked at her.

She couldn't mistake the surprise in his widened eyes.

"Ye were on the wall."

"I was."

"Ye refused to let me enter."

"Yet, ye are here." She waved a hand to encompass the chamber around them.

He studied her, his gaze moving boldly from her face down her body and back up again. It lingered on her shoulder. Nay, on her hair. He'd mentioned it before. She tossed her braid behind her and gave him a look that dared him to speak.

So, of course, he did. "I've never seen hair that color. Like honey with strawberries mixed in, but only a wee."

"Ye can thank my Norse ancestors."

"I will, as soon as I meet them." His attempt at a chuckle turned into a cough. "Not too soon, I hope," he added when he could again speak.

"My da will see about that," she told him. "But in the meantime, where are yer clothes?"

"I dinna ken. Perhaps the healer gave them to a seamstress to repair them."

"And clean them, too, I hope." She'd have to ask Siobhan.

"Aye, as do I. Speaking of cleaning, a hot bath wouldna go amiss. And aught to drink. I'm dry,"

Ailsa clenched her hands behind her back. She couldn't let him know how the image that his words brought to mind affected her. This man, without those plaids and sheets, soaking in a tub of steaming water while she washed his shoulders, his back, his chest. There was an image she would dream on tonight.

But not now. Now, he appeared to think it was his place to give her orders. That, she wouldn't tolerate. Still, he deserved an answer. "Nay until the healer gives ye leave. Yer injuries—"

"Aye, those." He shrugged, lifted a hand to his head, making muscles in his shoulder and arms flex, and huffed out a breath.

"Have ye recalled anything? Yer name?"

This time he took a deeper breath, making his chest expand and Ailsa's mouth water. But he looked away rather than answer her question. She swallowed and crossed her arms, trying to appear nonchalant as she waited for him to decide how much to reveal. She was certain he had to have begun to remember, perhaps not all, but something. In his place, she'd be cautious, too. He didn't know where he was, or who she was.

Perhaps she'd start there. "I'm Ailsa Sinclair," she told him and noted with satisfaction how his eyes widened ever so slightly at her name, then narrowed again. If she'd looked away, she would have missed the tiny change in his expression. He didn't want her to see him react. Interesting. "My da is Laird Sinclair," she added, but this time, he only nodded. "Yer turn," she prompted.

He pursed his lips. "Though 'tis impolite of me, I canna give ye mine. It has yet to come back to me."

"Nay? Yet ye seem to recognize my clan's name."

"Anyone would," he said, smoothly. "Sinclair is a proud and well-known name."

"And well-regarded?"

"Of course." He paused for a moment. "I suppose."

"So, ye dinna recall more than that?"

"It pains me to deny ye, lovely Ailsa."

Not half as much as her father would pain him when he returned. She expected she'd be in trouble for bringing this man into the keep, but her visitor would be even more at risk. Her father had little patience with mysteries.

CHAPTER 5

Anders fought to keep his expression unconcerned while he sparred with the lovely Ailsa. Sinclair! Of all places to wash up onto shore, injured and out of his right mind, he had to do it in Sinclair territory. He didn't know why, but being in the Sinclair keep seemed wrong to him. He hated that he didn't know what kind of wrong. Dangerous? A clan rivalry? Or was there a lass here whom he should remember? He didn't know, and not knowing could get him into even deeper trouble. He could find himself in the Sinclair dungeon long before his wounds healed, and likely without his clothes. He wouldn't last long there, but he could tell from the look on the guard's face visible behind Ailsa in the doorway that one wrong move and he'd be taken there whether Ailsa or the healer objected or not.

His condition when he arrived had been unexpectedly fortunate. He'd passed out and had been unable to answer any questions. He still couldn't answer more than one. His name was Anders. He felt confident of that much. But it might take more time than he had for the rest of his memories to return to him. "When will I meet yer da, the laird?"

She hesitated. "In a few days when ye are feeling better." She seemed reluctant to answer that question. Was the laird away? Was that why he'd been interrogated at the gate by his daughter? Was she the heir? Something about that idea made his heart beat faster and his belly clench. Was it from the idea of a lass being a laird? Had he seen that done somewhere else in his travels? What travels? How had he gotten here? And why?

The questions were piling up and making him frustrated and angry. Why couldn't he remember?

Despite having just woken up, he suddenly felt tired again, and the more he tried to force memories, the more his head ached. "Where is the healer?"

"I dinna ken. Do ye need her?"

"Aye, if I'm to have something to drink and a bath. Could ye find her, please?" Might as well be polite. He couldn't do much else. "And maybe some clothes for me, too?"

"I'll try," Ailsa promised and left him to wallow in his misery.

He didn't believe he usually did that. If he recalled anything real about himself, he wasn't a wallower. He took action. Frustrated by his inability to do so now, he lay down and arranged his covers as best he could to keep him warm. Why didn't the healer have a fire burning in here? He was freezing, damn it.

On some level, he knew that wasn't right. He shouldn't be this cold, but he had started to shiver. Where was the healer with a sleeping potion? Surely he'd feel better when he woke up. He might remember more then, too.

His teeth were chattering when he felt a warm hand on his forehead. He hadn't heard anyone enter the herbal, or worse, approach him. How long had he been out?

"He's taken a fever," the healer said to someone else.

Anders didn't want to open his eyes to see who was there.

"How bad? He wanted a bath and something to drink."

Ailsa?

"I dinna ken, but I'll do all I can to help him. Some willow bark tea to start, and watered ale will help him. Then let him sleep. The bath will have to wait."

"Shall I have the lads build a fire for ye? I brought clothes that might fit him, too."

"Fetch the lads. A fire will help. I'll need more plaids, furs, anything to keep him warm for the now. But we'll no' dress him yet. He's going to sweat this out or die trying."

Die trying? Anders didn't like the sound of that.

❧

LATER THAT AFTERNOON, Ailsa knew the minute her brother Boden returned from the hunt and got the news about the man she'd brought into the keep. She heard him stomping down the hall, ranting about an outsider in their midst. She gave Maighread, who was chopping herbs at one of her work tables, an apologetic shrug. In seconds, Boden burst into the herbal.

"What the hell were ye thinking bringing a stranger inside the walls?" He glared at her, then turned his frown on the man sleeping on one of Maighread's cots. "That's him? God's teeth, he's big. Have ye lost yer mind? Raghnall, too. He should have forbidden this."

"Ye werena here," Ailsa answered much more calmly than she felt. Her brother had worked himself into a fine sense of outrage, his prerogative to make decisions as heir and, as he saw it, man in charge while their father was away, had been ignored, and his ego was suffering. Answering him in kind would get her nowhere. "He collapsed in front of our gate. What was I to do? Let him die on our doorstep?"

Boden turned to the door and beckoned to the guard who'd moved into view, watching the argument. "Go get a few more men. I want him moved to the dungeon. Now!" Boden ordered.

"Nay!" Maighread's shout echoed around the room, loud enough to be heard out in the great hall. "Ye'll kill him for sure,"

43

she said more softly, but with as much conviction. "He's fine where he is. I can keep an eye on him. Raghnall put a guard on the door, so he's nay going anywhere. Especially off that cot for the foreseeable future. He's fevered, wounded, and canna recall who he is or where he's from. Ye put him below ground and he'll be dead before the laird returns. When someone comes looking for him and finds out Sinclair let him perish rather than care for him, how well do ye think yer da will react to that?"

Ailsa wanted to cheer. Maighread determined was Maighread unstoppable. Boden knew that, too. Thank goodness their visitor was sleeping under one of her potions. He didn't awaken, despite the noise and frayed tempers, to hear how close he was to being allowed to die.

"I'll toss him back into the sea first," Boden muttered. Clearly frustrated, he turned on Ailsa. "What are ye doing in here? He's a stranger, ye are an unwed lass. He could be dangerous. Da will kill him, and ye—and me—if he does anything to ye."

"Really, Brother? Look at him. How do ye think he's going to manage that? He canna lift his head."

"For today. What about tomorrow, or the next? Nay. This is madness. Ye are forbidden to come in here."

Ailsa planted her fists on her hips. "Ye canna stop me."

"I'm in charge while Da is gone. Ye must do as I say, or I'll lock ye in yer chamber."

Ailsa smothered a laugh behind her lips. "Ye can try. I willna stand for it. He's harmless, and until he isna, he will be cared for to the best of Sinclair's ability."

"Maighread's, aye, no yers, Sister. One of the serving wenches can help Maighread."

"Boden, ye ken better than that. If Mother were here, she'd help Maighread. I can do nay less."

Stymied, he swore and stomped out, his voice echoing as he berated the poor guard at the door. "That man will go to the dungeon as soon as he's well enough." He turned and looked back into the herbal, his frown sweeping from their visitor to Maighread and landing on Ailsa. "Or sooner if he causes any trouble."

୬

THE MAN'S fever lasted another day and a half. Ailsa fretted the entire time and left his side only when Maighread shooed her out to get some sleep. He was restless during that time, muttering and mumbling in his sleep, mostly incomprehensible sounds, but occasionally a word—or a name—would come through, such as *storm* or *crate*. Once he said *marry*, which stopped her heart. Had he meant *marry* or *Mary*, a woman's name? Did it mean he had a wife at home?

Once he started talking in his sleep, she had hoped his dreams would help him remember, or would give her clues about who he was. The fact that he recognized the Sinclair name made her certain that at the very least, he had recalled his own name and perhaps more. Sinclair looked to the Norse king and had poor relations with the clans all around them. No matter which clan he came from, there was a good chance her father would consider him an enemy.

"'Tis good to have yer help watching over this man," Maighread told Ailsa after the first day.

"I feel I owe it to him," Ailsa confided, "since I turned him away before he collapsed at our gate. I was afraid of what Da would say or do when he returns to find a stranger inside our walls."

"Yer da will have naught to say once yer mother hears of this, so *dinna fash*. I ken what ye are thinking lass, but ye did the right thing in caring for him, no matter where he is from."

"I still worry that Da will agree with Boden and want to put him in the dungeon."

"I willna allow that, no' yet. Nor will yer mother. If we're to find out who he is, he must heal and get strong again. That willna happen in the dank and dark down there."

Maighread's reassurance made Ailsa feel better, as did seeing how much better the wounds on the man's head, hands, and leg now appeared under Maighread's care. He seemed cooler and fretted less often, his sleep seeming to become deeper and more peaceful. Did he still dream? Of home? Of a lass named Mary?

Maighread looked down at him and sighed. "How can one man be so handsome? Shouldn't some of his beauty have been shared with other men who have little or none?"

Ailsa joined her. "I ken it doesna seem fair, but think on this. Why dilute such handsomeness among many men when we can enjoy it here, in this one?" Her fingers curled into the folds of her skirt. She might only be able to look and never touch.

Maighread put a hand over her mouth to muffle her laugh. "I like the way ye think," she said, stepping away from her patient. She picked up a bunch of herbs and several pieces of willow bark from a shelf. "I'm going to be here for a few hours making more of the potions I've used on our lad. That's enough time for ye to get a hot meal and a wee sleep, aye?"

Ailsa put a hand on her shoulder in gratitude. "It should. Have someone fetch me if ye need help before I return."

"I will. Now, go on and get some rest."

Ailsa took Maighread's advice and headed to the great hall for a meal. Expecting several people to approach her while she waited for food to be brought to her, she was dismayed that the first to do so were the two women most likely to spread rumors. "Who is the man the guards carried in two days ago?" The older of the two, Lorna, asked first.

"Why have we no' seen him since? Did he die?" Her friend Fingalina demanded and crossed her arms over her skinny frame.

Ailsa knew the less she told these two, the better. "Maighread is caring for him. He's been unconscious most of the time," she added with her fingers crossed under the table for the lie. Well, it was mostly true. He'd been sleeping a lot with the fever.

"Is he going to die? 'Twould be a shame," Lorna said. "I got a glimpse of him. He was quite handsome for a man in his condition."

"'Twould be nice to have a braw, new man in the keep," Fingalina added. "And a handsome one." She huffed out a sigh. "I hope Maighread is taking very good care of him."

"I'm sure she is," Ailsa said.

"Ye dinna ken who he is? Where he's from? I heard he could be a raider from Orkney. Ach, nay, what if the Norse king means to attack while the laird is away—"

Ailsa would have laughed—a lone Norse raider sent by their clan's main ally? But derision changed to relief when her friend Maesie, who worked in the kitchen and gardens, brought her food and shooed away the two busybodies.

"I ken ye are tired. I'll keep an eye out in this direction in case ye need me to chase anyone else away," Maesie promised. "Just give me a wave."

"Thank ye," Ailsa told her, "but those two were probably the worst."

"Wave if ye need me," Maesie repeated and went back toward the hallway leading to the kitchen and the herbal. And their mysterious guest.

Ailsa spent the rest of her meal enjoying her food, interrupted only by friends who stopped long enough to greet her. She went up to her chamber intending to get a few hours' sleep, but woke close to sunset. She dressed and went back to the herbal. "Maighread, I'm so sorry, I meant to come back before now, but I overslept."

"Ye needed the rest," Maighread said, turning away from the cabinet door she'd been behind while she looked for something within it.

"How is he?" Ailsa studied his sleeping form, still huddled under a pile of plaids and furs.

"Well enough. His fever is gone. He's still sleeping off the last potion I gave him to keep him quiet."

As she finished speaking, the man groaned and Maighread hurried to his side.

"So, ye are back among us," Maighread told him when his eyes opened and cleared. She put a hand on his forehead and nodded. "Ye'll soon be better. Yer leg is doing well and so are the rest of yer scrapes and cuts."

"Thank ye," he said on a deep exhale. "The fever is gone?"

Maighread nodded.

"Ye saved my life."

"Nay so much as that, I think," Maighread told him, "but ye'll enjoy it more now that ye are on the mend. Ailsa," she said and looked up, "would ye go to the hall and have one of the lasses bring a good meat broth and watered ale for our lad?"

"I'll fetch it myself from the kitchen," Ailsa offered, suspecting that he might need some privacy. She left the healer to help him. The ever-present guard stood outside the door and she could call for help from him if she needed it.

Cook had what the healer requested, and Ailsa added a request of her own. "Have ye enough water heated for a bath for our visitor tonight?"

"Nay, I dinna think so. I'll send the lads with a tub while more water heats."

"Please do. Maighread hasna said she'll allow it, so she doesna need it yet, but soon."

Cook nodded as she put a bowl of broth and several cups of ale and water on a tray. "Can ye carry so much, lass?"

Ailsa hefted the tray. "Aye. 'Tisna far, and the guard can get the door for me. Thank ye."

"Send word when ye want the bath."

Ailsa smiled and took the tray back to the herbal, pausing at the door to let the guard make certain she would be welcome. Maighread waved her in, so she entered and set the tray on the table where the man sat upright on a stool clad in the sheets and plaids he'd taken from the cot. He'd wrapped one around his waist and the other covered his back and shoulders like a shawl. "I've asked Cook to ready a bath for him. If ye approve, of course."

"*I* approve." He spoke up with enthusiasm, louder and with more energy than he'd demonstrated up to now.

"As do I," Maighread added. "Clean, ye will feel better, and yer wounds are healed over well enough."

"I'll go tell Cook," Ailsa said and turned to go.

"Nay, lass," Maighread said, stopping her. "I'll go. Stay here and make certain he drinks all of that broth. The ale he can drink as he wants it. Water, too. I'll send the lads in with the tub. I'll be back in a wee," she added and left them.

"Alone at last," the man quipped.

Surprised at his display of good humor, Ailsa grinned. "And ye with naught to do but eat," she said, pointing to the bowl in front of him. "Ye heard the healer."

"I did. I'm also certain I didna dream it, but heard ye say ye felt bad for turning me away. That ye feared what yer da would do. I'm grateful for yer care. Yers and the healer's. I dinna want yer da to be cross with ye for helping me. I will leave as soon as I am able."

"To go where? Do ye yet ken yer name?" Despite her earlier suspicions, the haunted look in his eyes told her he still didn't remember who he was or where he belonged. "Nay, ye canna leave until Maighread says ye may, and nay until ye recall enough to be able to go home."

"If I have a home." His mouth flattened into a thin line. "I recalled a name, or dreamt it. *Anders.* I dinna ken if 'tis mine, but ye may as well use it," he said and shrugged, causing his shawl to slip from one muscular shoulder. He pulled it back up, his gaze somewhere off in a distance only he could see. If he could.

"Anders. I like it. And dinna say that. Ye must have a home. A family. Ye came from somewhere." She gestured toward his clothes, neatly folded on a bench by the door, his boots underneath it. "My friend Siobhan is a seamstress. She repaired yer clothes and said they are plain but of good quality. I'd judge ye are nay a poor crofter from the boots alone."

"Well, that's a relief," he said and summoned a grin.

"Eat," she commanded, frowning at the tray before him. "Ye might be a boot maker, a fisherman or some other trade from a nearby village, or a warrior in service to a nearby clan. Someone must be searching for ye—or will be soon," she continued while Anders took a few sips of broth.

"Nearby clans? Who? Mayhap I'll recognize one of them."

"Gunn, Keith, MacKay, and Oliphant are the closest. We're tied most closely to the Norse king Erik and to Orkney."

He shook his head. "I dinna recognize any of them. No' as mine, nor as friends—or enemies."

"Is the broth too much for ye?" She changed the subject. She could see he had hoped one she named would elicit something … anything … from the void in his mind. Belly hollow with disappointment, she watched him set his bowl aside, frowning.

"Nay, 'tisna that. I dinna understand why I canna remember. The harder I try, the more empty my mind seems."

"Ye will remember," she said and put a hand on his bare arm. "Yer skin is warm, but not fever-hot. Ye must eat and get stronger. As yer body heals, so will yer mind."

He laid a hand over hers. "Ye ken this?"

"I pray 'tis so."

"Ye are a kind lass." He lifted his hand and stroked her cheek. "And a lovely one, too. In other circumstances, I would—"

A noise in the hallway stopped him. He dropped his hand.

Before she could blink, he stood and shifted around her as if to get between her and whatever was coming toward them in the hall.

"*Dinna fash*," Ailsa told him. "'Tis the lads with yer tub. The guard will let them in. Once ye finish eating, ye will be able to bathe."

Barely out of a fever, weak from days without food and enough to drink, and with nay weapons to hand, he'd surged to his feet and put himself between her and the door. To protect her. He moved like a warrior, quickly and decisively. She hoped he could remember something about himself before her father returned. Her father would want answers, and at the moment, Anders had none—not even certainty about his name. If Maighread was right that he was a warrior, Ailsa's father wouldn't quit until he had the answers he sought. No wonder Maighread was determined to keep Anders here.

As he slowly settled back down on the stool he'd vacated with such speed, she let her gaze rake over his chest and abdomen where the plaid around his shoulders gaped. She enjoyed the view, but had to shift her attention to the doorway as the door swung open and six of the older lads appeared with a large wooden tub. Two entered in front, two along each side, and two more carried it from behind. Maighread had sent the largest tub the clan owned. Ailsa wondered how many buckets of water it would take to fill it. Around a man as large as Anders, probably not that many. Cook might have had enough hot water ready when Ailsa asked her for the bath.

The lads took their time letting the tub down and positioning it, while staring at Anders. The bravest one of them spoke up. "He's the stranger?"

Ailsa nodded, embarrassed that they would speak about him as if he wasn't there.

"I am," Anders answered, surprising her. "Thank ye for bringing in the tub."

"Ye are a big one," another lad said, gaining confidence after the first lad spoke.

"Aye, but I think I'll fit in there," Anders told him and nodded toward the tub.

The lads laughed and went out the door.

His response had been the perfect one, acknowledging the lad rather than arguing, and making a jest out of the lad's observation. Anders had charm aplenty. And knew how to use it. What had he been about to say to her before the tub arrived? In other circumstances, he would … what?

Next, a parade of serving lasses entered with buckets of steaming water. Ailsa noted Anders nodded to them, but didn't smile. He pulled the plaid around his shoulders together over his chest and waited until the parade was finished and the lasses had gone before he let go and reached for the bowl to finish the broth.

Not that his circumspection had helped. Every lass had eyed him with interest, one after the other. In a few cases where a lass couldn't look away from him, more water landed on the floor than in the tub. The last one was so entranced, she dropped her bucket into the tub, sighed and left without retrieving it. The next lass in line pulled it out and took it with hers.

Ailsa's jaw clenched watching them admire him. Something about their behavior tensed her shoulders, too, and drew a line between her brows. Was she jealous? Or just embarrassed for his sake? "Ye'll be the talk of the gossip mongers in the clan in no time," Ailsa told him after the guard closed the door behind the hapless lass. Lorna had already gotten a glimpse of him when the guards carried him in from the front gate. She'd be furious when she heard what the lads and lasses who'd just been in here had seen. Ailsa would need to avoid her or she'd beg an introduction every chance she got.

"Let them talk," Anders said, but his expression betrayed concern.

"They will." She wondered what sorts of things the lads would say, and how different the lasses' comments would be. And how much of it would get back to Boden. Lorna was an irritant, but her brother could be a danger to Anders. "Take yer time," she told him. "Ye'll want that water to cool a wee before ye try it." There were several buckets of hot water and cold on the floor nearby to adjust the temperature of the bath.

Maighread returned and took in the large tub. "Ah, good. Yer bath is ready for ye." She put a stack of bath sheets on the nearby table and handed Ailsa a pottery bowl full of soap. "Ye'll do the honors, lass. Brana's bairn is coming. I dinna ken when I'll be back."

"What? Wait. I canna—" Bathe Anders? She felt her face go hot as her fingers grew cold. She wanted to. Oh, how she wanted to get her hands on those shoulders, that chest, but it wasn't proper. She wasn't the clan's lady with a husband to protect her honor, and he wasn't an important guest.

"He'll need help, and I canna stay to do it." Maighread plunged a hand into the tub. "The water is ready. Get to it. He can dress when he's clean."

"What about the wrap on his leg? His hands?" Ailsa didn't dare look at Anders, afraid he'd be angry the healer left this care to her, or worse, he was laughing at her.

"Unwrap them for the bath. I'll check them when I get back." Maighread gathered what she needed for the mother-to-be, left them and closed the door firmly behind her.

Ailsa gestured for him to take a seat at the table, bent and removed the cloth covering the gash in his leg. The wound looked much better than it had when he first arrived. "'Tis healing well," she told him, trying to distract herself. She was much too close to him, and to his lower half, covered only by a layer of linen and another of wool. She kept her eyes on his leg wound as she stood. His hands were nearly healed.

"*Dinna fash*, Ailsa. Turn yer back. I can get in the tub without help."

He probably could. She was tall for a lass, but he was bigger, heavier and stronger. "What if ye fall?" The idea that she could hold him up seemed preposterous.

"If I do and ye are beside me, I'll fall on ye. I dinna want to hurt ye. Stay here until I ask ye to come to me."

Ask her, not tell her. She liked that. "Ye are kind, as well." She saw heat in the smile he gave her, not at all like his earlier grin, but not a polite smile, either. He saw her as a woman, one he found as attractive as she found him. Or so she imagined.

"Turn around, lass," he said and moved to the tub, dropping the makeshift shawl from his shoulders onto the table as he went. She took a moment to admire the muscles that defined his back. It was as firm as his chest, wide at the shoulders and narrowing to a trim waist. When his hands went to his waist to loosen the plaid tied there, she turned away, but as soon as she heard him testing the water, she glanced around. Heavily muscled buttocks and legs matched the rest of him. When his head started to turn toward her, she looked away. Had he seen her looking at him? The swash of his body entering the water told her if he had, he had chosen to accept or ignore it. She hoped for the former, because she would see—and touch—much more of him soon.

CHAPTER 6

*A*ilsa peeking at his backside amused Anders, but he hid the pleased grin her curiosity aroused in him as he settled down into the deliciously hot water. In moments, it seemed his whole body melted as the heat penetrated sore muscles and the water dissolved the remaining sea salt from his skin. It took all his control not to groan aloud.

When he could speak, he told her, "I'm in, lass. I could use yer help to wash my hair." Damn, he should have turned around before he sat in the tub. She was behind him and he couldn't see her expression or her posture. Was she embarrassed to help him? Afraid? Or, he hoped, eager? He had dreamed of a beautiful lass to wash his back. Ailsa was even more beautiful than any lass he could have imagined. He was eager for her touch on his skin.

She came up behind him, brushed the top of his shoulder to let him know she was there, and ran her fingers across his head. "Yer hair is almost stiff with salt and sweat from yer fever." She soaked a washrag in one of the buckets and draped it over his head and neck.

Immediately, the heat and damp loosened his neck, and the

last vestiges of his headache eased on a moan. The broth had helped some, but this, and Ailsa's touch, did the rest.

"Did that hurt? How does it feel?"

He let go a sigh and leaned back. Her soft, warm middle cushioned the back of his head. "Better than ye ken, lass." Too late, he wondered how much she could see below the water's surface. He moved his hands to cover his lower half. And he realized he was probably soaking her dress.

"Can ye dunk yer head in the water?"

He didn't want to move, but he leaned forward and removed the rag, plunged his head into the water, and sat back up. Water dripped into his face as he pushed hair out of his eyes. The sensation disturbed him for a moment. Because he'd come out of the sea dripping wet? He picked up the wash rag and used it to scrub his face and its growth of beard. How many days' worth? He fingered the bristles and couldn't decide.

"That's good," Ailsa told him. "I'm going to use some soap. Let me know if the cut on yer head stings."

He dropped the washrag over his groin, leaned back and rested his arms on the top edge of the tub, depending on the sheen of soap on the surface of the water to help hide what was below it. Ailsa applied some soap and began working it through his hair, her fingers kneading and stroking his scalp, both soothing and arousing at the same time. Anders groaned aloud at the simple pleasure of her touch.

Immediately, Ailsa pulled her hands away. "Did I hurt ye?"

"Nay lass, just the opposite. Yer touch is worth everything I've been through since—" He stopped suddenly, searching for a memory of how he'd wound up injured on the beach. Nothing came to him.

Thankfully, Ailsa ignored his hesitation and went back to stroking his head. Anders marveled at how she affected him. When she traced soapy fingers into his beard, he leaned his head back on the edge of the tub and closed his eyes. The more she touched, swirling soapy hands down his throat and onto his chest, the more she aroused him. He would not have thought such a thing possible. His unruly groin proved he wasn't as weak as he'd first supposed. When her hands continued below the waterline onto his belly, he straightened up and pulled them out of the water. "I can manage the rest," he told her, "if ye will wash my back?" He made it a request. He had to, because what he really wanted was for her to continue going where she'd been.

"Of course," she told him with a wicked gleam behind her smile. "Lean forward."

She knew why he'd stopped her. He retrieved the wash rag and gave it to her, bent forward and wrapped his arms around his knees, grateful the position hid what her provocative smile had done to him. He'd hardened to the point of pain. If she didn't finish soon, he wasn't sure he'd be able to control himself.

Finally, the sweet torture was over and Ailsa poured warm water over his head to rinse away the soap. "Stand up and I'll rinse the rest of ye."

And let her see what she'd done to him? "If ye dinna mind, I'd like to soak for a while. The hot water is soothing. Move the buckets by the tub and I will rinse myself when I'm ready. It must be near time for a meal. Ye must be hungry. Go. Ye dinna need to watch over me."

"Ye could fall asleep in there and drown. Nay."

"If I slide down, water in my face will wake me, *dinna fash.* Besides, the guard is just outside the door. I can call for help if need be. And the healer could return soon."

Ailsa glanced toward the door. "I doubt she'll be back before morning. Brana is having her first, and that could take hours yet." She turned her gaze back to him. "Ye fear I willna like what I see."

"Dinna be daft, lass." He couldn't recall having been given any complaints. Then again, he couldn't recall much.

"I've seen a man before. I doubt ye are built any differently."

"I'm a big man, lass. Everywhere." He smirked, hoping she'd take the hint and leave without arguing further.

She didn't.

"Then ye have naught to fear. I willna laugh."

The more she goaded him, the more he wanted to react as he would when he and his brother went at each other. Wait. Brother? Of all times to have another memory emerge. Except it hadn't really. He had no name, no image, no idea if the brother was younger or older, whether they got along or fought constantly, nothing.

Ailsa's expression softened to one of concern as disappointment hollowed his belly, and must have showed on his face. "What's amiss, Anders? I'll turn my back if ye dinna want me to help ye, but I'll feel better if I ken ye can get out of the tub and dress without falling on yer face."

"Turn around. Ye are nay allowed to look."

"I would never—"

"Aye, ye would. I saw ye when I stripped and went to the tub." She colored prettily, didn't she?

"I …"

"Dinna think to lie to me, Ailsa. I will ken it if ye do."

"How would ye ken? We've barely met."

"Long enough, and I'm bare enough," he said to ease the sting of his demand with a jest, "so, turn about." He twirled a finger to punctuate his point.

She crossed her arms and huffed out a breath, but she did as he asked.

Anders stood and picked up the first bucket his questing fingers told him contained warm water. He wasn't looking forward to using any of the cold water, though if his thoughts continued to stray to the woman with her back to him, he might need one of them, or more.

He lifted the bucket and tilted it, letting the warm water

stream over his head and down his back. It felt so good to be rid of the itch from the dried salt on his skin. He picked up the next bucket and poured it down his chest, As he did, he glanced around. Ailsa faced away from him, but even the sight of her curves and glorious hair from the back made him hard. He gave in and reached for a bucket of cold water. That he dumped from waist high down his front, gritting his teeth on the oath the chill drew from him. But it did the job. When he caught his breath, he opened his eyes to Ailsa standing before him, a bath sheet held open just above her eye level. What had she seen?

"After three buckets of water, ye must be ready for this. I didna think ye could reach them."

Had she seen all of him? And what he'd done to tamp down his reaction to her presence? He couldn't see her face behind the bath sheet. "Thank ye, lass." He took the sheet and wrapped it around his waist, gathering the excess material in front. He still stood in the tub, so the end dragged in the water, but at least now, he could move without exposing himself to her.

"Put a hand on my shoulder," she advised, stepping close.

Touch her? How was he supposed to do that and not react to her again? "I can manage to leave a tub without help," he told her, hoping his gruff tone would encourage her to step away.

Instead, she took his arm. "Ye have a leg wound. Ye may no' be as steady on it as ye think. As long as I am here, I willna let ye fall."

There was no arguing with this lass. She reminded him of … someone. Who? Anders closed his eyes and fought for control, then put a hand on her shoulder and stepped out of the tub. "See? I am well. Ye can release me now."

Blessedly, Ailsa did so, but only to hand him another bath sheet. "Dry off. Yer clothes are clean and repaired, so ye can dress. Once ye can sit before me, I'll dry yer hair."

Her hand lifted as if she was going to reach for it, to stroke an errant curl off his forehead. He captured her hand in one of his. "I was right about ye."

"About what?"

"That ye are a kind lass. I appreciate yer help, but truly, I can manage the rest on my own."

"Ye might think so. Ye might even be able to, but I willna allow ye to risk it."

"Has anyone ever mentioned how stubborn ye are?"

"Only ye and everyone else who kens me."

Anders had to laugh at that, gratified that his chuckle made her laugh, too. Like the rest of her, she had a beautiful laugh. Sweetly musical and light-hearted. He wanted to hear it till the end of his days. Which might come as soon as her da got home. Especially if anyone found them like this, her standing so near, and him all but naked. "Turn yer back and I'll dress," he told her, doing his best to protect her and control the urges driving him toward taking her in his arms and kissing her senseless.

He longed to show her what he was made of. What he could do for her. If only he could remember when he'd learned how to please a lass. It wasn't fair that he couldn't recall the lasses he'd loved, though he felt certain there had been some. Perhaps even many.

A cold sense of dread filled the pit of his stomach. Nor could he recall whether there was a special lass in his life. He didn't think so. Surely he'd remember someone as important as a bride. But he vowed he would not risk hurting Ailsa if he wasn't free to care for her as she deserved. As she had cared for him. He must wait until he knew who he was and whether he was betrothed or married. He couldn't stand the thought of betraying any lass. Not Ailsa, and especially not any lass he loved enough to wed.

That certainty reassured him. Whoever he was, he cared about the women in his life.

Whoever they were. If there were any. Or if there was one.

But for now, he'd been standing long enough to feel his breath grow shallow and his legs weaken. He donned his clothes, sat on the bench and dried his feet, then put on his boots. "Yer souter did a masterful job of cleaning and repairing them," he remarked. "They've no' looked this good in years."

"Years? How many?"

He shook his head and shrugged. "I've nay notion. It just felt like the right thing to say."

"How do ye feel?"

"Clean, thank ye, and tired. A cup of that ale wouldna go amiss, I think."

She retrieved one and handed it to him. "Do ye feel up to something more than broth? I can ask Cook if she has any stew."

"Aye, that would help."

"Dinna move. I'll be back before ye ken I'm gone."

Little chance of that, Anders thought as he watched her exit and close the door behind her. She'd been away from him only for seconds, and already he missed her. What was happening to him? Was he simply grateful for her care? Or was there more to the desire for her he felt every time he looked at her, or heard her voice?

He rested his head on the wall at his back and closed his eyes, trying to remember a lass, any lass, from his life before he arrived here. Any clue that he would be free to pursue Ailsa. In a moment, he glimpsed a lass with chestnut hair toss a hawk into the air, but his memory followed the flight of the raptor and didn't return to the lass, so he never got a clear look at her face. Suddenly, he saw himself. But the memory, or the vision, was strangely … wrong. He saw the man clearly, as if he was looking at another person, not the imperfect view of himself in the distortion of a polished metal mirror or a reflection at the edge of a loch. What did that mean? Who were these people?

The door opened, breaking his concentration. Ailsa entered

with a tray, the mouthwatering scent of rich meat stew reaching him immediately. She set the tray on one of Maighread's tables and beckoned him over. "Come, eat. This will make ye feel better. Cook guarantees it." The scent of the stew was all the invitation he needed, but Ailsa's grin had him on his feet faster than he thought himself capable.

After he ate, Ailsa toweled his hair dry and combed it out, another pleasure but one that nearly put him to sleep. She stood with him and walked a few circuits of the chamber at his side.

"I'd take ye outside," she said, "but I'd have to explain about ye to more of the clan. They ken someone was carried in, but since ye ken so little about yerself, there's been naught to share with anyone else. Rumors are swirling though, as ye might imagine. And another dozen lads and lasses saw ye today."

Anders wished he had more to tell her, enough that he could be seen with her without causing comment.

"Besides," she continued, "if ye are seen walking about, Da may decide ye belong in the dungeon or out of Sinclair altogether. Maighread doesna think ye are ready for either. So, we'll keep ye safe in the herbal as long as we can."

Anders was grateful, but the prospect of spending long days ahead within these four walls was as unwelcome as the notion of being consigned to a cell in the dungeon. Still, he saw the wisdom. He hadn't recalled enough to be certain anything he said would not make his situation worse. With Ailsa's help, he had to believe he'd soon be himself again. Whoever that was. Memories had come to him in his dreams, even day dreams he had to content himself with when he was left alone in the herbal. With no clothes, he had no way to leave it until now, and there was a guard on the door at all times. As grateful as he was for the care he'd been given, he wondered how long he could stand to remain here.

"Do ye recall where yer home is?"

"South, I think," Anders told her as they made another circuit of the chamber, a frown of concentration revealing his struggle to dredge up memories.

"Nearly all of Scotland is south of here," she chided, then smiled, letting him know she was teasing. "That's a lot of countryside for ye to claim."

"Mayhap I am the lost and forgotten king of Scotland."

She snorted at that.

He looked out the open window at the low hills in the distance and the edge of a cliff and the water below it on the opposite side of the window's view. The light was turning golden, a sign that the long, late summer day was near its ending. He turned his gaze back to her. "'Tis so beautiful here, I canna think why I would wish to leave."

He hoped his expression would tell her he wasn't talking about the scenery.

§

STELLAN and his men rode into the MacKay bailey in late morning. The stable lads took their horses, freeing Stellan to collect the herb packets his men carried and take them to the MacKay healer, then search out Seamus. He didn't have to look far. Seamus walked into the herbal as Stellan was finishing with the healer.

"There ye are," Seamus said by way of greeting and clapped him on the back. "I was told ye had arrived."

The healer told Stellan, "We're grateful for the supplies ye brought. I'll get to work." She stepped to one of her tables and began breaking the packets' wax seals and dumping their contents into a large wooden bowl.

Stellan looked from her to Seamus. "Is Anders here?"

"Nay. Why would he be? Did he come with ye? And get separated from ye?"

Stellan frowned at that news. Seamus didn't know about the

race. He couldn't. Stellan and his men had left the morning after Seamus' courier had brought the news. The courier was still at Sutherland, as Mariota's guest, or perhaps on his way home to MacKay.

Stellan noticed the healer's interest, so he told both of them what her request had sparked, and that Anders had chosen to sail to MacKay.

"That's daft," Seamus exclaimed. "And bloody dangerous."

The healer stopped what she was doing and joined them. "What happened on yer way that ye think he'd arrive first?"

"We were delayed by a mudslide after the storm two nights ago," Stellan told them. "We wouldha been here yesterday but we had to make our way around it. With good weather and favorable conditions in the Pentland Firth, Anders should have beaten us here. But perhaps they had to put in somewhere along the way because of the same storm that delayed us."

Seamus' expression turned serious. "We havena seen him yet."

Where was Stellan's twin? If only their boyhood connection was still strong. But it wasn't. It had become tenuous, strengthened only by extremes of emotion or danger. He hadn't felt Anders reaching out to him with a sense of peril. That gave him some comfort. Perhaps they'd been delayed by the storm two nights ago and put into shore to wait it out. If the seas were still too rough to attempt the Pentland Firth, waiting was their wisest course. That, or turning for home, depending on Stellan and his riders to reach MacKay.

Not knowing rankled. Something Stellan couldn't name told him there was trouble.

"Ye'll stay for the night," Seamus offered as he gestured for Stellan to precede him out of the herbal. "Have a few good meals and a night or two in a soft bed before ye return to Sutherland, aye? Perhaps tomorrow will see Anders' *birlinn* arrive."

Seamus' offer made sense, and after nights of camping in the wind and rain, the idea of a night in a warm bed tempted Stellan.

His men deserved the same indulgence. But he couldn't ignore the sensation in his gut of some nameless trouble tied to Anders. "We'll impose on ye for a meal and a change of horses," Stellan agreed as they entered the great hall and the scent of roasting meat and watered ale hit his nostrils, making his stomach growl, "but I'll feel better if we ride east along the coast and see if we can spot them."

"If ye go too far, ye'll find yerself in Sinclair," Seamus warned while gesturing him to a seat with the rest of his men and signaling for a meal to be brought to them.

"I ken it, but that border is more than a day's ride away—nearly three to Sinclair's Girnigoe Castle, aye? We'll chance it. I dinna like that Anders is late."

Seamus nodded. "I dinna recommend crossing the border into Sinclair. The auld laird isna a friend of yers—or mine. Or any of the northern clans, truth be told. He looks to Orkney and the Norse rather than his closer neighbors. While ye search, I'll send a man to Sutherland to tell yer da what ye are doing."

Stellan almost told him not to, but if anything had gone wrong, their father would have to be told. He'd be furious, and Mariota would be frantic without some news if he and his men didn't return on time. He'd promised to be back in her bed in a sennight or a wee more, but now he didn't know when they would be able to return home. "I appreciate the offer, Seamus. Da and Mariota will, too. Thank ye."

While they waited for their food, Stellan described the area of the mud slide that had delayed them and the route they'd used to get around it. Seamus' courier would need that information to avoid the trouble they'd found along the way, and wondered if the courier who had brought Seamus' original request had started yet for home.

Once they were served, Seamus said, "I hope ye willna be gone too long, but ye'll have provisions to last a sennight to supplement what ye can find on the hunt. We could do with fewer coneys." He grinned, then excused himself to go speak to their cook about packing supplies for a week's travel and left them to their meal.

Stellan appreciated the care and cooperation. Mariota had chosen well when she named Seamus to replace her as Laird MacKay. While Stellan ate, he talked over tactics and routes with Tormund, his other men, and a MacKay scout Seamus had sent to answer their questions.

All too soon, they were ready to go. The MacKay stable lads who had taken their horses when they arrived were already shifting their saddles, tack, and belongings to fresh mounts.

With a grateful farewell to Seamus, they left the MacKay keep and headed east along the coastline. Seamus' scout had told them where the rivers were safe to cross and warned them of bogs. He would go as far as the Sinclair border with them. After that, they would be on their own to travel as quickly as they were wont to do.

The countryside consisted of low, rolling hills, sandy bays, cliffs, and rugged insets where a boat might hide. It was not always easy to see down to the coastline. They risked standing on the edge of a cliff to peer down to the sea or what passed for a beach more times than Stellan wanted to recall.

The rest of the day passed more slowly than he would have liked. He kept his gaze on the sea, hoping to spot a Sutherland *birlinn*. He saw nothing but endless water and sky. Disquieted and disappointed, he called a halt as the late summer darkness fell, and they made camp.

"Anders' *birlinn* could get by us in the dark," his friend Tormund remarked.

"If they do, Seamus will send a ghillie after us." Stellan hoped for exactly that. It would be the best outcome he could imagine.

MARIOTA WAS CROSSING the Sutherland bailey from the weaver's workroom back to the keep when a MacKay ghillie arrived.

"Lady Mariota," he cried when he saw her. "Well met. I have news for the Sutherland laird." He slid off his horse and handed the reins to a lad who'd run out from the stable. "Walk her a wee to cool her," he told the lad. "Please see she gets water and food. She's traveled far."

"Aye, I will," the lad promised and led the horse away.

"What news, Bron? Is Stellan well? And his men?" Anxiety made her heart flutter, and the babe in her belly shifted in response.

"Aye, they're well. There's nay harm in telling ye the news I bring before I speak to the laird," he added as they entered the great hall and Mariota gestured him toward the laird's solar. "Anders' ship hasna arrived yet. Stellan has gone to ride the coast and try to spot them."

"Ach, nay!" She suddenly needed to sit down.

Bron stopped and took her hands, squeezing them between his. "*Dinna fash*, milady. It doesna mean there's trouble, only that they have traveled more slowly than they wished."

Mariota wanted to believe that, but all she could think about was how the idea for this contest had come from her. From an innocent remark as they rode along the waters below Dunrobin. Guilt made her chest hollow out. What if Anders was lost at sea? Stellan would never recover from the loss of their men, much less his beloved twin.

"Milady?" Bron's concerned tone snapped her out of her misery.

"Aye, the laird." She led him in and introduced him. At Sutherland's nod, she took a seat to the side of his work table.

Sutherland stood. "Ye have news? From Mariota's expression, I willna like it."

"'Tis only that Laird MacKay wished to keep ye aware of what has happened. Stellan and his men arrived well, though delayed by a storm and mudslide. Anders' ship had not arrived by the time I left MacKay," he continued.

Sutherland sank to his seat, his face going gray.

"It may have arrived there by now, Laird Sutherland. But even before I left to come here, Stellan rode out immediately to travel toward Sinclair along the coast to see if the *birlinn* is still on the way or beached, and to look for yer men. The MacKay is sending men after Stellan to pass along information. He will send news to ye as he learns more."

Sutherland didn't speak, but he clenched and unclenched his fist several times, and deep furrows divided his brows.

He looked anguished, but Mariota feared he was also tempted to throw out the MacKay man. The news Bron brought was not his fault, and he'd made a long, dangerous ride to bring it to them. She counted on Sutherland to remember that fact before he spoke.

She held her breath until Sutherland's brow smoothed and he nodded.

"Ye are welcome to our hospitality. Food, drink, and a place to sleep until ye wish to return to MacKay. I thank ye for bringing me this news."

"I wish 'twere better, Laird," Bron told him.

Mariota was again amazed at Sutherland's restraint. This news was potentially terrible. Heartbreaking. She could barely keep her seat. If Anders was lost at sea—something she had teased him about and that she now even more deeply regretted— and if Stellan went too far east and was taken prisoner by Sinclair, perhaps even killed, the Sutherland laird and clan might never recover from the loss of the twins. She wanted to pace, to give voice to her fears, but she would not do that in front of their father.

Still, her mind kept spinning out how different the future they'd planned would be without her beloved husband. Her son would be heir, but who would train him? His only remaining uncle, Cameron, was wed to the Rose chief Mary Elizabeth and would not want to return permanently to Sutherland. The current Sutherland might be too old by the time her son came of an age to begin his training—training that Stellan was meant to begin. She fought tears of fear and regret. The Sutherland arms master was a good man, but he was not the father. Stellan looked forward to undertaking his son's early training. She would be strong for the twins' father and for her son, and for the child she carried.

Mariota rose and took the MacKay ghillie out into the great hall where she had a serving lass take charge of him. Then she returned to the solar.

Sutherland had not moved while she was out of the chamber. He still stared off into space, and Mariota most certainly did not want to know where his thoughts took him. Her own were too dire.

"I must send Sutherland men north to Sinclair, and call in Rose and Brodie reinforcements to keep Dunrobin and all of ye safe," Sutherland said.

He was planning to go after his sons. "We dinna yet ken what we are dealing with," Mariota reminded him "God willing, both of the twins are safe at MacKay by now. Seamus will send news." She thought he would argue with her. She even hoped he would. But all he did was slump in his seat.

"Ye are right, lass. 'Tis too soon to call in our allies."

"Still, 'twould be wise to prepare missives to send. Just in case." He was right that they would need men to reinforce the men—and her women archers—on Sutherland's walls if he and most of his warriors headed north. But without knowing where Anders and Stellan were, taking an army north to Sinclair could incite the very violence they wanted to avoid.

She put a hand over her belly, breathing deeply for her bairn and to calm herself. Where was Stellan? Still safe in MacKay territory? Or venturing into Sinclair in search of his twin, heedless of the risks he took? Those questions made her heart hurt. She didn't want her children growing up without their father. Nor could she imagine life without Stellan. She didn't want to try, but if the worst happened, she would do what she must. She always had.

CHAPTER 7

A few hours after Ailsa finished her morning chores, ate a quick meal with her friend Siobhan, and settled a dispute between two of the maids charged with cleaning in the keep, she nodded to the guard and opened the door to the herbal to check on Anders. He sat on a stool, her favorite book of Highland myths and sagas open on the table before him in a pool of morning light from the herbal's small window. He'd requested something to read to alleviate his boredom. He'd told her he liked myths, or Makars' poetry, but he would not be opposed to learning more about Sinclair history. She thought he needed something more diverting than Sinclair history, which bored her to tears, so she'd started with tales of mystical creatures. When he wasn't reading, he paced the chamber, walking in circles and figure eights around the tables Maighread used for her pots and potions, claiming the movement helped him get stronger. He certainly seemed improved over the day when he came out of the fever.

His concentration on what he read was so deep that he didn't react to her presence and greet her as he normally would. So, she took advantage of the chance to stand quietly in the doorway for a few moments, look at him and imagine his kiss. He would be gentle and yet persuasive, and he would light a fire in her body that might never go out. She wanted his kisses, his arms around her, his body pressed to hers, his scent filling her nose, making every sense she possessed sing in excitement and longing. For him.

Ailsa couldn't help letting her imagination run, inspired by the tales Anders now read. She'd grown up with the idea of the fae, both fanciful and frightening, as a mystical part of her world from the lore of the Highlands. She'd learned more on her family's visits to Orkney. And like most lasses, the desire for magical love in her life had never faded. Looking at Anders, she had to wonder if a man as beautiful as he was a gift from the seelie, or if he could be a selkie. Had he left his sealskin hidden somewhere in the forest above the bay? He'd come from the sea, after all. She couldn't imagine what she might have done to deserve such a boon. He was the most handsome, funny, and gentle man she'd ever known. He'd been kind to her and to the healer, even when he was in pain and frustrated over his lack of memory. Had he lost it after being touched by the fae rather than because of the wound on his head or his time in the cold sea?

He bore his protective confinement in the herbal with grace, which continued to amaze her. But being free of fever and clean had to have something to do with his improved mood. In the days since he'd arrived, he'd made remarkable progress. He moved as if his leg no longer pained him, and his scraped hands had responded so well to Maighread's poultice that they were nearly healed.

Ailsa wanted him well and able to care for himself. And in full possession of his memory. There was much about him that she wanted to know. Needed to know if she was ever to act upon the feelings for him that filled her. But she dared not start something she didn't want to stop. Not when her brother was ready to throw Anders into the dungeon, and getting too close to her would put him in danger from her father. And not when he couldn't remember whether he had a wife or bairns. Surely he would remember them first—and he hadn't.

Though she worried what his lack of memory would mean for Anders. And for her. How would he leave Sinclair when he had no idea who he was or where to go home? Would her father let her wed a man with no memory of who he was, where he came from, or whether he was already wed, and a man whose clan he could not name?

Or was her friend Siobhan correct that Anders remembered and was hiding what he knew?

He finally looked up from his book and saw her. A smile lifted the corners of his mouth. "Why are ye standing there, Ailsa? Come. Keep me company."

Given her earlier thoughts, the steps she took toward him felt like steps through more than distance. What was she approaching? A man? Or one of the fae?

He stood and held out a hand to her and she paused. He looked just as she had dreamed, just as she had told him she hoped to see him reach for her someday. Her heart beat faster, but she gathered her courage and took the remaining steps to reach him and lay her hand in his. He felt warm and real. Here was a man, not one of the sith. A man she cared for, perhaps too much too soon. That was her mind speaking, not her heart. Somehow, though she'd barely noticed it happening, Anders had stolen her heart away.

He hooked the next stool with his foot and pulled it closer to his, then guided her to a seat.

"How are ye today?" She knew the answer before she asked the question, but those were the only words she could summon while he gazed at her with such admiration.

"I am better every day. Especially when I see ye, Ailsa. Do ye have any news?"

"I wish I did. Naught has happened. My parents have no' yet returned, but should soon."

"Perhaps I could be allowed to wander about the castle for a while? I appreciate the books, but I tire of these walls."

"I ken ye do, but—"

"Ye fear yer da's reaction. He will find out about me, lass. Sooner or later, I will have to face him."

"If ye wander about, Boden will hear about it. Even if he does naught to punish ye—if Maighread keeps him from taking ye from here," she said and gestured at their surroundings, "I fear he will take Da aside as soon as he arrives. If my brother gets to him first, he will be set against ye before I have a chance to speak. Da will be angry that I let ye in. I dinna want that to happen until I have a chance to prepare him."

"Prepare him? Why? Have I done aught to make ye think I pose a threat to Sinclair? What will he think one lone man can do?"

"I dinna ken, but Boden thinks ye are a threat. Da may as well."

"Ah, we're back to that. Lass, I will leave now if 'twill keep ye from having to bear any punishment for my presence here."

"'Twillna matter," Ailsa said. "Ye are here now. Besides, ye have yet to ken where ye are from, or where to go."

Anders shook his head. "I begin to dislike a man I've yet to meet."

"My da? Or yerself?"

His widened eyes betrayed surprise at her perception. "Both, perhaps."

She dropped her gaze for a moment. "I would be glad for ye to stay," she told him, then covered her mouth with one hand as she looked up at him.

The warmth of a blush rose up her throat to her face.

Anders' gaze turned molten as he admired her. "I'm pleased to hear ye say that. Once I am stronger, I would—" He stopped suddenly, then took a breath. "But nay. I canna promise anything. Do anything." He traced his fingertips over her face ever so gently. "Ye are so lovely, so tempting. But I dinna ken if I belong to another. I wouldna wish to harm ye. Or her. If there is another."

Unable to resist, she traced her fingertips over the back of his hand, then pulled away. "Ye are also wise," she said, but she didn't meet his gaze. His eyes were as dark as hers must be when her hands lifted toward him again, but she pulled them back without touching him and stepped back. She had to keep her distance. Anders was right.

"I think ye are quite strong enough," she told him. "I dream of seeing ye well and strong, kenning who ye are, and holding out yer hand to me."

"Ye dream of me?" He held one hand out to her. "I can do that now, Ailsa."

His words gave Ailsa an odd feeling in the pit of her stomach. Hunger, but of a very different kind. And hope?

Her cheeks warmed again. "I'm spending most of my time with ye. 'Tis no' surprising ye'd remain on my mind even when I try to sleep."

"So, I keep ye awake, but when ye do sleep, I'm in yer dreams. A lesser man might think ye have come to care for me."

"Ye mustna say things like that where others can hear. I'm caring for ye every day. If 'twere to get back to my da, I fear ye wouldna like what he did about it. Ye mustna antagonize him, Anders. He is the Sinclair. He could have ye killed."

"My alternative is to remain hidden away, like the least favored neep in the bottom of a bin in the pantry. Is that it?"

"Or face the consequences before I have a chance to smooth the way."

He cupped her face and traced his thumb across her lower lip, a frown drawing down his brows. "Then I hope ye are very good at smoothing." He leaned in, his gaze pinning her in place for endless moments, as if, after he'd promised not to harm her, he fought an overwhelming urge. Or was he giving her time to deny him? She couldn't. Nor could he. Her lips parted as his touched hers, firm, yet soft, just as she'd imagined. His scent surrounded her, and the feel of his kiss made her want to taste him. She traced his lips with the tip of her tongue, and his answering groan spurred her on.

He slipped his hand behind her head, tightened his grip, holding her mouth to his while his tongue stroked hers. Her body answered with a bloom of heat behind her breasts like a rose bud bursting into full flower. Her nipples tightened as she moved closer to him, and the friction of her clothes shifting over them sent small shocks through her body. The pulsing sensation broke the thrall his kiss had spun within her. They were doing precisely what they'd sworn not to do.

She leaned away, and he dropped his hand. For a moment, he looked so forlorn she took pity on him. "I'm sorry."

"Nay, I am. I shouldna have done that, but ye ken I want ye, lass. I must … I will do better controlling myself."

"What if I dinna want ye to?" Her heart was still pounding, her center felt empty and needy—for him. For Anders and all he could give her. She met his gaze, looking for his reaction and saw only concern, not eagerness in his eyes.

"Dinna say that unless ye mean it—and ye understand the consequences. I dinna ken who I am. Or if there's a lass waiting for me."

An uncertain sense of regret filled her, smothering the fire within her. How could she have such strong feelings for a man she barely knew? A man who was in fact, unknowable. She couldn't fathom the frustration and dismay he must be suffering, wanting her, and not knowing what his life was like before he came here. Her own frustration angered her. What was she thinking? "I'm sorry, Anders. I … I hadn't considered how ye would feel about that possibility."

"I dinna ken how to feel, lass. When I see ye, when ye are near me, all I want is ye."

"Why?"

Her question made him stop and look aside for a moment. When his gaze returned to her, he smiled. "Ye are beautiful. And kind. Ye helped save my life, and when ye could have let others care for me and forgotten I exist, ye continue to come to me, every day. Ye speak of protecting me from yer brother and yer da. From my own worst impulses. Ye are an exceptional woman, Ailsa. How could I no' have feelings for ye?"

"'Twas never my intention to trap ye—"

"Ye havena. Ye have shown me who ye are, as beautiful on the inside as ye are on the outside." He caressed her face again, almost reverently, then smoothed back her hair, his touch warm and gently possessive.

"But even if there isna anyone waiting for ye, becoming involved with the laird's daughter could put ye at grave risk, and I dinna want to do that. I havena worked hard to see ye heal only to lose ye when my da returns and finds out about ye."

"What can we do?"

"I have another idea. If ye would like to meet a few more Sinclairs, I have two or three friends ye might enjoy. I trust them. I could bring them here, to ye." And they might be valuable allies if such were ever needed.

His whole demeanor changed at her words. Straightening, he gave her a wide smile that appeared only a little forced by regret for what they had done—or was it for stopping so soon? "I would appreciate that. I will never turn ye away, lass, but meeting more of yer folk 'twould be welcome."

WHILE AILSA WAS out of the herbal, Anders took care of his private needs. He ran a hand through his hair, trying to distract himself from the desire to sink into the depths of her blue eyes and learn everything there was to know about her, the urge to touch her full lips again and taste her, the memory of the silky feel of her skin on her delicate cheek and the weight of her head in his hand. Anders couldn't believe he was still alive, and that he was being cared for by such a lush beauty as Ailsa. She entranced him, just like one of the fae in her book, and like the humans they captured, he feared he would never be free of her.

He could barely breathe with wanting her. He needed to touch her, to press her body against his and take her mouth. The thought was sweet torture. His pulse pounded in his throat like the slap of oars on deep water. He wanted more, but he didn't dare.

He should not have taken such liberties with her. He had vowed not to and had already broken that vow. His lack of control shamed and angered him. That kiss was his fault. He must do better to protect her from himself—and from her own desires. She wanted him. He had no doubt of that. But he would not hurt her—nor ruin her—and leave her. She deserved better of him—or of any man.

What would it mean for him when her father returned? Ailsa's words reminded Anders that Sinclair seemed to his imperfect memory to be an enemy, or at least not an ally. He could not pursue anything closer with her until he knew more about himself. Despite her objection, Ailsa might be developing feelings for him, but her father wouldn't care about that. He'd only care that she'd been in danger from an enemy under their roof.

The rest of their conversation disturbed him as much, if not more.

Anders could think of many things one man inside Sinclair's walls could do. Open a gate to invaders. Dishonor Ailsa, or kill the Sinclair heir. Escape and tell their enemies how to get out—and into the keep. Any of those would cause chaos. The Sinclair would have reason to be concerned about Anders' presence here. Boden was right, though Anders would never say that to Ailsa. If he did, she might begin to agree with her brother that he belonged in the dungeon. For as long as he could, he must continue to appear and behave as if he was harmless. At least until his memories came back and he knew how truly dangerous he was—and could be.

But Ailsa was no fool. She could think of those same risks. Why did she continue to protect him? What would her father do to her when he found out, especially after her brother blamed his presence on her? If Anders had any idea where his home lay, he'd find a way to leave and remove the jeopardy he presented for her. But in his current state, even if he got outside Sinclair's walls, he could wander for days, still be picked up by a Sinclair patrol, and wind up right back here.

He shook his head to force himself back to reality. He had no answers and wasn't likely to get any today. Running made no sense, despite how much he wanted to protect Ailsa. He would have to protect her by his presence rather than his absence. And by keeping his hands off her. Making friends among other Sinclairs was a good way to start.

It felt good to be clean, and if she brought back three lasses, he would want to look the best he could to impress Ailsa's friends. Alliances worked, even on the personal level. He rubbed a hand over his chin. He needed a shave, but that would have to wait. That or just allow a short beard to grow. He didn't think he'd ever worn one. He could only hope he would not embarrass Ailsa. She had offered to fetch her friends, so he must look presentable enough. As he was would have to do.

He hadn't seen Maighread yet today. She seemed content to leave his care to Ailsa, whom he wanted more than any lass he'd ever known, and he'd known quite a few. He had? A brief sliver of memory showed him faces, as if the lasses danced around him and he had only a moment to regard each one.

None looked familiar. None spoke their name. There wasn't time.

The more glimpses of faces he saw, the more convinced he was that he would remember his past. He would know who he truly was and where to go. Where to take Ailsa to make a home and a life with her. If he survived. And if she wanted him after he found out who he was.

Voices in the hall alerted him that he was about to meet more Sinclairs. He took a breath, stood and faced the door. He was in his element around people. He knew that, but not how he knew it. He appreciated that Ailsa would risk so much for him, possibly exposing her friends to their laird's wrath. He hoped someday to be able to help her make friends among his people, too.

The herbal's door opened. Ailsa entered first, followed by a shorter, dark blonde lass who took one look at him and paused. One of two men following bumped into her and pushed her forward, followed by another man, before Ailsa entered.

"Everyone, meet Anders. Anders, these are my friends Maesie, Murdo and Tasgall. Maesie works in the kitchen and kitchen garden, and she's also an herbalist learning from Maighread. Some day, she may become the clan's healer."

Maesie stared intently at Ailsa, at him, and then back to Ailsa, as if to communicate something she didn't want to say out loud. Anders suspected whatever it was would have amused him.

"Murdo is a fisherman and expert at weaving nets," Ailsa continued, unaware of Maesie's interest. "Tasgall is a Sinclair guard."

Anders was enjoying the introductions until Ailsa named Tasgall, the shorter, stockier of the two men, as one of her clan's guardsmen. Tasgall's gaze on him was direct, even penetrating, but not hostile. Not yet.

"I'm pleased to meet all of ye. I wish I could tell ye what my skills are, but they are hidden from me for now."

"Ailsa told us," Maesie said. "We're sorry ye canna remember who ye are. I canna imagine what that must feel like."

"'Tis no' the most pleasant experience I've ever had," Anders told her. At her surprised expression, eyebrows lifted, he laughed. "No' that I would ken, I suppose." Strange, but it actually felt good to jest about what had happened to him.

"What do ye recall?"

Ah, so Tasgall went right to the meat of the matter. He had a guard's instincts and wasn't afraid to use them.

"Little enough. A name. Mine, I suppose. I'm using it, at any rate. Odd bits and pieces, a few images of people I canna name, places I dinna recognize. I hope those glimpses mean 'twill all come back to me."

"The people ye see might be family or close friends," Maesie suggested.

"Aye, I've thought about that. 'Twould make sense, but so far, they havena introduced themselves."

Maesie gave him a quick grin.

Tasgall continued his interrogation. "Can ye describe the places ye've seen?"

Anders shrugged. "Forests, hills, a stretch of coastline on a bay that might be yers. Naught distinctive."

"But important enough to come back to ye," Murdo said, the last to speak up.

The fisherman was tall with long, well-developed muscles from hauling nets, Anders supposed. "Or common enough." He shrugged again. "I'm sorry but I dinna have the answers to yer questions. So, tell me, what is life like at Sinclair for ye?"

The conversation went on long enough that Maesie left to fetch cider and ale for them, as well as cheese and bread. While she was gone, the conversation lagged until Tasgall asked Murdo about his last trip to visit a lass he was sweet on.

"'Twas a wild ride," Murdo told them. "The Pentland firth was in a foul mood, and the tide was against us, but we were determined no' to have to walk from an easterly landing all the way to Thurso."

"Ye have a lass in Thurso? A MacKay?"

Tasgall's question made something tingle on the back of Anders' neck. There was something buried in his memory about MacKay.

"Aye, she's in Thurso, but no' a MacKay. A Lamont. Her da came down from Orkney."

What about MacKay and the Pentland? It seemed important, but like many things, it remained just out of reach.

"We took nets and such to sell in the market there. And Cook asked for some herbs she thought I'd find in one of the stalls."

Ice slithered down Anders' spine. He almost had it. Sailing the Pentland to MacKay territory. And something about herbs for a healer.

"Did ye find them?" Maesie asked.

"Aye."

"Did ye see yer lass?" Anders had to ask to cover the struggle going on in his head.

"Aye," Murdo answered, coloring a little. "I did."

"A good visit, then. How was the firth on yer return?" Anders hesitated to ask, but there was something about that body of water than meant something to him.

"As rough as ever. We had to wait for the storm a few nights ago to pass before we could come home." He paused and frowned. "Once we turned south, we chased a *birlinn* also headed south but closer to the coast. It might have come through the firth ahead of us or down from Orkney. The odd thing was how slowly they traveled, but they were seaworthy and didna signal for help, so we passed them by. Now that I think about it, I saw the same *birlinn* south of Sinclair bay headed north again as we were unloading our ship."

Anders fought not to let his reaction show on his face. Tasgall was watching him while he listened to Murdo's story. To him, it sounded as if the crew of the *birlinn* was searching the coast for something. Or someone. Him? The sense of secrets about to be revealed within himself held Anders still. He couldn't have moved if Tasgall had come at him swinging a claymore.

Maesie's sudden chatter with the guard outside the door ripped the edge of elusive memory away. Anders blinked away his dismay as the guard opened the door and she came in carrying a tray. Some revelation had been close. So close he could almost touch it. But it was gone.

Still, her timing saved Anders from Tasgall's inspection, his attention stolen by the kitchen maid.

"This should help any dry throats among us," she announced as the guard closed the door behind her. She passed out cups.

Anders took his with thanks and sipped. Cider. Sweet and restorative. Probably the perfect thing to settle the blades pricking at this belly. So many hints, but nothing that built a complete story. Not even a single complete picture.

"What did I miss?"

Maesie's question pulled Anders out of his thoughts on a flash of annoyance. Perhaps he'd just missed the reason he was here. That edge of memory had felt that important.

"Murdo has a Lamont lass in Thurso," Ailsa announced.

"I dinna have her," Murdo corrected, "but I hope someday she will be mine."

"How did ye meet her? And why have ye never mentioned her to us?"

Ailsa's questions sent the conversation into safer territory, letting Anders set aside his emotions and relax enough to enjoy the cider Maesie brought—and to enjoy looking at Ailsa. He never tired of the way light played on her bright tresses. Not quite a Norse blonde, nor a Highland red, but something in between—a beautiful blend of her heritage.

An image of himself with a dark-haired lass suddenly rose before his eyes as if he looked at them from only a few feet away.

As the conversation continued around him, he couldn't shake one question. How could he see himself as if he was outside his body? Or two questions. Was the *birlinn* Murdo saw searching for a missing man? Him? And third, was the dark-haired lass in his visions his wife?

❧

AT MIDDAY, Raghnall, the Sinclair guard captain sent Tasgall to fetch Ailsa to the bailey. "We caught this lot in the woods above the bay," he told her when she arrived, gesturing to nearly a dozen men standing clustered together and surrounded by Sinclair guards.

"Who are they?" They looked tired. Worn, bedraggled, and hungry. But they stood straight, with shoulders back, determined to put on a brave front.

"There's a *birlinn* beached down the coast a ways," he told her. "They willna say much, but I believe they're the crew."

More strange men? Ailsa's belly quailed as she imagined how her da would react to this. Anders' situation had just become more complicated, especially if they came from the *birlinn* Murdo had seen sailing their coastline.

"What are we to do with them?"

"The only place to keep them safe and ensure they dinna cause trouble is—"

Ailsa held up one hand to stop him. "I ken what ye are going to say. The dungeon."

"Aye." Raghnall's tone told her he wasn't eager to do it either, but they couldn't allow that many strangers to run freely within their walls.

She didn't want to put them down there.

"Who speaks for them?"

Raghnall pointed. "That one. The eldest, Tomas, seems to be their spokesman, if not their captain. They refuse to say why they are on Sinclair land except that the recent storm forced them ashore, but that was days ago. They should have gone on their way by now, unless their *birlinn* is damaged."

"Tomas," Ailsa said as she moved closer to them and introduced herself, "is yer *birlinn* seaworthy?"

He shrugged and nodded.

"So, 'tis? Or ye are no' sure?" Had they come through the Pentland Firth in the storm? If so, they were lucky to be alive.

Tomas shook his head. "We havena tried to float her."

"Were ye looking for someone?"

His head came up at that, but he didn't answer.

"My guard chief insists ye go into the dungeon," Ailsa continued, hating to say the words. "I would object, but ye havena identified yourselves to him." At least until her father got home and decided what to do with them, Raghnall was right. There was no place else to put them. "But ye will be well cared for. I give ye my word ye will have food and drink and warm blankets."

"Fer how long, lady?" Tomas traded a glance with another of his men. They both looked concerned, but she supposed in their position, she would, too.

"Until the laird decides what to do with ye."

"Let us go, lady, and we willna be any trouble to ye."

"What's this?"

Ailsa fought not to cringe at Boden's bellow. Raghnall frowned, telling her he had not sent for her brother, despite him being, as he'd insisted to her over Anders' fevered form days ago, in charge. Raghnall knew Boden's temper could be trouble. She took a breath, turned to face her brother and calmly told him what they knew.

"A dozen men, roaming Sinclair land?" He glared at the men. "Already ye are trouble. I willna allow ye to leave. Ye must wait for the laird's decision."

Tomas looked as though he wanted to say more, but kept his thoughts to himself.

Still reluctant, Ailsa nodded to the guard captain. Raghnall and several of his men escorted their prisoners down the stairs that led to the dungeon, Boden nipping at their heels. He could brag to their father that he had done his duty and confined them in the dungeon. Maybe he'd be satisfied with tormenting them and forget about Anders. Watching them go, Ailsa crossed her arms and fretted. Who were they? Did they have any connection to Anders? Tomas wouldn't say, but it seemed clear to her that they had stayed on land looking for someone. Murdo had mentioned a *birlinn* sailing up and down the coast. Theirs? The coincidence was too compelling. Would Anders remember Tomas if she mentioned that name? Another thought made her gasp. She and Maighread had assumed Anders was injured in the storm, but what if he'd been attacked by these men? If they were his enemies rather than his friends, how could she find out without betraying him?

CHAPTER 8

*D*espite Ailsa's hope, Anders' visit with her friends earlier that morning hadn't cured his frustration at being confined to the herbal. Given what he'd heard and how he thought it might apply to him, the visit had made him even more restive and anxious to get outside. Was Maesie working in the kitchen by now? If he could talk the guard outside his door into letting him out of this chamber, he might be able to convince her to let him wander about the walled kitchen garden, even if he had to do it with the guard on his heels. Moving about would strengthen his injured leg. And he might learn more about how to escape the Sinclair castle.

Ailsa had left with her friends, and he didn't know how long she'd be gone. Surely she had duties for the clan to deal with.

Mind made up, he opened the herbal door, expecting to be challenged and ready to plead for some time outside. Where was the guard? Had something happened to call him away? Anders hadn't heard any shouting, but the herbal window didn't look out onto the bailey, and with the door closed, even voices in the great hall were muted.

The hallway was empty. He closed the door behind him and

headed for the kitchen. It was a busy hive of activity, and he didn't see Maesie, but he could see out to the kitchen garden through an open doorway, so he simply walked in that direction. With each step he took, he inhaled the tempting scent of roasting meat, baking bread, and some sort of stew. The kitchen fell quieter and quieter as he moved through it. By the time he reached the open doorway, silence reigned, and his stomach was grumbling.

"Are ye hungry, lad?"

Resigned, he turned and looked at the Cook, a middle-aged woman of generous girth. She was frowning at him, but the lasses who were supposed to be preparing the next meal with her all had their gazes on him, too, only they were smiling. And sighing. Then hiding their smiles behind bashful hands.

"Ye'd be the lad Maighread and Ailsa have been caring for, aye?" Cook asked. "Maesie described ye to us."

Anders gave her his best smile and a shallow bow. "I would. My name is Anders. Thank ye," he said and paused to let his gaze travel the kitchen to take in every lass working there, "and all of ye, for taking such fine care of me. Yer good food has helped me heal all the faster."

At his acknowledgement, the lasses began to trade glances with each other, sigh more sighs, and send more admiring glances his way.

"I'm of a mind to spend some time outside on such a pretty day," he added. "I will take care no' to step on any of yer garden, Cook. I ken how important it is." That seemed to win her over, at least a little. She nodded, gave him a thin smile, then clapped her hands. "Back to work with the rest of ye. Now."

Anders knew he'd better move on or she might be calling for guards with her next breath.

"Have some stew and fresh-baked bread, at least, before ye go wander about, aye? 'Tis time for the midday meal."

Or maybe she would not. "I would enjoy that, Cook. It smells delicious." But if he tarried here and the guard found him, he'd never get outside.

"Sit down, over here," she said and pointed to a small, square table off to the side.

He knew when he was boxed in. He may as well enjoy the meal she offered, even if it meant missing out on where he'd wanted to go. He dared not give the clan's Cook any reason to distrust or dislike him. Hers was an important voice in clan life. She could be an ally.

In moments, he was happily spooning up a rich venison stew, soaking up the sauce with warm, buttered bread, and washing it down with ale. "I canna recall the last time I ate so well," he told Cook when he finished.

She laughed, making him certain she knew about his memory loss.

He gave her a sheepish grin, stood, and took her hand. "Thank ye for yer care. I do appreciate it." He lifted her hand and kissed the back of her knuckles.

"None of that, my lad. I'm easily yer mam's age."

He gave her a gentle smile. "I wonder if she can cook half so well."

Maesie entered the kitchen as he spoke. Anders supposed she'd been in the great hall helping to set up for the midday meal.

"Ach, Maesie, come show Anders the gardens ye are so proud of."

"Of course," Maesie answered and hurried over, mouthing, *what are ye doing out here?* while the cook turned away from her and back to him.

Cook shooed Anders away. "Out with ye. Enjoy some sun while the day lasts."

Grateful that wherever the guard had been when Anders looked out the herbal door, the man hadn't bothered to check on his charge when he returned to his post or he would have found his missing prisoner by now. Anders stepped out of the kitchen with Maesie and took a moment to let his eyes adjust to the bright sunshine. The day was as warm and lovely as it had appeared from the herbal's window. He exhaled a sigh of relief to be out of doors, out of the same four walls. He would always remember how well he'd been treated there, but he was past the point of needing to be confined. Now they did it for their safety, not his health. Boden thought he could be a threat. Perhaps others did, as well.

Maesie took a few steps down the path from the kitchen door, stopped and beckoned for him to follow her. She walked the paths between the planted beds, some now harvested and empty of anything green, others wilting from the cooling changes in the weather, and others more suited to cold still thriving. But frost would damage even those. "A few weeks or a month, I think, 'till the frost." She took a deep breath. "Ye can smell it. The trees are starting to show their colors and drop their leaves. The scent in the wind is different when it blows from the land side."

Anders had never thought of the scent of the air being a harbinger, but the way Maesie described it, it made sense.

He stepped down onto the gravel path that ran straight through the garden toward what he assumed was a postern gate. He could see the tops of trees on the other side. How difficult would it be to escape through that gate? What lay on the other side?

"'Tis a very large garden," he remarked. "'Tis yer responsibility?"

"For the most part, aye. Maighread also tends some of it. She and Cook have taught me well, but there's always more to learn. We collect some herbs from the fields and woods, even near the seashore, but many will grow quite well here."

"I'm impressed," Anders told her. This far north, the growing season had to be even shorter than it was at home. Like many, the garden was laid out to take advantage of a southern exposure, surrounded by walls that collected heat during the day and kept the garden warmer at night. It also served to keep out pests such as coneys, deer, and other hungry animals.

As they walked the paths between planting areas, the lasses working in them ceased harvesting some things and plucking weeds from around others and stood. Maesie introduced each one. Anders enjoyed meeting them and learning a little about the work they did, but his gaze kept straying to that postern gate. It seemed familiar. This was really no different than the gardens at … where? Suddenly, images of expansive and well-tended gardens filled his mind, the sea off to one side, a castle up on its ridge and the fortifications behind them on the other. More gardens lay inside the castle's walls. He could picture them even if he could not place them. Relief flooded him. He'd been right. For his memory to come back, he needed to get out, see more, and meet more people than he could sitting in the herbal.

Finally, they neared the gate set into the wall farthest from the kitchen. Anders asked, "Where does this go?"

Maesie shrugged. "We've an orchard in the next area. Beyond that is the keep's outer wall."

Anders stomach fell. Another barrier. He fought to hide his reaction, asking, "What of the orchard? What do ye grow?"

"Trees that bear fall fruits, apples and pears, to harvest. They're a wee more hardy than the summer fruit trees, though we have cherries and such. The first frost, if 'tis light, willna do much to them, but we will soon harvest all we can. As the sun comes round to autumn, the forest throws more shade on this side of the keep, so the plants dinna grow as well."

"The forest's trees are close enough to do that?"

"Aye. No' like near the main gate. On this side, the forest is much closer." She opened the gate from the garden into the orchard. "Follow me."

Anders marveled that she led him through the orchard so casually, not stopping until she found a spot with a clear line of sight beyond the orchard wall. He could see the tops of firs and pines close by over the wall, and touches of gold or red as well, in scattered hardwoods.

"Ye can see the fruit is near to ripe. We can start picking in a few days, I think," she said, her gaze on the fruit trees rather than the trees visible over the wall.

He couldn't resist one question. The answer might mean freedom when the time was right. "Do ye ever go outside the walls? Ach, of course ye do. Ye said ye gather some herbs and such from the forest and near the seashore."

"Aye, we do. If we're going far, we take a guard with us and go through the main gate where ye came in."

Had she just said what he thought she'd said? If he understood what she implied, there was a postern gate on this outer wall that they used for quick trips outside while staying near the keep. They only used the main gate if they were going farther afield. Though he hoped Maesie was trying to give him the idea that escape was close at hand from here, he still feared she was mistaken. He would never be given the chance.

But Anders held tightly to that bit of knowledge. He might yet need it.

❧

AILSA FINISHED SPEAKING to the clan's new guests—or prisoners, she wasn't certain how she would describe their actual status. In her mind, they'd done nothing violent that warranted them being considered prisoners, but the dungeon was no place for guests, either. She didn't like that they were concealing their clan affiliation, but she could think of many reasons why stranded sailors might be inclined to do so. To protect themselves. To protect their clan from retaliation for some perceived slight. But also to conceal a purpose less aboveboard than trying to recover from a storm.

Well, for the time being, they were safe where they were and she would see that they had some comforts. It was the best she knew how to do until her parents returned.

Her brother could be a problem. He probably would be a problem, but Raghnall could help distract him. She hoped.

Stymied, she headed back to the herbal to see how Anders was doing. The guard stood by the door, his back to the wall, looking bored. She greeted him, then went inside the herbal and closed the door behind her. And froze. Anders wasn't there. Frantic, she whirled around, feeling ridiculous while she looked in every corner and under every table. She eyed the small window for a moment, then snorted. There was no way a man Anders' size could squeeze through that and drop a dangerous distance to the ground below. Yet he'd gotten by the guard.

Or perhaps not.

The guard looked too bored to have known he was guarding an empty chamber. If he left on a comfort break thinking that Anders was asleep inside, and Anders happened to look out the door while he was gone … aye, she could see it happening that way. She mentally retraced her steps. Nothing had seemed unusual in the great hall. He hadn't gone that way, which meant he'd made his way to the kitchen.

Cook saw her arrive and came over. "What *fashes* ye, lass?"

"I, ah, was looking for Anders, but he's no' here."

"He ate a hearty meal a while ago and is walking in the gardens outside with Maesie."

Relief made Ailsa reach for the nearest tabletop to steady herself. "Thank goodness." Chances were good that Boden hadn't seen him. Yet. Anders hadn't wandered out into the bailey or even out of the keep, though the guards, had they noticed him in the usual comings and goings of the clan, would have stopped him. "Thank ye, Cook. I'll go find them."

When she stepped out into the sunshine, she paused to let her eyes adjust, then swept the gardens with her gaze. Anders was impossible to miss, following Maesie through the gate from the orchard back into the main garden. Not only was he the only man within its walls, taller than the lasses working there, and much taller than Maesie, he had the power to draw her gaze no matter where he was. Sunlight brought out glints of red in his dark hair, and poured over his broad shoulders. He looked so perfectly formed, that save for his sun-kissed skin, he could have been carved from marble by some Italian master like the drawings in one of the books in the clan's library.

Now that he was in her sights, she reminded herself that he could be perfectly irritating, as well. She stalked across the garden path to him. "Hello, Maesie. Anders, what are ye doing out here?" She fought to keep her tone light. Maesie was not at fault in this escapade of his.

"I was just showing Anders around the gardens," Maesie said, stating the obvious.

"That was kind of ye," Ailsa told her. "But I need to speak with him. Thank ye for taking care of him."

Maesie nodded, gave Anders a quick smile, and hurried back to the kitchen.

"Ye are angry." Anders studied her with that direct gaze that seemed capable of reading her mind.

"I'm … not sure what I am. I was frantic when I didna find ye in the herbal. And even more so with the thought ye might have overpowered the guard and gone to the great hall or outside in the bailey. I'm relieved ye were in Cook's and Maisie's company."

"'Twas nay a problem. The guard was away when I happened to open the door. So, I took advantage of the opportunity. Cook and her helpers were kind, as was Maesie. Lasses always like me, and I them."

"How do ye ken … never mind." She frowned at the bemused expression on his face. That didn't sound like another memory, just something he knew in the same way he recognized the name Sinclair. Just how many lasses had he been friendly—or more than just friends—with? How many had he remembered? An unfamiliar sensation soured Ailsa's stomach. Was she jealous? "Lasses talk. Yer appearance here will be all over the keep before the evening meal is served."

"So, there's nay reason to stay in the herbal."

Frustration made her clench her fists. "Ye ignored my caution about showing yerself. When my brother sees that ye are well enough to be out here, he will think ye no longer need Maighread's care in the herbal. He will have ye moved to the dungeon and Maighread willna be able to contradict him. The dungeon is nearly full. Ye willna like being down there among so many strangers."

She paused to let that sink in, then added, "And what do ye want me to tell my da, the Laird, about the strange man wandering about Sinclair by himself? I warned ye about this."

Anders expression changed from confidence to consternation in a blink. "Is he back from the Orkneys?"

"Nay, no' yet. Soon, I think. But he's no' yer problem right now. Boden is. And perhaps those men in the dungeon. Do ye ken someone named Tomas?"

Anders' face went blank, then he shook his head. "Nay, I dinna think so."

She huffed out a sigh. Perhaps that was good. Perhaps not. He might recognize Tomas if he saw him, but if the new strangers were hostile to Anders, she didn't want them to see him. "I had hoped to break the news about ye to the laird privately, and to have Maighread with me so we would keep ye out of the dungeon. Ye being out here has made that much more difficult to do."

He ran a hand through his dark hair, frowning. "I'm sorry lass. I wasna thinking."

"Mayhap that blow to yer head did more than hide yer memories from ye. It stole yer sense."

The creases on Anders's forehead deepened and he shook his head. "An unsettling thought, to be sure."

"I'll walk with ye back to the herbal."

"The guard will think I left with ye. Will that no' cause a problem for ye with yer brother?"

"Mayhap. I'll deal with Boden if I must."

"Ailsa, I am sorry. I …" He looked up, letting the sun hit his face as if it was the last time he'd feel its warmth there.

Ailsa's heart broke for him. "If I could restore yer memory, I would. If ye kenned where home was and wished to leave, I would help ye. But I canna. All I can do is give ye time to heal and keep ye out of trouble until ye are well."

"I dinna make it easy." He gave her a heart-melting smile.

She gave him a laugh in reply. "Ye dinna. But ye already ken I think ye are worth the effort."

"Ye are worth more to me than anything else I may have."

She looked him up and down. "Well, the boots are likely worth something, but I'd no' get much for the clothes."

He laughed at that, then gestured her forward.

Despite his earlier despair at leaving the garden, he entered the kitchen with a smile on his face. That made Ailsa feel only a little better. She was returning him indoors to confinement. No matter how pleasant she tried to make it, it was little better than the dungeon if he was not free to leave it.

"Ailsa, come quick!" Excited shouts drew Ailsa from the kitchen late that afternoon. Had their new captives escaped the dungeon? She ran out to the bailey and instead of having a problem to deal with, happily joined the mob who greeted her parents and their men with shouts and cheers. Ailsa pushed through the crowd to them and hugged first her father, then her mother, welcoming them home. But she also whispered to her mother, "We must speak. Without Da. Soon."

Her mother nodded. "I'll come to yer chamber," she promised before the crowd pulled her away and everyone headed indoors.

Maighread had said her mother would be an ally. For Anders' sake, Ailsa was counting on it.

Less than an hour later, a soft knock announced her mother's arrival.

"What is so urgent, Love?" She closed the door behind her and took a seat on Ailsa's bed while Ailsa paced before her.

"We have a guest." Ailsa told her what she knew of Anders, how he came to them, what his injuries had been, and that Maighread approved of him. "And he canna recall who he is or anything about his life before making his way to our gate. Only the name we think is his."

"My, that is interesting," her mother said. "Where is he?"

"In the herbal. At first he was too injured and ill to be anywhere else. As he got better, both Maighread and I thought it best to keep him there until Da got home. Boden wanted to put him in the dungeon, but he wasna well enough for that." Now that he was, she didn't want to say more. Ailsa paused and clenched her hands in front of her. "I have feelings for him. He's a good man, Mother. I'm sure of it, no matter where he comes from or why he wound up here."

"I must meet this good man," her mother said and stood. "Now."

Ailsa's muscles tensed with worry. So much depended on her mother's sympathy and willingness to help. "I hoped ye would say that." On the way downstairs, she added the news about the men in the dungeon. "I dinna ken if they are connected in anyway. Since they arrived days after Anders, I doubt it. But 'tis a strange coincidence."

"Yer father will deal with them. Once we ken what he uncovers, we'll ken what to do."

At the door to the herbal, Ailsa paused and looked inside while her mother greeted the guard. Anders was again reading, but Maighread looked up and noticed them. Ailsa beckoned her to come out into the hall, and closed the door after her.

"Welcome home, Lady Sinclair," Maighread told Ailsa's mother.

"'Tis good to be home, thank ye. Ailsa told me we have a visitor under yer care. What can ye tell me about him?"

Maighread glanced Ailsa's way before turning her attention back to the Sinclair lady. "He arrived injured and no' in possession of himself. He had a gash on his head and nay memory. He has regained little in the days he has been here, but part of that time was spent suffering with a fever. He is healing and regaining his health, and I have hope that with time, he will recover his memory and ken who he is." She paused and added, "He's been nay trouble. I like him."

Ailsa smiled at that comment. It was high praise coming from Maighread, who generally reserved her opinions of others to herself.

Her mother studied Maighread for a moment, then cocked an eyebrow at Ailsa's smile before turning back to the healer. "Is he well enough to leave the herbal?"

"In body, aye. Though I would object strongly to seeing him sent to the dungeon. His condition could worsen there. And I canna believe being confined there would help him regain his memory."

Ailsa frowned. "Ye havena heard about the men Raghnall brought in this morning? They're down there now." She added what she'd seen and the little she knew about them.

"I stand by my words, even more so now that ye tell me that. He wouldna be fit to defend himself from other men."

Ailsa doubted that, but she suspected Maighread didn't believe it either. It was a convenient excuse to keep Anders out of harm's way.

"I will advise my husband as ye suggest. My daughter seems to be taken with yer guest. He has told ye naught else about himself?"

Maighread shook her head.

Ailsa shrugged. "He hasna recalled much beyond his name. Nay clan name. He thinks he comes from south of here. We dinna ken much else."

"South of here?" Her mother chuckled, clearly as bemused by the territory that claim encompassed as Ailsa had been. "He's a puzzle, indeed. Well, let me meet him."

Ailsa opened the door but stood back to let Maighread enter, then her mother. Anders set his book aside and stood, questions in his gaze as it shifted between the three women. Maighread went straight to her work table. Ailsa stepped up beside her mother and made the introductions.

"I've heard yer tale from my daughter and our healer. I wish to hear it from ye, Anders."

"I'm pleased to meet ye, Lady Sinclair, and will answer as best I can. First, though, thank ye. I've been well treated during my stay. I appreciate Sinclair's hospitality."

Ailsa watched with interest as he set about charming her mother, telling her what he could, which wasn't much. As he had to her, he apologized for not being able to reveal more about himself, and repeated that as yet, he had no more answers to give. When his gaze shifted to her, she gave him a supportive nod.

"Ye say ye sometimes see images in dreams. What sort of images?"

Anders pulled his attention back to her mother and shrugged. "Faces mostly. Some scenery. Trees, water from the deck of a sailing vessel. The beach below this keep, I think. Never enough to help."

"What about yer parents, lad? Do ye recognize them among the faces ye see? Do ye have a wife or bairns of yer own among them?"

Ailsa held herself still, trying not to distract Anders. Her heart constricted painfully, and she feared he'd see her reaction in her eyes. Her mother trying to jog his memory was one thing, but asking if he had a family of his own waiting for him somewhere should have gotten more of a reaction that it did. That knowledge was important to both of them, but her mother's question didn't seem to help. Anders looked more crestfallen, and more frustrated the more he tried to summon answers that would satisfy her.

"I'm sorry, Lady Sinclair. I dinna ken." His gaze shifted from her mother to her, grief and apology written plainly on his face. She hoped her mother didn't recognize how much that lack hurt both of them.

"I'm sorry ye are going through this," Ailsa's mother told him. "It must be vexing. Maighread recommends ye remain in the keep until ye ken more about yerself. I will make arrangements for ye once I've spoken to the laird."

"Lady—"

"*Dinna fash.* I dinna propose to allow ye to be sent to the dungeon. Maighread will keep ye under her care as she sees fit."

Anders bowed his head in acknowledgement. "Thank ye for that."

"Ye are welcome, Anders. Ailsa, attend me, please."

Ailsa followed her mother, but glanced back in time to see Anders give her a smile. He knew she had influenced her mother. His acknowledgement warmed her. He didn't take her efforts for granted. She nodded and went out, closing the door behind her.

"What did ye think, Mother?"

"He is everything ye said, Daughter. Handsome, too, and clearly taken with ye. I saw how his gaze kept moving back to ye each time he finished answering my questions. But as complicated as his situation may be, if ye are harboring such feelings for him as I think ye are, yer situation is complicated, as well. Among the agreements yer laird and father reached with the Norse king for the clan, Sinclair has received an offer to betroth ye to one of the king's sons. Yer da intends to speak to ye about it, but I must tell ye he is in favor of the match."

Ailsa's belly twisted. She clamped her lips together and shook her head. "I … Mother, I dinna think I can accept. No' now. Da will be angry, but how can I?"

"Yer da will be angry at first, and disappointed the agreement he worked hard to make favorable for Sinclair may no' suit ye. But Daughter, ye mustna tell him nay. No' yet. Ye are infatuated with Anders. As ye find out more about him, especially if he recalls a wife and bairns, ye may find that attraction will fade. Ye must take the time to honor yer da's intention. I will support ye as far as I am able, but if ye back yer da into a corner, and I ken ye are capable of doing that, I must stand with my husband and laird. Remember that."

Ailsa's vision swam, tears filled her eyes but she refused to shed them. "I will do my best."

"Do better than that, lass. 'Tis important."

CHAPTER 9

*A*nders watched Ailsa and her mother leave the herbal, grateful that one worry had been lifted from his shoulders. He would not be sent from the herbal to the dungeon.

As soon as Ailsa and her mother left the chamber, Maighread busied herself gathering together supplies of poultices and wrappings.

"Thank ye, Maighread, for taking care of me, and for anything ye did to convince yer Lady to continue extending me hospitality."

"Ye did that yerself, lad. Ye have manners, ye do. The Lady noticed. I had my say, and Ailsa spoke up for ye as well. Ye have friends here."

"Ye canna ken how much that means to me." He gestured at the supplies she was putting in a bag. "Are ye going somewhere? Has there been a battle?"

"Nay, lad. Some strange men have been put in the dungeon. I'm off to see to any injuries they may have."

She headed out before Anders could open his mouth to ask another question, leaving him alone to think. More strangers? Now he recalled Ailsa mentioning them while she berated him for leaving the herbal. At the time, he'd been smarting from his own thoughtlessness and her censure, and had missed the significance of her statement.

Could they be from the *birlinn* Murdo mentioned? Is that how he wound up on that beach, washed overboard and lost from the ship in the storm? Why couldn't he remember? The name Tomas meant nothing to him. Should it? He began to pace, trying to stimulate some hint of answers. But nothing came. He needed to see those men. To speak to them. He might be part of their crew and they could tell him who he was.

That thought stopped him. Ailsa said Sinclair didn't get along with its neighbors. If they were from nearby, they could be in danger in a Sinclair dungeon. Sinclair might see them as enemy spies, arriving under the cover of the storm to find out what they could about the Sinclair holdings and castle. They'd be hanged.

And if he was one of them, Lady Sinclair's protection would not be enough to keep him from hanging right along with them.

But if Lady Sinclair was truly going to be an ally, she might have ideas of her own to help him. Ailsa trusted her. He trusted Ailsa. He had no choice but to give her mother a chance.

He should focus instead on finding other ways to stimulate his memory, such as his walk in the gardens earlier. The change in scenery seemed to have helped. Where else could he go? Who else could he talk to? Maighread had worked wonders for him. Thinking about Lady Sinclair's questions, Anders struggled to imagine his family. A father, a mother, a brother, but no images came to him. Did he have a sister? More siblings than one of each? A best friend? Nothing.

But as he considered how much trouble he and the men in the dungeon might be in, faces started to come back to him. A man standing at the tiller, studying the sky. He closed his eyes and let the image expand until he saw men seated at the oars, fighting to turn their *birlinn* to a wee beach they'd spotted in a lightning flash.

Were they the men in the dungeon? If they were with him and they'd stayed in the area trying to find him, he needed to see them, to let them know he was alive, if not entirely well. To find a way to get them all out of here. But how? He was in no shape to free them.

He needed to talk to Ailsa, to enlist her help to find out who they were. If they were in danger here, she might be able to help in freeing those men or convincing her father to let them go. And to let him go with them.

But could he trust her? He'd had this concern ever since she told him about Sinclair's lack of nearby allies. Would she stop seeing him as an injured guest, as a friend, as a man she was attracted to? He'd rather be a potential lover, and possibly something even more important. Could he leave her? He didn't want to, but he might be forced to. She might hate him and betray him to her father.

Could he take that chance?

And could he ask Ailsa to risk helping more strangers? He couldn't predict what her father would do to her.

Frustrated, he resumed stalking around the herbal, his thoughts running in circles as fruitlessly as his feet.

AFTER SUPPER, Ailsa's father called her mother, Boden, and the guard captain Raghnall with her into the laird's solar to hear why Sinclair had filled with strangers during his absence. Her father wasn't happy, but after Raghnall mentioned the beached *birlinn* and nearly a dozen men combing the woods looking for shelter and trying to avoid the castle, Boden spoke up.

"I think they meant to spy on us."

"'Tis likely," the laird replied. "Why beach on Sinclair land if they didna mean to do that?"

"They claimed some of them needed some time on land after

getting tossed about in the storm a few nights before we found them," Raghnall explained. "They didna want to name their clan, but seemed most eager to leave rather than to pose a threat."

"They looked worn," Ailsa interjected. "I wanted them treated as guests despite their reluctance to name their clan, but Raghnall insisted the only safe place to put them was the dungeon, and Boden also insisted. So, I have seen them provided with a few comforts, such as warm bedding and the same meals as the rest of the clan."

"A waste, if ye ask me," Boden said. "They're here to cause trouble."

"They havena had any chance to do so," Ailsa argued, "and if Raghnall's men hadna found them, they might have been gone from our territory by now."

"Might have," Boden parroted and snorted.

"Ailsa's instinct was a good one," her mother said, speaking up for the first time. "If they are truly strangers and potential allies, we dinna want to make enemies of them, and if they are from a hostile clan, it harms none to show them kindness that may improve relations between our clans."

Her father listened as her mother spoke, but didn't react. "I'll see them tomorrow," he said and dismissed her and her brother.

Ailsa could see that her father was tired from the trip down from Kirkwall. Her mother, too. Likely they would share a dram and talk a wee before heading up to bed. She hoped they slept well so her father's thinking would be clear on the morrow.

She could also see the walls closing in on Anders. Her father would speak to the men in the dungeon, and would likely conclude he was somehow connected to them. She harbored that suspicion herself, but since Anders couldn't remember anything, she couldn't confirm it. Nor would her father be able to. And if Anders wasn't one of theirs, they wouldn't know who his clan was. Ailsa suspected that he was someone important in his clan, even a clan chief's son, given his manners, his intellect, and the quality of his boots. But if he belonged with the men in the dungeon, she knew she'd best keep that idea to herself. He wasn't well enough to withstand a harsh interrogation such as Boden would want to deliver, and his lack of memory would frustrate her father, especially after what her mother had told her about the betrothal offer he came home with from Orkney. Da would resent the presence of another man, one who'd captured Ailsa's interest, and perhaps her heart. Was Anders important enough in his own clan to compete with a son of the Norse king?

If only he could remember who he was.

As she moved toward the solar's door, she fretted. Had her mother told her da about Anders yet? Had Raghnall? Surely Boden had. Hadn't he? Ailsa worried that he suspected Anders was lying about not recalling who he was or where he came from. She'd been surprised Anders hadn't come up in the conversation. Perhaps they had yet to tell her father. Or perhaps Mother kept Boden quiet.

She needed to speak to her mother again, in private.

Boden grabbed Ailsa's arm as soon as they were outside the laird's solar with the door shut behind them. She tensed, trying to hide the irritation her brother's presumption caused, then pulled her arm free. She was headed for the great hall, up the stairs and to her own bed. She didn't need to listen to him rant about dangers from their guests.

Boden glared at her and crossed his arms.

She glared back. "What?" She planted her fists on her hips, daring him to make a scene that would draw their parents out of the solar to intervene.

"Ye didna tell Da all ye ken, did ye? We've another stranger within our walls, one ye are hiding."

Ailsa's stomach dropped to her boots. "I'm doing nay such

thing. Ye saw him," she reminded him, waving a hand in the general direction of the herbal. "Maighread is caring for him." She had to brazen it out, but it was a risky strategy. Boden wouldn't protect Anders.

"A few of the lasses are whispering about the handsomest man they've ever seen walking about in the kitchen garden. Some are jealous that ye are keeping him to yerself. Your secret is out, and Da will soon ken about him. What do ye say to that, Sister?"

Damn, her brother must have been talking to some of the lasses who worked in the kitchen gardens. So, he was jealous, was he? At nearly eighteen, Boden had been eager for female attention for years. But his combative personality and short temper tended to make the lasses keep their distance from him—as much as they could, given that he was the heir. "Why would I tell ye anything? Ye'll only run to Da."

"I'm the heir. 'Tis my job to protect Sinclair."

Ailsa looked around, waving her hand toward the great hall as she did so. "And a fine job ye are doing, Brother. Sinclair still stands, and to my certain knowledge, no one has died lately. Da is still laird and mother is still lady and chatelaine."

"Ye have a lover hidden in the herbal. And he's no' one of us."

Ailsa's laugh came out sounding more like a shriek. She pressed her lips together and silenced it to keep from drawing their parents out of the solar, though she enjoyed how her derision infuriated Boden. But really, a lover? If only he knew how she wished for that, and how impossible it seemed. "A mysterious stranger is my lover? Ye've been in the whisky again, have ye?"

Boden stepped back from her, consternation flashing in his eyes for a moment before he went on the offensive again. "Suppose I go tell Da right now?"

"Suppose ye are wrong? How embarrassed will ye be?" Should she tell him that their mother knew all about Anders and had met him already? Nay, not yet. Let him keep digging until the hole was deep enough to swallow him and his obnoxious accusations.

"How embarrassed will Da be for yer Orkney betrothed to find ye are ruined?"

This time, Ailsa didn't hold back her shriek of frustrated outrage. "Ye are a fool, Boden. Accusations like that will come back on ye."

"I doubt it. I saw a man sleeping on a cot. I havena seen him on his feet."

Ailsa snorted. But maybe he had a point. If she showed him Anders in the herbal with Maighread's sharp eye on him, maybe he'd drop this nonsense. She couldn't deny Anders being here. He'd made certain of that when he visited the kitchen and the gardens with Maesie. But she could prove they werena lovers and silence her brother. "Come with me."

"To the herbal? Or have ye moved him to a chamber upstairs? Near yers?"

"Ye will see." She led him to the herbal and opened the door. Anders sat across from Maighread, reading while she chopped herbs for some potion. "There is yer stranger, brother. A stranger only to ye. Maighread kens him well and has cared for him since he arrived injured, as ye saw already."

"A problem, milady?" Maighread's gaze shifted from Ailsa to Boden and back again.

"My brother insisted on meeting our guest. Boden, this is Anders. Anders, this is my brother, the Sinclair heir, Boden."

Anders stood and offered his arm. Boden, shorter by a hand's width, took it, looked up, and tightened his grip. Why was everything a contest to him? Anders appeared to match the pressure Boden exerted, but did not push past it, though he could have. "I understand ye like to hunt. Perhaps once yer father meets me, I'll get a chance to join ye," Anders said as he and Boden ceased their contest of strength.

Ailsa could have burst out laughing at how smoothly Anders showed Boden he was unimpressed.

"Dinna count on it," Boden answered curtly, his color high

and his jaw tense. "Maighread," he said, acknowledging her presence before he turned to go. "Ailsa, a word."

She and Maighread traded a glance. Ailsa shrugged and followed Boden out into the hall. "Are ye satisfied, Brother?"

"I'll be satisfied when he's in the dungeon or gone. A man like that has nay business moving freely about this keep."

"A man like what?" Once again, Ailsa's temper started to climb, tensing her muscles and making her clench her fists. "He hasna moved freely anywhere. He's been injured and ill with fever, only lately has he recovered well enough to sit at a table, as ye saw."

"He was seen in the garden, or have ye forgotten that?"

Ailsa quailed. She'd been so intent on defending Anders that she had.

"He's a warrior, no' a fisherman," Boden continued. "Look at him—nay man that size is an innocent stranger."

Her only hope to divert Boden was to go on the offensive. "Ye are jealous."

"Dinna be ridiculous. I am the Sinclair heir."

"Then dinna ye make ridiculous accusations, Boden. Da willna respect anything else ye tell him when he finds out how wrong ye are."

"I'll see about that," Boden said. "I think I'll go tell him now."

"He and Mother are going to their rest. I suggest ye dinna," she warned.

With a final smirk, he sauntered away, leaving her fuming in the hallway. Bringing him here was a mistake. She hadn't hoped to forge a friendship, but at least some sympathy from her brother for Anders' plight would have been nice. She should have known sympathy was beyond Boden's ability. His delusions had only worsened when he got a look at Anders.

She waited a moment before following to make certain he wasn't trying to sneak back to the solar. When she saw him climbing the stairs to his chamber, she heaved out a relieved breath. But the relief lasted only a moment.

Raghnall entered the great hall while she watched Boden disappear at the top of the stairs. She hurried over to him. "Have ye told Da about Anders?"

Raghnall frowned and shook his head. "Nay, lass. I assumed ye wouldha done so already."

"Nay, no' quite yet. The arrival of the men in the dungeon has distracted everyone. Da kens about them, and plans to speak to them tomorrow, but Anders never came up in the conversation."

"What are ye asking me to do, lass?"

After sparring with her disagreeable brother, Ailsa's eyes filled at Raghnall's kindness. He had called for her instead of Boden when the strangers from the *birlinn* had been brought inside Sinclair's gates. He trusted her.

She blinked back the wetness in her eyes. "Let me tell him. I promise I will do so tomorrow—early. I willna allow him to blame ye for Anders' presence, or ye no' telling him yet. Maighread backs me, as does Mother."

"I'll leave it in yer capable hands, lass."

For the second time tonight, relief made her blow out a breath. "Thank ye."

She had to tell their father about Anders or her brother would. He wouldn't obey their mother.

Ailsa was still furious that Anders brought this about by refusing to stay in the herbal, though she also understood his frustration. But he'd created a problem for her and a jeopardy for himself. Boden would paint Anders' presence in the worst possible light, and that would be hard to recover from. Her father couldn't be charmed.

CHAPTER 10

*E*arly the next morning, Ailsa knocked softly on her parents' chamber door. She was at her wits' end with the conundrum her brother presented, much less what their father would hear whispered around the clan about the *other captive*. Her mother answered, a shawl wrapped around her shoulders over her night rail. "Is Da up yet?"

"Nay, lass. He is still abed. The journey home tired him."

"Can we talk in my chamber? I dinna want to disturb him."

"Of course."

They settled in Ailsa's chamber. After she told her mother about her brother's knowledge, she asked, "What am I going to tell Da?" Ailsa wanted to wail the question like a wean confused and angered by something out of her control. But she was years past that sort of behavior. With Boden out of the keep hunting the day Anders arrived, she had been left in charge of Sinclair and had made a decision to save a man's life. She shouldn't feel so anxious. But she kept picturing herself walking into the laird's solar and telling him, "*Ach, I forgot to mention the man I have hidden in the herbal.*" He'd be on his feet and shouting for Anders to be fetched before she had a chance to explain how he got there. And

113

why. And her da would be within his rights to punish her and to execute a man who refused to answer his questions. Would he listen to her long enough to understand that Anders could not comply? She needed her mother to be there, but she also wanted to face her father as an adult. In this case, she wasn't certain how to do that. If he brought up the betrothal agreement in the midst of all this, she might lose her mind.

"Ye'll tell yer da the truth, lass, as ye told me. He'll have to meet him. To question him. He willna be happy."

"Aye, I ken that. I most fear he'll assume Anders belongs with the other men in the dungeon. Maighread believes he willna fare well there."

"Yer da might be right to assume he's one of theirs."

"I ken it. Truth to tell, I've had the same thought several times since the other men were brought in. But I believe him. Maighread does, as well. And he's come to mean so much to me. I ken it makes little sense."

Her mother stroked her hair and smiled. "It makes perfect sense. Ye feel responsible for him. Ye saved him. And aye, he's as handsome as any man in Scotland, and much more attractive than most. Ye'd be blind if ye didna see that. Ye have cared for him, and he has been appreciative of that care, aye?"

Ailsa felt herself blushing. "Aye. I still want to protect him."

"Nay, lass. Well, aye, that, too, but he's well enough ye want him able to protect *ye*. 'Tis natural, this attraction."

"That doesna help me deal with Da. He'll be furious if he thinks I've come to care for Anders. And he for me."

"Has he?"

"I think so. But he's cautious. He still doesna ken who he is or what ties he might have to others."

"I honor him for his caution. But 'tis time to bring him out of hiding. I will find a chamber for him in the keep. Getting out of the herbal and living among us may help him more than staying there any longer."

"'Twould. He is bored. I brought him books and a few friends to talk to, but …"

"But 'tis nay enough. I understand." She paused. "Did ye ken yer da had to fight to win me?"

"What? Nay. Tell me." Was her mother about to tell her there was hope for her and Anders?

"My da didna approve of the match. He wanted me to wed the MacLeod heir. But I had my heart set on yer da, and his on me. We wouldha hand fasted and run back to his clan, but before we could do something that would have put Sinclair and MacLeod at odds for generations, Mother convinced Da that the match was meant to be. Yer da may understand more than ye think, despite being invested in the betrothal with the Norse prince." She hugged Ailsa and moved toward the door. "If he doesna, Maighread and I are used to convincing him to see our way when we think 'tis important enough."

"But I am nay longer a wean. I must be the one to speak for Anders."

"Ye will, but ye will have help. We women do naught of importance alone. I'll go rouse yer da and tell him ye need to speak to him before anyone else does. Go down to his solar, and bring Maighread, too."

After her mother left, Ailsa spent a moment thinking about how she would begin to explain Anders to her da, then left her chamber. Her knees shook the entire way to the herbal to collect Maighread and to the laird's solar to talk to her father. Her mother was there with him, and smiled a welcome. Her da waved her to a seat. "What is this about, Daughter?"

She refused to face him sitting down. Once she'd explained how Anders came to be with them and what had happened since, she stood silent, barely breathing, waiting for her da's reaction. It helped that she was flanked by her mother on one side and Maighread on the other, who repeated what she'd told Ailsa a few days before, that Anders might be better, but the dungeon was not the place for him to finish healing. It was a show of support that she deeply appreciated. But the look in her father's eye still worried her.

"I will speak with him," her father said. "But more urgently, I must see the ship's crew as they are reputed to be of sound mind and should be able to answer some questions." He turned to Maighread. "Ye can corroborate all that my daughter has said? The man Anders has posed no danger to the clan?"

"Of course, Laird. 'Tis why I'm standing here."

"And ye, Wife, have met this paragon, I suppose, yet ye didna tell me."

"Ye are being told now, Husband, as is proper for the laird to be informed of a guest in the keep."

"A guest, eh?" He eyed his wife, a glimmer of a smile touching his eyes but not quite moving his lips. "Very well, call him what ye like, but I'm disposed to putting him with the other guests as soon as Maighread is comfortable that we willna kill him by doing so. See that he doesna cause me any trouble or he *will* move to the dungeon with the others."

Ailsa nodded solemnly and left the solar with Maighread. Her mother stayed behind. Ailsa wished she could hear what else her mother would say to her father, but perhaps her mother would tell her later. She took hope from how well he'd accepted their united front. For now, Anders could stay in the keep. She couldn't wait to tell him the news.

Stellan was losing hope. They'd ridden for the better part of three days, their gazes constantly moving between the sea, any beach that might be below them, and the forest and fields around them up on the cliffs. Seamus MacKay had not sent word that Anders had arrived, late but alive. They'd seen no sign of a *birlinn*, not Anders' craft, and not any others. Stellan had taken special care as they rode along the stretch of the Pentland Firth, but they spotted no wrecked ships, and no one wandered about the woods or glens they traversed. They might as well be alone in this part of Scotland.

But that wouldn't last. They were well into Sinclair territory by now. Perhaps as close as less than half a day's easy ride to the Sinclair keep and the coast that lay to the north of Sutherland's stretch of coastline.

If they didn't find Anders and his crew soon, they'd have no choice but to inquire of the Sinclair laird. He was as likely as not to toss them into his dungeon rather than listen to them, and Sutherland would be without both heirs. Stellan could just imagine what their father would say about this. Except for the mission to help the sick bairn at MacKay, he would never have allowed the trip on the northern seas surrounding Scotland. As it was, Stellan had delivered the herbs their healer needed a day later than should have been necessary to make the trip overland. It seemed they had been ill-fated from the start.

So, where was Anders?

Tormund rode at his side, his gaze landward as Stellan's remained seaward. The men with them did much the same, focusing on one side or the other and changing positions now and again to give their eyes a rest by looking at something different to analyze. "We're moving faster, Stellan," Tormund said. "Are ye in a hurry to greet Laird Sinclair?"

Stellan pulled back on his reins and slowed down a little. "Nay. And aye. We shouldha found something by now."

"Ye think they were captured and are waiting at Sinclair for rescue?"

"I think if he's there, by now Anders will have had his way with most of the lasses in the keep."

Stellan still had no sense of his twin, but he refused to think that was because of anything other than distance. Any other alternatives were too awful to contemplate. Anders lost at sea along with his crew and *birlinn*. Nay, that could not have happened. They had to have made it as far as Sinclair Bay, which meant they were alive in the care of the Sinclair clan. Or its custody. Either way, they would be alive. And they could be rescued. Or ransomed. Or both clans could go to war over them, in which case, Stellan would happily dismantle the Sinclair keep stone by stone until he retrieved them. "We keep going. Right to Sinclair's gate if need be."

Tormund, silent for a moment, quietly said, "I think ye are about to get yer wish."

Something in his voice made Stellan turn his head to look at Tormund before his gaze tracked to what had captured Tormund's attention.

"I see. No one touch a blade," he ordered. "Keep yer hands where they can see them."

Sinclairs, at least ten of them, perhaps more deeper in the trees. Too many for the small Sutherland party to fight unless their lives depended on it. So far, they'd made no hostile move, but at that thought, one of their men rode forward. "Who are ye and what are ye doing on Sinclair land?"

"We're searching the coast for a lost *birlinn*," Stellan answered, carefully not revealing his clan.

"A lost *birlinn*, ye say? We seem to have found one."

Stellan's heart lurched in his chest. "Where? With its crew?"

"No' far from the Sinclair keep, and nay, no' with its crew."

Stellan squeezed his eyes shut. It was a foolish thing to do in the face of an enemy patrol, but the pain that lanced through his belly could have been caused by the man's sword in his gut rather than his words. *Anders!* His mental shout was powered by the anguish and fear filling him. *Where are ye, Brother?*

The silence, both physical and within his mind, was unnerving.

He felt Tormund shift beside him. "Have ye seen any strangers along the coast?"

Tormund's question dragged Stellan back from the agony within him.

"Nay."

"Then we must continue to search," Stellan ground out. "As soon as we find our men, or what happened to them, we'll leave Sinclair. Peacefully."

The Sinclair patrol chief signaled to his men. They rode slowly out of the woods and surrounded the Sutherlands. "Ye'll come with us and speak to the laird. He'll decide what to do with ye."

Stellan was torn. He wanted to continue what they'd spent the last three days doing, looking for his brother and his crew, despite its futility. Becoming prisoners of Sinclair would prevent that. If Anders and his men were not there, going with the Sinclair patrol would be a mistake. But before they showed up, he'd nearly convinced himself the Sinclair keep had to be where the Sutherlands were. He glanced at Tormund, who nodded. Stellan turned back to the Sinclair scout, took a breath and said, "Aye, we'll go with ye. We dinna want any trouble. We just want our men back."

"Ye dinna ken if they're even alive."

He was right, but Stellan hated to hear the words spoken.

"How long have ye been away from the Sinclair castle?"

"Three days on patrol along Sinclair's borders south and east," the man answered. "We turned for home this morning, and now we've caught up to ye."

Hope bloomed in Stellan's chest. "So, they couldha been found, but ye wouldna ken it."

He nodded. "For yer sake, I hope they have been. Let's go."

Stellan flicked the reins and got his horse moving, following the patrol chief, grateful that Tormund stayed by his side. The Sinclair had been cordial, but if anything changed and they had to fight, they might not win, but they'd take as many Sinclairs to hell with them as they could.

THE NEXT MORNING, Lady Sinclair drafted Ailsa to help her and Cook inventory the keep's provisions. "Since we now have so many strangers with us, someone will surely come looking for them. Until then, we must feed them. And if trouble comes with their clan, we must be ready for a siege. We must have food on hand for people and animals to last several months. That means we must be certain to have a good supply of flours, grains, vegetables and the like, as well as the meat the men will bring from the hunt."

"A siege? Truly? Why would we no' release them?" Ailsa asked. "They've offered nay hostility."

"Nay, they havena, but neither have they revealed their clan. And they are no' like Anders, who says he canna recall his. They are hiding who they are. Why?"

"Because they want to leave without causing trouble?"

"Once they do reveal their clan, yer da willna release them. He'll try to ransom them. That will bring their clansmen."

Ailsa crossed her arms. "What if they dinna agree to pay a ransom? What then?"

"We must hope it doesna come to that."

"What does Da hope to gain by antagonizing a strange clan?"

"Gold? Cattle? That *birlinn* they abandoned along the coast? There is much Sinclair could benefit from."

"Or many Sinclairs could starve to death over the winter before a siege gets resolved." Ailsa's belly hollowed at the thought of the possible hardship facing them. "Da should talk to them, then let them go."

Her mother ignored her. "Cook, ye ken what to do. I need a list of supplies and amounts, the status of harvesting the kitchen gardens and orchard, how long they're likely to last. The laird has sent men out to hunt, so ye will have a good supply of meat to salt, and as long as the weather cooperates, the lads will fish. The stable master and head fisherman are aware. If trouble starts, the orchard may be denied to us since it lies outside the inner wall. 'Tis too soon to harvest much ripe fruit, damn it. Still, I hope if that wall is breached, the attackers dinna destroy the trees."

Cook nodded, her expression grim.

Ailsa listened with dismay a heavy weight on her chest. There was so much at stake."What else must be done to protect us?"

Lady Sinclair turned to her. "Yer da is meeting with Raghnall and the keep's craftsmen, the blacksmith, stonemason, and such. They'll ensure we have sufficient weapons and ironmongery on hand, and that any weak spots in the walls are repaired." She crossed her arms, clearly worried. "We canna ken how long a siege might last. 'Twill be hard on all of us if it lasts into the winter."

"And the men in the dungeon? Hardest of all on them?" Ailsa hated to ask the question, but the course her father seemed determined to set Sinclair on was a path that would lead, at least, to trouble. At worst, to many deaths. No wonder her mother looked fraught.

"'Twill depend on who those men are, what yer da demands of their clan, and whether their clan will negotiate for them," Ailsa's mother told her while Cook put her lasses to work helping with her stores. "I'm going to take one of the lads with me and count what we have in the buttery. The spirits housed there will help keep morale up, but they can also be used as weapons to drop fire on troops below our walls."

Ailsa took Maesie out into the garden to estimate what would be ready for harvest and when while Ailsa took notes. Her mother's words kept running through her mind. Not only were they preparing to ensure people within Sinclair's walls survived, they could drop fire onto a clan outside. And let the men in the dungeon starve. Or worse. She'd always known such was possible, but never thought to see it happen. The reality of it made her want to weep.

"Ailsa! Are ye listening to me?" Maesie demanded, clearly cross with having to keep repeating what she told her.

"Sorry, aye. Nay. I ken we have to finish this, but I'm *fashed* about why. Da shoulda let those men go."

"But he didna, so we have a job to do."

"Aye, we do." Ailsa prayed they never had to depend on the stores the clan had saved to get through a siege and the coming winter.

CHAPTER 11

After another hour of work in the garden, Ailsa was ready for something to drink and some shade. Helping the clan survive what her mother feared was coming gave her a sense of accomplishment, but didn't keep her dress from sticking to her back. The warmth in her face told her the sun had reddened her skin. But her fatigue evaporated when she came inside and discovered that her father was about to question the new captives.

He nodded as she joined the group headed out into the bailey, accepting her presence.

She was thankful she and Maesie had finished before her father decided to do this. It gave Ailsa another chance to ensure her orders for their comfort were still being followed and had not been rescinded by her brother. She wouldn't put it past Boden, who was also in the group with her father. He was quick to judge, and if someone was in the dungeon, his philosophy was that they must deserve to be there and suffer for it.

Raghnall and a few of his men stood off to the side at the guard post, keeping an eye on everyone. More of his men waited at the top of the stairs. Ailsa knew the prisoners were not armed.

They'd been searched before they were brought inside Sinclair's gates. But that didn't make them helpless. The iron bars between them and the Sinclairs did.

The men were unharmed. Her and her mother's early morning meeting with her father had accomplished what she wanted for Anders and for these men. But for how long?

How they answered her father would make the difference, and if this did not go well, she would not be able to help them. All they'd told her and Raghnall was that they wanted to be released to go home. If they refused to tell her father where they came from and why they were on Sinclair land—a reason he could accept as the truth—she feared he would deal harshly with them.

"I'm Laird Sinclair," her father began. She appreciated that he kept his tone mild, even friendly. "Ye have met my guard captain Raghnall, my son and heir, Boden and my daughter Ailsa, aye?"

"Aye, we have, and we're grateful for the comforts yer daughter insisted we be given," the older man answered.

"And ye are?"

"Tomas." He named the other men without hesitation, but first names only. As before, he didn't mention a clan.

"What were ye and yer men doing in Sinclair territory?"

"We didna intend to be. We were sailing by when a storm blew up. Some of the men dinna have their sea legs for weather like that. By the time the sea calmed, they were exhausted. As were we all. We put to shore to rest."

"'Tis a believable tale, Tomas, but ye are no' telling me everything. What is yer clan?"

Tomas shrugged. "Our clan has naught to do with our presence here, Laird Sinclair. Only the storm and the rough seas. There is naught more to tell save that we needed fresh water. Our barrels were either lost in the tossing or sea water got into them."

"Sea water and no' rain?"

"Likely both, Laird Sinclair."

"Ye said ye were sailing by. From where? And where were ye bound?"

"Around to the isles. I thank God the storm caught us here and no' in the Pentland or we wouldna have made it out alive."

"So, ye came from—?"

"The storm blew us south."

Ailsa's stomach was starting to knot. Tomas was being evasive and her father was starting to toy with him like a cat with a mouse.

"Ye dinna sound like Orkneymen."

"I didna say we are, Laird—"

"Sinclair. Aye, I ken my name. These are all yer men?"

Tomas' eyes widened for a split second, then he dropped his gaze. "Aye, laird."

Ailsa clenched her fists at that evasion. Her father's question could be taken more than one way. But she knew he hadn't been asking if any of the men in the dungeon did not belong with Tomas' group. She was certain Tomas had not interpreted it that way, either. Had Tomas simply been surprised by the question? Or had Anders also been on their *birlinn*, and her da's question made Tomas hope Anders was here?

"Very well. Since ye willna answer me fully, ye will remain where ye are until ye do," her father told them, making Tomas frown.

"Laird, we'd like to go home. We've wives and bairns who'll be anxious for our return."

"How long they wait is up to ye. Unless ye are willing to tell me the truth, they will have to wait a wee longer." He signaled to Raghnall, then caught Ailsa's gaze and lifted his chin toward the stairs.

The message was clear. They were leaving. Or she was. Nay, he was also waving Boden out, and moving toward the stairs himself. Her da had learned all he needed to for now. But what had he learned?

Once they were back up in the fresh air of the bailey, he stopped them and turned to Raghnall. "Their reluctance to reveal their clan concerns me. But that also tells me they may be useful to us. I believe there was much that Tomas carefully didna say. They may have been headed from Orkney and around the Pentland before the storm caught them. Or something else entirely. I do believe him when he says they didna mean to land here. Ailsa, I strongly suspect yer Anders is one of theirs, whether he kens it or nay."

Ailsa nodded, reluctant to answer. But the time was right, and prevaricating to her da would only make things harder for Anders. "I have wondered about that, but Maighread insists he'll be harmed in the dungeon." She cut her gaze to her brother, who, as she suspected, was glaring at her. Because of her early morning meeting with their father, she'd stolen his chance to spring the news about Anders on him and blame her.

"I've already agreed he can stay in the keep as long as he causes no trouble. He's yer responsibility."

She met his gaze, determined to show him he could count on her. And respect her. "He has been since he collapsed at our gate."

"Good, ye ken what to do."

"'Tisna safe to have a man that size in the keep," Boden objected.

"I've given my permission," their father said and turned away, headed for the keep's heavy oaken door.

Boden turned to Ailsa with a smirk. "I'm glad Anders is yer problem. When he does something violent, it'll be ye that Da punishes."

IT HADN'T TAKEN Anders long to settle in to his new chamber. His relief at not being consigned to the dungeon felt like an escape of a sort. He had a hearth, a warm bed, and comfort that would not be available anywhere else. As Ailsa had pointed out, he had no belongings save the clothes on his back and one change of clothes she had found for him when his clothes were being repaired, but never used. And though the four walls here were much like the four walls in the herbal, at least the view from the window was different.

He crossed to it and compared its width to his size and shape. Unless he was sorely mistaken, the window was large enough for him to squeeze through, should he decide he needed to. That thought cheered him. Aye, the drop to the ground was long enough for him to break a leg or worse. Even if he didn't get hurt, how would he escape the guards' notice and get free of Sinclair's walls? If he'd misunderstood what Maesie had implied about another postern gate on the outside of the orchard, the only other way out was through the main gate. Even the seaside walls dropped below the cliff to the beach, or at best to shallow water. A fall from there would be as damaging or deadly as a fall from the land-side walls.

Those thoughts kept him pacing, alternating between worries and gratitude for his new abode until he heard a knock on his door. He opened it, expecting a new guard to introduce himself.

Ailsa stood in the open doorway. "I need to speak with ye."

"Come in. Thank ye for this." He waved a hand to encompass the room. "'Tis good to have a window large enough to allow in fresh air." Not to mention a slice of view of what happened in the bailey—and a possible way out if all else failed, by climbing down the tower. It surprised him that the Sinclairs would allow him such access, but Ailsa—or her mother—had worked magic.

"Aye, some of Maighread's potions can make yer eyes water," she said as she crossed to the chair by the hearth. "She's asked for the mason to expand the window in the herbal, but he's yet to make time to do it."

"I heard some excitement in the bailey a while ago," he mentioned, hoping for more information than he'd been able to glean from the noise. He sat on the edge of the bed, across from her, so she didn't have to crane her neck looking up at him. Being alone with her was giving him ideas. He wanted to pull her from her chair onto his lap, then lay her down on the bed and finish what they'd started in the herbal. But he couldn't. Not just because he'd promised. Because he still couldn't remember if he was unattached.

"Do ye recall my telling ye the dungeon was full?"

Anders frowned. Why was she asking about that? Had her father changed his mind? Was she here to see that he was escorted down to join them? "Aye, I do. Why do ye ask?"

"Ye didna ask who might be there. There are nearly a dozen men who put to shore after the storm that brought ye to us. They might be yer clansmen. Or they might have been hunting ye."

He folded his arms over his chest, pondering her surprising suggestion. What if he had been hurt while being hunted? That would change everything. He could be an escaped prisoner of his own clan, or any number of other things. Were the men he'd seen in his flash memory of being on a boat now also in Sinclair? His vision of them had not given him any sense of trouble. He'd thought he was just part of their crew. Once again, he cursed his lack of memory. Glimpses and hints did not help him, not when peril surrounded him. And the fact that he had a memory that might fit with those men? But the glimpses he'd gotten hadn't shown him bound, or bound to an oar. He'd bet he was crew. He'd be wise to keep that to himself for now, but their predicament angered him.

"Ye should ken that the men in the dungeon might recognize ye. If Da finds ye do belong with those men, he'll move ye there. Maighread willna be able to prevent it."

Anders had turned to look at the window while Ailsa spoke. He was glad of it now. She couldn't see his face and the irritation on it. There was trouble, and he might wind up in the middle of it. Likely those *were* his men. His problem was now compounded by their presence—and how to get all of them, himself included, out of Sinclair.

"They're being taken care of," Ailsa continued, still unaware of the effect her words were having on him. "Treated more as guests than prisoners, with good food, water and blankets."

"So, ye made the decision to put them in the dungeon?" This time, Anders did turn to face her, and he let his displeasure show in his expression.

Ailsa frowned.

Anders realized in all the time he'd been in Sinclair, he'd never once shown her this side of him. Yet she needed to know he was a real man, with real feelings. Not just hopes and longings, but irritation and even anger.

"Raghnall advised it," she said. "I had to agree. There just wasna any other place to put that many men."

"Ye couldha let them go."

"The Laird was away—but we kenned he would want to speak with them. Boden wouldna let them go either, so nor could I." She stood. "My father will send for ye soon. Mother, Maighread and I spoke to him. He agreed no' to send ye to the dungeon unless ye cause trouble."

Anders sighed. Another worry eliminated, though looking at Ailsa made Anders want to cause the kind of trouble that could get him killed. He dared not—for her sake. As long as her father kept his word, he'd keep his hands to himself. The rest of him, too.

"Why now?"

She shrugged. "Ye are different. They wouldna identify themselves save for first names. Ye canna. A man named Tomas seems to be their leader. But so far, they willna name their clan. I dinna ken what they're hiding, or why, but 'twillna help them with my da."

"Lass, if they ken me, they could take me home."

"Is that what ye want?" Her face fell. "Of course, it is. Ye have a life somewhere. No' here."

"But here, I have ye to console me," he told her, trying with his tone to tell her how much she meant to him. He couldn't use the words he would say if he knew he could have her. If there was no one else in his life. "No' as much as I could wish for, but leaving ye would be … difficult."

She wrapped her arms around her middle. "Seeing ye go would … hurt."

"Ailsa." He reached for her.

She raised a hand. "Nay, dinna say it. We will deal with that possibility if it comes to pass. I will be happy for ye, but heart-broken as well. And sad that I didna get to ken the real ye, with yer memories intact."

"This is the real me," he said, stood, and reached again for her hand. "All we have is now. Nay the past, nor the future. I am the man ye ken. The rest is history and possibility. Nay more than that."

"Nay? The rest is family, and friends, and possibly a lass of yer own. We canna forget that."

He leaned forward and pressed a kiss to her knuckles. "I havena. I willna, or ye'd be in my arms instead of standing there."

She gave him a wan smile, pulled back her hand and turned toward the door. "I should go."

"Aye, if ye must. 'Tis no' what I want. Nor ye, I think."

She took a step toward the door, turned back to him, leaned in and kissed his cheek. "Nor I."

AFTER RIDING under escort most of the rest of the day, Stellan wasn't happy about entering the Sinclair keep as a prisoner, but it was the only way to discover if there were any men being held here, and if they were Sutherlands. The *birlinn* the Sinclairs found might not be the Sutherland *birlinn*, but the coincidence was too great to ignore. The guard hadn't indicated it was wrecked. Perhaps he didn't know. But if Anders had time to beach it, he and his men were somewhere in Sinclair territory. Or here, in this keep.

He still hadn't sensed any distress from Anders, so if he was here, he was in no immediate danger. That gave Stellan some comfort as they passed under the iron-barred portcullis and entered the Sinclair bailey. Tormund exchanged a look with him that he couldn't mistake. This was risky. Perhaps even foolish. If Anders was here, Sinclair held the future of Sutherland within its walls, both heir and spare, possibly along with a significant number of its most valued men. Sinclair could demand of Laird Sutherland anything he wished, and probably get it.

Another man approached their guards as they dismounted.

Stellan stayed on his horse, so the rest of his men did the same. For a moment, Stellan thought the new man would be enough of a distraction that the Sutherlands could turn their horses and ride out, but he dismissed the idea. The Sinclairs would remount and be on them in moments. They knew their territory. The Sutherlands didn't. And they wouldn't leave any of the men imprisoned behind.

"What have ye here?" The new man frowned at the Sutherland prisoners, still astride their horses.

"Men we picked up in the woods a few miles west. Looking for a missing *birlinn* and its crew."

"They've come to the right place." The man turned to regard them. "I'm Raghnall, the Sinclair chief guard. Ye lot may as well dismount. Ye're going nowhere until the laird gives his leave. I'll take ye to yer men. Filib, go tell the laird we've caught a few more fish." He paused and eyed them again. "Nay, no' fish. Fishermen, I'd say." He laughed at his own wit.

Stellan fought not to roll his eyes. "They are here—the *birlinn*'s crew," he said, relief a warm blanket thrown over the cold uncertainty of allowing himself and his men to accept being captured.

"Aye, I believe so. Ye will be the judge of it, or they will, once they see ye." Raghnall studied him for another moment. "One of 'em looks a lot like ye. Like brothers, aye? Laird Sinclair will be pleased to hear that."

Anders! His twin was here! Stellan fought to keep the jubilation bubbling in his chest from his face. He dared not look at Tormund, but hoped he and the other men had kept their expressions impassive, too. A lot alike? He must look rougher than he imagined after several days of riding. He rubbed his bristly jaw, then swung a leg over his horse, dismounted smoothly and stood calmly, waiting for Raghnall's next move. Inside, his gut was churning with the need to take action. *Anders was here.* And Sinclair had to know about the Sutherland twins. Tales of them had spread around the Highlands since their boyhood. The price for their lives and freedom had just escalated, probably drastically. But at the moment, he didn't care. He wanted to see Anders and the rest of his men, to make certain they were well cared for and unharmed. As valuable prisoners, it behooved Sinclair to see they remained that way.

"Come along," Raghnall said and waved Stellan forward. Sinclairs escorted the rest of his group, but Raghnall stayed by Stellan's side as Stellan got the last glimpse of daylight he expected to see for the foreseeable future, and they descended the stairs.

Voices revealed the presence of prisoners below. Stellan recognized most of them. But he didn't hear Anders, which surprised him. His brother would normally be in the thick of any discussion. Raghnall had seen him. Where was he?

Stellan and his men entered the dungeon hallway, the several conversations among the prisoners there ceased, replaced by shocked expressions, perversely amusing him.

"Ye're late arriving at MacKay," he announced, then more softly added, "Where the hell is my brother?"

A few men paled at that question. Tomas glanced around, stood and approached the bars of the cell that held him and three others. "Stellan, lad. I must beg yer forgiveness. The news I bear is the worst possible for ye to hear." Tomas looked aside and pressed his lips together, then continued. "We lost him during the storm. Swept overboard by a rogue wave. We spent days searching up and down the coast before we came ashore to search for him on land. Some of these lads' men," he said and gestured toward the Sinclair guards, "found us and brought us here. If Anders is still alive, he's out there, somewhere."

If Raghnall hadn't mentioned having seen his twin, Stellan's heart would be in pieces. As it was, he felt sadness and anger for the pain in Tomas' and his other men's eyes. They didn't know.

He whirled on Raghnall and stepped close. "Ye didna tell them the man they searched for, the man they mourn for," he said, took a breath and shouted, *"has been here the whole time?"*

"What?" Tomas' voice rang clear above the outcry from the other men. Joyous whoops and cheers made the walls ring. "Anders is here?"

Raghnall pushed Stellan away from his person. "Until I saw ye, I didna ken he was one of yers," he said to the group, then turned back to Stellan. "But I have bad news. Yer brother was hurt. A blow to the head. He has nay memory of who he is."

Stellan took a step back and reached for the bars behind him, needing their support, his desperate grip holding himself up. Without the cold iron in his fist, he'd be on his knees. "None?"

"He remembered the name Anders, but didna ken if 'twas his own, but that's what he's been using. Ye lot never admitted ye were missing a man. A man named Anders. Other than that, I dinna ken. I havena seen or spoken to him in days."

"How has he been cared for?"

"Our healer, and the laird's daughter Lady Ailsa, allowed him inside to be cared for when he collapsed at the gate while the laird and lady were gone to Orkney. Yer brother made his way this far on his own, though he was in bad shape."

"Dear God," Tomas muttered.

Stellan now understood why he'd felt nothing from his twin. It could be that his twin was all but gone. No longer present in his own head. "I must see him."

"When the laird allows it."

Stellan released his grip on the bars and grabbed Raghnall. "Now."

Raghnall inclined his head to his men. They opened a cell door and pushed Stellan's escorts inside. Two of Raghnall's men pulled Stellan off him and shoved him inside another cell. "Ye will be well-treated," Raghnall announced, "as yer other men have been. But make no mistake. Ye are prisoners of Sinclair, no' guests. The laird will decide when and where and how ye spend the rest of yer time here."

And possibly the rest of yer lives. Raghnall left the words unsaid, but Stellan heard them, all the same. He gripped the bars of his cell and swore at Raghnall. "Damn ye, take me to Anders."

"Ye will see him," Raghnall promised. "When the laird gives his aye."

CHAPTER 12

Anders wasn't surprised when, rather than Ailsa, one of Sinclair's guards fetched him to meet with the laird. He didn't expect she would be privy to their conversation. So, he was surprised when she greeted him at the door to the solar.

"Da's inside," she told him. "I was going to talk to ye earlier and bring ye here, but Mother wanted a word with me." She nodded to the guard who'd escorted him downstairs and the man moved away.

"Is everything alright?" Anders' knew this interview was crucial. Had something happened to harm his chances of coming out of it alive?

"Aye. I just wanted ye to ken that Da will question ye closely. Ye must answer as best ye can. Mother, Maighread and I are on yer side, and Mother will speak to him in yer favor, but ye mustna lie to him."

She seemed especially concerned for him, yet nothing he could see had changed.

"I willna." It was the only answer he could give. It might not be true, but she didn't know that, and he hoped he would not have to lie—or stretch the truth too far—in the coming interview. His supply of answers was slim indeed.

"Let's go in," she said and reached for the door.

He grasped her arm before she could touch the handle. "Ye have come to be very important, very special to me."

Her gaze asked the question he dared not answer—not here and not now. How special? How important?

"Ye must remember that, no matter what happens," he added, wishing he could answer the question in her eyes.

At her nod, he released her arm.

She opened the door and stepped through. "We're here, Da. This is Anders. Anders, my father, the Sinclair Laird."

"Sir," Anders said. He would have said more, but knew from his experience with his own father that it was best to wait for the laird to speak. That bit of knowledge came to him like others had, lacking a face or any context. But his father's lesson in respect gave him a warm feeling in his chest. It might yet save him.

The Sinclair sat behind his work table, Lady Sinclair and Maighread sat on the other side. He was a large, imposing man, but Anders sensed more curiosity from him than malice.

"Anders, ye are a puzzle."

"To myself as well, Laird Sinclair."

"Ye have spoken to my wife as well as my daughter and our healer."

"I have." He moved his gaze from the laird long enough to nod to Lady Sinclair and the healer. He would have turned to Ailsa as well, but given the way she could capture his gaze, that would have taken his attention from her father for too long.

"Ye have persuaded them to yer cause. That is quite an accomplishment."

"Sir?"

"They have advocated for ye, argued for ye to have a chamber and a measure of freedom not normally granted to a stranger within our walls. I have agreed to their demands on yer behalf, but with reluctance. I warn ye. Dinna do anything ye will come to regret."

"I wouldna expect to, Laird Sinclair."

"Lying to me will be yer first and last mistake. Now tell me, what do ye recall of yerself?"

With that question, Anders was on familiar ground. He told the laird what he'd told the man's wife. The faces he'd glimpsed but could not name, the places that could be anywhere, none of which he could identify. Even the name he was using was a guess. The first one that came to him. "Meeting yer people, moving from yer herbal to another part of the keep, those have made new glimpses appear to me. But I still dinna ken enough to put the pieces together. To ken who I am."

He knew his voice conveyed sincerity. He was telling the truth.

Sinclair listened to him with a crease between his brows. Was it a frown of disbelief or a sign of concentration? Either way, he'd listened closely, and watched the same way.

Anders felt studied, examined, and found lacking. He didn't like the feeling.

The laird remained watchful for a few moments after Anders fell silent. His gaze shifted from Anders to his wife, and to his daughter. "I will speak plainly. Since ye arrived, ye have been given extraordinary freedom for a stranger in our keep. It may no' seem that way to ye, but 'tis true. So far, ye havena abused that privilege. But let me make myself clear. I'm told ye have spent considerable time with my daughter." He held up a hand, silencing Ailsa's quick intake of breath. "I'm speaking now, Daughter." He turned narrowed eyes back to Anders. "Hear me well. I dinna care if feelings have developed between the two of ye. If ye ruin my daughter, ye are a dead man. Even if her feelings lead her to … cooperate."

Anders didn't risk a glance at Ailsa. He wanted to know how

she reacted to her father's threat, but any move on his part would only make the man suspicious.

"Ye have swayed the womenfolk, but I warn ye, I am no' so easy to influence." He leaned forward and now Anders could see the determination in his gaze. "Now, there are men in my dungeon who may be able to identify ye. They may ken ye and try to protect ye—or may have been searching for ye to capture or kill ye. Either way, I will have the truth of who they are, and who ye are."

Anders was suddenly grateful that Ailsa had warned him about those men. If she hadn't, he would have reacted, and his reaction would have told the Sinclair too much about his hope that they could help him. "I canna speak for them, but I would tell ye more about myself if I could."

"See that ye recall what I have said as the rest of yer memory comes back. Have I made myself clear?"

"Perfectly, Laird Sinclair."

He waved a hand. "Ye may go."

Anders nodded and glanced at Ailsa. She motioned toward the door, letting him precede her out. Once the door was closed, Anders stopped her. He took her father's threat seriously, but as long as he had a say in it, he had no intention of staying away from her. He wanted to ask what she made of her father threatening him if he ruined her, but since he would never harm her that way, he asked, "What do ye think he learned from that?"

"I dinna ken. I'm sorry for his threats. Ye have treated me with naught but honor."

Anders nodded. "I wanted to ask ye what ye thought, but didna wish to cause ye any discomfort."

"Ye can be honest with me, Anders. Always."

"I have, and I will. And ye with me, lass."

She reached out and took his hand, squeezed it, then let it go. Anders tensed as his body reacted to her touch, wanting more than the touch of her hand on his. Much more. But her father's threats were too fresh in his mind, and he knew being caught alone with her, touching her, would be dangerous.

"Forget my da's threats," she told him. "He wants to protect me."

"As he should."

She waved that away. "We need to get ye to the dungeon to see the men being held there. I'd rather ye had the chance before ye must do it with Da present. Once those men see ye, I dinna ken what will happen, but I believe much will change. I'll escort ye back to yer chamber. Give me a few minutes to arrange something."

❧

AILSA'S FRIEND Tasgall caught her as she came back down the stair. "Ye willna believe what I just saw. Ye need to get Anders down to the dungeon right away."

"What do ye mean? What did ye see? I was about to find ye and ask for help doing just that. "

"I think 'tis best if ye see for yerself. Fetch the lad, and go through the kitchens. Raghnall is going to be talking to yer da as soon as he can get away from the guard who noticed a weak spot in the outer wall."

"A weak spot?"

Tasgall grinned. "'Tis likely naught, but 'twill keep Raghnall busy for a few minutes and delay him from fetching yer da. Now go."

Ailsa ran back upstairs and in moments had Anders moving. The great hall was empty when they crossed it. If Raghnall wasn't still outside, he was in with her da and time was short. Tasgall's grin had made her eager to see what excited him, so she hurried Anders along.

Anders came with her willingly enough. She was glad his leg had healed well enough by now that he could keep up with her, but his expression was puzzled. "What do ye think yer da will do?"

"I dinna ken, but ye would rather meet these men without him, aye? Apparently something has happened to make that meeting urgent."

They cut across a back corner of the bailey and went down the dungeon stairs. Tasgall met them at the bottom. "Ye probably have only a few minutes. Dinna waste them."

He stepped aside.

Anders turned to Ailsa. "Perhaps ye should wait at the top of the stairs in case yer da comes. Ye might delay him. At least ye can claim ye dinna hear what was said below."

She nodded and turned to go, but paused as he moved away, ascended a few steps and stopped again. What had Tasgall been talking about? Unable to resist, she went back down and followed Anders far enough to see the men in the cells.

Anders stood, transfixed, his profile to her as he looked at a mirror image of himself behind the bars of a cell. A twin! These *were* his men. His clan. His family.

The realization made her heart leap in her chest with joy for him. They could help him much better than she could. And they could take him home, where he belonged. Where familiar people and places would help restore his memories. But that thought also saddened her, making her body feel too heavy to support as she quietly stepped away. With a hand on the stone wall beside her for stability, she ascended a few more stairs, but she couldn't bear to move out of earshot. She had to know. The rumble of voices followed her up as the shock of the reunion wore off. Cheers and glad cries of Anders' name made her smile, despite her knowledge that this might be the end of any chance the feelings they seemed to share would grow into a love both real and lasting like her parents'.

❧

ANDERS' first view of the men in the dungeon stopped him cold. He knew them. All of them. And himself. He'd been right about his name, the part he'd been using. He was Anders Sutherland, minutes-younger twin to the laird's titular heir. Memories flooded back, from the ill-fated night when he was swept overboard in a storm to the next morning crawling up the hill and begging … begging! … for entry into Sinclair. And further, to the discussion with his father about making the trip, daily events and familiar people at Dunrobin swooped through his mind like startled birds bunched together and swirling against the arrival of a hawk, diving and twisting, leaving him breathless and weak. All the way back to the man standing before him, but as nine-year-olds, swearing a blood oath to each other that they would always return to Sutherland and would rule it together some day.

Now that they both stood in the Sinclair dungeon, would they ever have the chance?

"Thank God ye are here," Stellan said, softly. Even reverently. "Damn ye, ye are alive!" His voice rose as he reached through the bars to grab Anders and pull him closer for an awkward hug and the men around them threw off their shock and cheered. When the noise died down, Stellan pounded on his back. "A perfectly good *birlinn* and ye couldna stay on it?"

Anders took Stellan's face in his hands. His twin. The face in his dreams, his visions. Not his own, but his brother's. "I'd forgotten how much ye look like me."

"Ye mean, ye look like me," Stellan insisted. "I arrived first."

Anders grinned, his pulse steadying at Stellan's humor. He made a fist and took an easy swipe at Stellan's bristled jaw. "How long have ye been looking for me? Weeks, from the look of ye."

Stellan sobered and dropped his hands from Anders' shoulders. "We rode for three days from MacKay. Always watching the coast below us for any sign of ye men," he said and glanced up to take in the Sutherlands in the other cells, "or a wrecked *birlinn* that would at least tell us where to search for bodies."

Anders grabbed one of the bars between them and held on. "Thank ye Brother, and the rest of ye, too," he told them as he twisted around, his gaze moving from Stellan to Tormund to Tomas to the others and back to Stellan. "Seeing ye has brought me back to myself. I remember ye and why we made this ill-fated trip, all of it." But he kept his grip on the cold iron, the only thing anchoring him to the ground. He had his memories back! All of them? He didn't know or care at this moment. He had his brother, men of his clan, his past, present and, he prayed, all their futures, once again.

"They ken who we are now, since I arrived," Stellan said. "Who ye are. Everyone kens about the Sutherland twins. I think Sinclair will demand a king's ransom from Sutherland for our release. We'll be here a while, but we should be safe."

"Privately, we grieved for ye," Tomas said, joining the conversation when Anders turned away from the hope in Stellan's eyes. There was so much at stake. The future not only of Sutherland with its heirs in unfriendly hands, but Sinclair's as well. Each of them knew the Sutherland laird would not let this detention go on for long. And if the twins' lives were lost while in Sinclair, Sutherland would destroy Sinclair and damn the consequences.

But Tomas was speaking.

"Since our search of the coast failed, we believed ye were lost at sea. We dreaded telling yer father and brother. We believed if ye were here, someone would mention ye, and feared asking because we would have to reveal more about who we are to an unfriendly clan. Worse, once they brought us down here, we hoped to hear ye in another of the cells, but of course, we didna. We asked when we were brought down if we were the only prisoners, and they told us aye."

To protect him from more unfamiliar men in case they were enemies searching for him? Or to keep the new captives off balance and ignorant until more about them came to light? What else didn't they know? Anders' crew quietly filled him in on their search for him and told him they'd heard the Sutherland *birlinn* had been confiscated by the Sinclairs.

They conversed in low tones that Anders hoped did not carry up the stairs to any Sinclairs waiting above, including Ailsa and Tasgall. He told them briefly about how confusing the memory loss was. How frustrating to see bits in dreams and visions and not recognize anyone. "But I ken ye all, and yer names. If I'm no' entirely back to myself, I am close. Seeing all of ye helps, and so will going home. I'm no' betrothed or married, am I? I keep seeing a lass with a hawk."

"Mariota, my wife," Stellan told him, frowning, while all the other men laughed.

Anders laughed, then laughed some more, unable to contain the elation that filled him. He feared he might look like he'd lost his mind rather than just his memory, but his joy broke through his efforts to quell it in front of the men. He was unattached. He could love Ailsa. He *did* love her. He could have her if he could convince her—and gain her da's permission—to wed with him. If she would have him. She cared about him. She had spent hours, days, caring for him. She was attracted to him. Having lived his life as a man who enjoyed being with women, he knew those signs very well. But did she love him? He thought she must. He hoped so, but he swore before he left Sinclair, he would know. And he would have her promise to wed with him.

"Why would ye remember her and no' any of the other lasses ye are, ah, more closely acquainted with?" Stellan asked when Anders calmed down.

"If I kenned that, I might have remembered more before now."

"Will they put ye in here with us?" one of the men asked.

"The healer has insisted I remain in the keep to help my recovery. They have treated me very well. I canna complain other than there's little difference between being a guest and being a captive. I still think I'll be more useful there."

"How so?" Tomas asked.

"I can see and hear more there."

Stellan nodded. "How they have treated ye is to their credit. Now, how do we get out of here?"

"I've seen much of the keep and have a few ideas for where and how to get away once we find an opportunity. 'Twillna be easy. We must wait and watch and listen."

CHAPTER 13

As they talked, Ailsa's hopes broke into smaller and smaller pieces. Like pottery flung against a stone wall to burst into shards able to slice open any flesh that came near them. Like her heart.

She heard enough to know Anders lied. To her and to her parents. He had regained his memory, and he was plotting now to escape without her.

She had been wrong about him. About his feelings for her. His laughter when she heard his brother tell him he wasn't betrothed or married told her he took none of it seriously. He didn't have any feelings for her. He'd used her. His kindness, his calm, all an act to make certain Sinclair cared for him as he needed until he healed in mind and body and he could escape.

Now that his fellow clansmen were also here, they complicated his plans. But she didn't doubt Anders' lies would continue until he got what he wanted.

Freedom.

Not her.

Standing halfway up the stairs, Ailsa heard the commotion of her father coming across the bailey with some men. The time for Anders' reunion was up. So was her loyalty to him. She didn't know what her father would do when he saw the brothers together, and she no longer cared. She had to protect her friends. She beckoned Tasgall toward the stairs as she mounted the rest of them. "Get below. Ye are on guard," she hissed, knowing if her da thought he'd had anything to do with Anders being here, it would go badly for her friend.

Tasgall hesitated. "He'll take it out on ye."

"Better me than ye," she hissed again to keep her voice from carrying. "Go."

She headed up the last few steps as Tasgall vaulted down the stairs and took up the guard station at the bottom. His arrival wasn't missed by the Sutherlands.

"What's going on?" Anders asked him.

"The laird is on his way."

ANDERS TURNED to face the stairs. "Ailsa is still up there?" What would her father do to her when he found out what she'd done?

Tasgall didn't have to nod.

"Why are ye here, Daughter? This is nay place for a lass." The laird's voice boomed down the stairs.

"Dinna be angry, Da. I brought Anders to see if he would recognize the men being held here. Or if they kenned him."

Anders couldn't see the laird, but he could imagine the expression on his face.

"We'll discuss this later," Sinclair snarled. "Get yerself back to yer chamber and dinna leave it until yer mother comes for ye." As he came down the steps, he muttered, "Damn meddling lasses," over and over again.

But he went silent when he saw Anders standing next to Stellan.

Then he broke into a feral grin. "Well, that explains every-thing. The famous Sutherland twins." He studied them for a long moment, then asked, "Which of ye is the heir?"

"I am," they both said together.

"Come, now, ye canna both be heir. 'Tis said the elder is serious and solemn—and married. The younger is lighter of spirit and fond of the lasses. 'Twould be hard in yer current state to discern which of ye is more solemn, but I ken one of ye is fond of my lass. So, ye are truly Anders, and the man in the cage is the heir, Stellan." He leaned his back against the cold stone wall near the guard station where Tasgall stood silent and studied them. "'Tis quite remarkable. Ye look exactly the same, save for ye, Stellan, living rough the past several days. And ye," he snarled, turning to Anders, "living well under my roof, cared for by my healer and my daughter. Claiming to have lost yer memory. A convenience to avoid answering questions, aye?"

"Nay, 'twas gone, and to some extent, 'tis still uncertain."

"Just like that? Since ye left my solar? I'd best call the priest. 'Tis a miracle."

Anders didn't appreciate the sarcasm in his tone, but he understood it. "It happened when I saw my brother and our men. 'Tis that new, and that unexpected. I dinna yet ken how much I'm still missing."

"Perhaps more time spent with them will provide the answers ye seek."

"Da, nay!" Ailsa's shout communicated her understanding of what her father proposed to do, and her objection to it.

Sinclair spun around to face the stairs. "I told ye to leave, Daughter. Go. Now." He turned back to Anders. "Consider yerself lucky. If I hadna given my word to Lady Sinclair and Maighread, I'd throw ye in that cage with yer twin, but I promised no' to lock ye in down here. That doesna mean I canna lock ye up somewhere else." He glanced over his shoulder. "Tasgall, take this Sutherland up to his chamber and lock the door. Post a guard."

Tasgall moved forward. "Ye heard the laird. Come with me, Anders."

"I will, because I, too, made a promise no' to cause trouble for Sinclair. But I heard what ye said to Ailsa. She isna to blame for my being here. Dinna punish her for something I convinced her to do."

Anders noted Tasgall's frown at the lie over the laird's shoulder and was glad Sinclair hadn't seen it. He moved forward past Sinclair and let Tasgall give him a light shove toward the stairs, more for show than impetus.

"Is this how ye treat yer guests?" Stellan asked.

"Sutherlands? Dinna name yourselves guests. This is a dungeon, one that can be much worse for yer men and ye than it has been up to now."

With that, he started up the stairs after Anders and Tasgall.

"What are ye going to do with us?" Anders asked where he'd paused near the top of the stairs.

"Naught. Ye are going to make Sinclair very rich when yer da pays the ransom for ye and yer men. He'll be eager to do so when he sees the missive I plan to send. He canna refuse me anything I want, nay when I have his heir and his spare. If he fails to respond as I require, I can also send him a matching set of heads."

Tasgall, above Anders, stumbled on the last step. Anders shifted to cover for him as Sinclair began to chuckle, then to laugh outright, the sound echoing in the stairway as they emerged into sunlight coming from the bailey into the short hallway that led outside. Anders had never been so glad to see the sky. But also never so angry that his twin and his men were locked away below ground. Under threat. They were going to get out of here. He would find a way, and they would do it before Sutherland gave up whatever price Sinclair demanded—or Sinclair grew tired of waiting and they lost their heads.

"Why did ye do such a foolish thing?" Lady Sinclair demanded when Ailsa opened her chamber door to her mother an hour later. "Have ye lost yer mind? Yer father is furious. Anders is confined to his chamber. Ye may leave yers only to help me with the preparations for a siege," she said as she advanced into the room, forcing Ailsa to keep backing up. "People say yer da threatened to send the Sutherland laird the heads of his heir and Anders. Do ye see what ye caused?"

The backs of Ailsa's knees hit her bed in time for her to collapse onto the mattress instead of in a heap on the floor. "He did what?" As angry as she was with Anders, she couldn't bear the thought of him being dead. She should have turned him away. Mayhap his men would have found him and left the area before Sinclair guards picked them up. But he'd been in such terrible shape, with no memory of who he was or where he belonged. Without Sinclair help, she knew he might have died that day.

"Ye heard me."

"He canna do that."

"Dinna be naive Daughter. Of course he can."

"Mama, he canna. I … Anders …" Hearing Anders plot with his men—men he knew well—came back to her like a kick to the gut. She didn't want him dead, but he didn't deserve her loyalty, either.

"Ye have a betrothal offer from the Norse King. Which do ye think entices yer da more? The lesser son of an enemy clan or the *Norse King?*"

Ailsa dropped her face into her hands. "What have I done?"

"Better question. What are ye going to do about it?"

Ailsa lifted her head and met her mother's gaze. "What do ye mean?"

"Ye'd best be thinking about what Anders is worth to ye and what ye are willing to use to bargain with yer father to save his life. And if that is what ye want, to make him yers. There are plenty of Sutherlands in the dungeon. The laird can sacrifice a few and still get the payment he's demanded." Her mother knew nothing about what she'd overheard Anders and his men saying in the dungeon. She still believed in the *good* Anders.

"Ye would stand by—"

"I'm his wife, no' his warlord. He will do as he sees fit for the clan."

"And start a war."

"Sinclair has a powerful ally."

"Sutherland does, too, many of them." A chill skittered down her spine. Even her mother might be willing to sacrifice Anders. Did he deserve that?

"I should agree to wed the Norse prince. Then Da would have all the gold and cattle from the Norse king that he will demand of Sutherland. He could let them go. And still keep their *birlinn*. Without bloodshed. Without harm to the men in our custody—"

"Without harm to ye as well?" Her mother sank down beside her on the bed. "Daughter, we are discussing things that are no' in our purview. I ken ye have feelings for Anders, and he for ye. I havena spent much time with him, but I have seen the way he watches ye. He's a man who's never been in love before, but even as his memory and his old life come back to him, I think ye may remain the most important thing in his world." She slapped her hands on her knees and stood. "Or ye did until his twin arrived. 'Twill be interesting to see how he solves that dilemma."

Her mother's words shocked her into reconsidering.

Whom had he betrayed? Really, no one yet. Save her. She'd thought his interest in her was real—and she'd been wrong. But the rest—his kindness, his concern for others, were real. She could think of many times she'd seen him demonstrate his care for other people. Unless that was as false as the way he treated her.

Nay, she hadn't been so blinded by her own fantasies to

mistake that. She had overlooked that even here, a prisoner of Sinclair, he had a duty to his clan. To his twin. She'd seen and heard that fealty in what he'd said in the dungeon. Their discussion had nothing to do with his feelings for her.

Her heart lifted as her mother's observation came back to her. Had she judged Anders too harshly?

CHAPTER 14

The day looked to be fine outside, with a warm breath of air slipping in the window and out again, like the world was breathing. Anders enjoyed the sensation, but guilt tainted his pleasure, as well. None of his clansmen in the dungeon could feel this, or see the bright blue sky. For two days, Anders had paced the dimensions of his chamber, front to back, side to side, again and again, until he thought he might go mad with the need to act. The Sutherland heir languished in the Sinclair dungeon. And Sinclair held even more Sutherland men. Men the clan needed. Himself included.

He had no doubt Sinclair had sent his ransom demands by his fastest horse and most experienced courier. They were probably in Sutherland already. He hated to think how his father was taking the news that both he and Stellan were here, and that much more than the *birlinn*'s crew were being ransomed. Mariota would be frantic for Stellan. Would she ever again see her husband and father of her children? How could their good intentions to take needed herbs to MacKay have gone so wrong?

How long before Sutherland would arrive with an army at his back to demand the return of his men?

Anders was under no illusion that his father would willingly pay a ransom. He was much more direct than that. And with the coalition of allies he'd amassed, Anders didn't think Sinclair could stand up to him, even if Sinclair managed to get Orkneymen or the Norse king involved. Sinclair was in for a siege at best, a battle at worst that would see its keep destroyed, its men killed, its innocent women and children hurt—for what? And if it came to a fight, Anders didn't give the Sutherland prisoners a chance in hell of living through it to walk out Sinclair's gates as free men.

Sutherland knew that. So did Sinclair.

Anders wanted to talk to Stellan. Between them, they could argue courses of action, pros and cons, relative dangers, and find a way out of this. But he didn't have that luxury. The only people he could speak to now were Maighread when she came to check on him, whoever brought his food and removed his *chanty*, Tasgall when he had the guard duty on Anders' door, and, he hoped, Ailsa. He missed her already, and he didn't blame her for what her father was doing. He doubted she approved, but he had no way of determining that. As he'd feared, she was avoiding him now that she knew who he was.

What would she think of him, Stellan and the other men when Sutherland showed up in force to retrieve them, at great risk to her clan? Would she blame him? Had he ever told her why he and his men had been sailing by in time to get caught by the storm? Perhaps if she knew, she'd understand he never meant any harm. None of them did. Would he ever get the chance to tell her? And after what she now knew about him, would she care?

A GATE GUARD brought a missive to Mariota that a courier had just delivered for the laird.

"Where is he?" Mariota asked. Usually, they would offer a meal and a place to sleep, but the guard shook his head.

"He left." He shrugged and turned to go.

Puzzled, Mariota thanked him and went to find the Sutherland. As expected, he was in his solar, but the door was open. "Laird?"

"Come," his said without looking up from whatever he was reading, spectacles perched on his nose.

"This just arrived, Laird," she said and handed him the missive.

He eyed the seal with a frown, glanced at her, then cracked open the parchment's seal and unrolled it. As he read, his face went white, then redder and redder. Mariota sank into a chair. "What does it say?"

"'Tis from Sinclair. He has the *birlinn* and its crew. He demands cattle and gold for the return of the men. But he'll keep the *birlinn*."

"Does he say how many men? Are they all there? All well?"

He shook his head. "He doesna say, save that he does have Anders. He wants a boon for their safe return, or he'll throw them back in the sea—without the ship."

The relief Mariota felt at the news that Anders was alive evaporated in an instant. She gasped. "Surely he doesna mean—"

"Surely he does, lass. Sutherland and Sinclair have been at odds for generations."

"Anders and his men wouldna be there if there hadna been trouble of some sort. What happened to Highland hospitality?"

"Sinclairs and Sutherlands, lass." He sighed and set aside his spectacles. "There's more. Stellan and his men are also in Sinclair. They were picked up by a patrol while searching for Anders and his men, as Seamus told us he would. Save for yer son, Sinclair holds the future of Sutherland. Now, we must use the missives ye wisely advised me to prepare, to call on our allies."

Mariota dropped into the seat behind her. Her chest was

suddenly so tight, she couldn't get enough air. Stellan, captured. All her fears crashed out of her mind and into her body at once, making her heart race. "We're going to war?"

"With enough support, we will mount a siege. Sinclair will expect that, and likely started preparing even before he sent this missive." He picked up the parchment, frowned at it, and dropped it back to the table top. "Rather than do what Sinclair demands and pay him, I'll bring a thousand men to his walls."

"What's to stop him from killing the hostages?" She put a hand on her belly.

"No' a damn thing, lass, and that's why we will tread carefully. I ken we will risk some of the Sutherlands that Sinclair holds, and I dinna want to do that, but I will have to. Sinclair will reserve Stellan and Anders until the very end, since he kens their value to Sutherland. Ye can take comfort in that."

Cold comfort, to be sure, but Mariota would cling to it until all hope was gone for the rest of their men, and for them.

"We will take most of our warriors," he continued, "save for a few to man the walls with yer ladies ye've taught archery." He waved Mariota's objection to silence even before she could speak. "I willna let lasses go with the men. If it comes to fighting, they will be at risk of death—or worse than death. Seamus will bring MacKays soon after from the west to flank Sinclair. Rose will sail across the Moray firth, and even Brodie, if we need them, will come later, or come here to reinforce the guard. That is how we planned it. That is how ye wrote it in the missives we will now send. Ye will coordinate all the clans' movements from here, and keep lines of communication open. In the meantime, at Sinclair, we'll talk. Or try to break in. Or help the lads break out."

"They have both twins." Those words kept echoing in her mind.

"They do. I have thought it inevitable ever since Seamus told us Stellan had headed into Sinclair searching for the lost *birlinn*. He would not give up until he found them, or he was stopped."

Suddenly, he looked twenty years older. Stellan's heir was in the nursery with his nurse. Their second child was still in Mariota. But the fact that the next generation of Sutherland lairds was already in place didn't make the possible loss of his heir any easier to bear. She could see that, even amid the agony that thought caused her. "I'm so sorry," she said.

"Sorry for what, lass?"

"I never should have questioned whether anyone had ever found the fastest way to get to MacKay."

"'Tisna yer fault lass. I agreed to the race. It served our alliance with MacKay to ensure the herbs they needed to save the bairn reached them as quickly as possible. No one could foresee whatever befell the *birlinn*. But we now ken at least some of our men survived and where they are. We will do all in our power to get them back."

❧

TWO DAYS LATER, Ailsa stood on the battlements in the afternoon sunshine. The wind blowing off the North Sea behind her, salt-filled and chill even for late summer, teased wisps of hair from her braid. They wrapped around her head and tickled her face or stung her eyes.

Her father and brother stood nearby, and guards lined the walls, separated by only a few feet from the men on either side of him. A show of force that Sutherland appeared to be paying no attention to.

Instead, Sutherland was setting up tents in the woods where they'd be sheltered from arrows fired from Sinclair's high walls. She got glimpses between tree boughs of tent fabric, Sutherland plaid, men carrying arms and shields, and could hear shouted orders and the neighs and whinnies of horses being tied off somewhere further into the trees.

There was no conversation on the wall. Sinclairs watched

grimly as her father's prediction came true even sooner than anyone expected. Sutherland must have set out the same day the Sinclair's missive arrived. Her father quietly asked Raghnall if all the hunters were back inside the gates. Raghnall's gruff, "Nay," was his only reply.

So, there were at least a few Sinclair men out there. Men who knew the forest better than the invaders. Men who could harass the Sutherland forces from the rear, then fade into the trees. The hunters might not be armed for battle, but they were armed for boars. Ailsa didn't see much difference. As long as their supply of arrows held out, they might be a factor in Sinclair's favor.

What could Anders see from his window? Not much, she was sure. But he'd know something was going on. The stakes had just gotten higher—for all of them, Sutherlands and Sinclairs alike. She wished she knew what to do about him. She still wrestled with her feelings for him and the sense of betrayal she'd felt after hearing him conspire with his brother and their men. But her mother's words, and Tasgall's favorable opinion of him, confused her.

When her father turned to Raghnall, Ailsa feared what he would do. "Move Anders to the dungeon with the other men," he ordered. "With that force out there, I dinna want a Sutherland free to move about within our walls."

"Aye, laird. I'll see it done now." Raghnall went to another of his men and conveyed the laird's order.

Ailsa crossed her arms, dismayed at Anders' impending change of state, but also confused about how to feel about it. Now that she knew he'd lied to her, now that she knew he was a Sutherland, she could no longer trust him. Putting him with his other men would simplify guarding all of them, and keep the rest of the Sinclair keep safe from anything Anders might have been tempted to do to aid his clan outside their walls. Like finding a way to help them get inside. From the dungeon, he was powerless to act, but he would also feel betrayed, promises made to him broken.

Surely he'd know that the arrival of a siege force changed everything.

But Tasgall had told her he had lied to her father to protect her. What was she to make of that? She shouldn't feel what she felt for Anders, not any more. But he'd gotten into her heart. He'd been kind, gentle, friendly, curious, all things she valued and admired. He was the most beautiful man she'd ever seen. Even his twin was less in her eyes than Anders. He cared for her, too, she'd been sure of it. But was that also a lie? If so, he'd not only fooled her, he'd fooled her mother. Ailsa didn't think that was possible, but perhaps she'd been wrong. She blinked wetness from her eyes. This is what she deserved for letting a stranger into her heart. He broke it. How much more would he break before he left Sinclair forever?

CHAPTER 15

$\mathcal{A}$nders could see some of the display of men and arms on the Sinclair battlement from his window. The wall towered above him by enough to block his view of the forest beyond, so he couldn't see what had Sinclair up in arms. But he didn't have to see to know. Sutherland had arrived.

From his vantage point, it was impossible to know how long it would be before the fate of the men in Sinclair custody would be decided. There was certainly the potential for a grand battle, but he knew his father and he'd met the Sinclair, so he hoped he was right that both men would try to negotiate and avoid war.

Boden was a problem. How much would he affect his father's thinking? Anders worried that Sinclair might think he could win by, as he'd threatened, starting to kill his prisoners one by one, thinking Sutherland would cave in after a few weeks and turn over the ransom. But Anders knew that would set off Sutherland, and both clans would get the battle they hoped to avoid. It all depended on patience and how much influence the Sinclair's women had over him. Sutherland travelers had come to Sinclair seeking hospitality. Not this.

Sutherland would be setting up for the siege no one wanted

but everyone expected. Did the men in the dungeon know? Perhaps Ailsa or Tasgall would tell them, but perhaps not. Unless they overheard conversation between guards, they'd remain ignorant until a battle began.

Tasgall was likely on the wall. Anders didn't know where Ailsa might be at a time like this, but he wanted her safe, wherever that was. He wasn't sure how Stellan would react now that he'd had time to think about Sinclair's threat to their men. With Sinclair on guard against forces outside its walls, that could set off an ill-conceived escape attempt that would get Sutherlands killed.

Still, if he was right about what Maesie had implied, all they had to do was get outside the outer orchard wall. The forest loomed closer there. With less likelihood of being spotted, especially if they could make it out at night, they would stand a much better chance of reaching Sutherland's lines alive. He had no idea how to accomplish such a feat with so many Sutherland men at risk, and all of them save himself in the dungeon. It would take help from at least one Sinclair, and now that he was known to be a Sutherland, he wasn't sure whom he could trust. Not even Ailsa.

It might take too much time, but he knew how to get down to the beach. Were any of their Rose or Brodie allies sailing the area around Sinclair Bay? If he and his men could launch the Sutherland *birlinn*, they'd have help just offshore. Getting across the open glen to the woods, though closer, might be too dangerous.

Somehow, they would figure a way out and how to do it. Or die trying.

Anders wanted Ailsa, not war. How could he convince her to trust him, or to help him escape with the rest of the Sutherlands, go home with him and marry him there, all without risking her life?

ᥫᩚ

"WE ARE Sutherland's first line of defense," Mariota told the couple sitting around the table in the laird's solar soon after the midday meal. They were parents of one of the lasses interested in training in archery. Brighde and Nan, two of her best friends at Sutherland, were also present. They were both team leaders and trainers who had learned their archery skills from her. "Any young lass may train with us. They will be posted on the battlements where they will be as safe as can be in an attack against us, but able to help defend the keep."

"I ken ye began training lasses soon after ye arrived here,' the mother said, "but I dinna think 'tis the right thing for a lass to do. Certainly no' my Daviana," she added with a snort.

"Now, dear," her husband began, but a glare from his wife silenced him.

Mariota traded a glance with Nan. Their daughter had approached Nan about joining the training. She wanted to help defend her home and her people, like her friends were learning to do. The younger members of the clan were well aware that the laird and his sons were away from the keep and there was trouble with another clan.

"Training gives the younger ones a sense of safety, and of being ready to contribute to the success of the clan," Nan said. "They may never fire an arrow at an enemy or while hunting for game to feed their family. But they will be ready if they are needed. Yer daughter wants that same chance. And because several of her friends have already begun, she kens well what the training involves. She wants to be with her friends, no' be left out, or looked down upon because she isna doing the same as they are."

"Surely there are plenty of other lads and even lasses for this," the woman objected.

"Aye, there are, and many of them are already training. Just as the lads also train in hand-to-hand fighting and with other weapons. It makes them stronger and more confident. This does much the same for the lasses."

"'Twould be good for Daviana, dear," the husband ventured. This time, the wife didn't glare at him, merely glanced his way then back to her hands, frowning.

"I wouldna bring this decision to ye," Mariota continued, "save that Daviana herself asked Nan if she could train her. She's a good lass. We would be grateful to have her join in."

The mother's expression softened. She looked up, first to her husband, then to Nan and Mariota. "Very well, we will try this. If at any time Daviana changes her mind and wishes to cease—"

"She may do so, of course," Mariota told her. "Why don't ye go give yer daughter the good news. She can join the other new lasses in a beginning session with Nan in an hour."

"Today?"

"Aye, there's nay better time to learn than the present."

The couple stood and the woman nodded, her expression, if not enthusiastic about the idea, at least accepting. "Very well. She will be there." They left the solar.

Mariota sat back with a sigh.

Brighde smiled. "I can see that ye were a good laird by how ye dealt with that mother's concerns."

"I wasna laird long enough to be good or bad. That was simply acknowledging her fears and showing her the respect a caring parent deserves."

"Whatever 'twas, I'm glad it worked," Nan told her. "Daviana was most eager."

"I hope she's still eager after she develops some blisters and scrapes."

All three chuckled at that.

One of the guards poked his head in the door. "Another missive, Lady Sutherland."

Mariota held out her hand. "Thank ye." She cracked the seal and read, then nodded. "All is well so far." She set it aside. "I got one yesterday from Seamus with the same news. He and his men arrived and were deployed with Sutherland. All is quiet. Sutherland and Sinclair have traded missives, and there has been some shouting over the wall, but no violence. Yet. That gives me hope that all this will soon be over. Sinclair is still going alone. There has been nay sign of Orkneymen or Norse ships."

"When will ye respond to the Sutherland?"

"I'll write a reply when ye leave for training. I need to advise him that Brodie has sent men here, and that Cameron is home and will remain for the duration to be the senior Rose and to help me. I havena discussed with him what he would do about Rose if the worst came to pass. His responsibilities lie there, no' here. He is nay longer heir to his father and brothers." Her son was. Cameron knew that as well as she did. "We will need to have that conversation at some point. Since he just arrived, I dinna want to make him feel unwelcome."

"That will complicate everything," Nan said, frowning. "What would his position be, in that case?"

"He could become regent for my son."

"Why would he?" Brighde asked. "He has a smart former laird for a sister-in-law. Ye are capable of doing what needs to be done."

"I'm sure we'll discuss that. But I hope he will also foster my son, both sons if the bairn I carry is another lad. I imagine Mary Rose will be glad to have him. Or them. I dinna wish to create a rift with Cameron."

"It sounds as though ye are planning well," Nan told her and took her hand, knowing how sad it made Mariota to look toward the day not only when Stellan might not be there, but her son as well, sent away to foster.

"Ladies," a male voice said.

Mariota looked up and fought to keep her expression neutral. "Cameron, come in. We were just finishing." Had he heard them talking about him? It pained her to look at him. His resemblance wasn't as close to Stellan's as Anders' was, but he was cut from the same cloth. From the back, or in dim light, she might mistake him for either of his older twin brothers.

Nan and Brighde stood to leave. "'Tis good to see ye, cousin," Nan told him, "despite the circumstances."

"Aye, and good to see ye, too." He waited while the two women left, then entered the solar. "Mari, I need a moment of yer time."

Cam took a seat across from Mariota. "I want to send a missive advising father to withdraw and leave the fight to his men. He should be here, no' risking his neck in Sinclair."

"Ye do ken yer da, aye? He's exactly where he believes he needs to be, negotiating laird-to-laird with the Sinclair."

Cam nodded, his jaw clenching and unclenching a few times before he spoke. "I ken it willna work, but someone needs to talk sense to him. Aye he's the Sutherland, but he's also of an age where he shouldna be camped out in the woods in enemy territory for weeks—even months. What will a winter in those conditions do to him?"

Mariota shook her head. "I ken ye love him, but ye dare no' send it, Cameron. 'Twill make him more determined to stay, and it might lead to impulsive and unwise action. Trust yer da," she told him. "In my estimation—and experience, he is a truly wise man."

"Mine, as well. Still, I canna help thinking Sutherland would be better served to have him home." He paused and held up a hand. "No' that I dinna think ye capable. Clearly ye are. I see how ye are preparing for trouble to come here, and I am impressed. I just dinna want to be the last man in my family of my generation left alive—or without Da if aught happens to the twins. Yer son is years away from stepping into his grandfather's and father's place. And my life is now at Rose."

Mariota pressed her lips together. Any response she might make would sound dismissive, or even disparaging. Cameron was trying to help. She tamped down on her irritation and spoke. "I would like to send Beathan to ye when 'tis time for him to foster away. If ye and Mary are willing, of course."

Cameron smiled. "We would be honored, and would take care of him as our own."

"I hoped ye would agree. When he returns home, Stellan will be happy to hear that is settled."

"May that day be soon," Cameron said and stood to go.

"One more thing," Mariota said, stopping him before he stepped away.

"Aye?"

"I appreciate yer counsel, Brother, while we are without yer da and my husband. Thank ye for coming to help us."

Cameron studied her for a moment, then his lips lifted in a grin. "I see. Putting me in my place, are ye, Sister? Very well. I ken my role and I accept it. Ye have only to ask and I will give ye as much sage advice as I can muster."

Mariota rewarded him with a grin of her own, relieved that he hadn't taken offense. "We understand each other."

He gave her a quick bow and left the solar.

Mariota watched him go, letting her imagination play with the notion that he was Stellan. It was easy to do. Their resemblance was strong. But no man was like her Stellan. She hoped he'd be home soon.

ANDERS WAS of two minds about his new accommodation. He was happy to be with his twin and their men, but unhappy about being behind bars. Sinclair had effectively pulled his teeth. He could no longer discern what was going on in the keep, nor could he keep the captive Sutherlands informed and ready to move if a chance presented itself. And it was cold. Ailsa had provided blankets and Maighread had insisted Anders have several more. But there was no warming hearth in the space, only torchlight to provide a meager source of heat and light, and fewer of those since the siege started. Worse, save for one, those torches were removed at night to the area where the guards stayed.

Sinclair had made it clear it wasn't willing to negotiate the ransom demand except to increase it, since he now knew he held the Sutherland twins. Anders feared they were in for a long and hungry stay at Sinclair. He worried that his men, and the men who came with Stellan, would be sacrificed if food stores got too low. Why feed enemy clansmen ye didn't need when ye had yer enemy's most precious pair in your hands?

He couldn't fault the logic, but it kept him up at night. Ailsa hoped things would never go that far, but he could see doubt in her eyes when she visited, and the beginning twinges of fear that all of this would not be over soon.

It made him love her all the more. Whether she feared for her people or his—or both—it showed that she truly cared about those around her. And the fact that she spent every spare moment with him, no matter how exhausted she was, warmed his heart. He wanted her to rest, but even more, he wanted her with him.

"I've time to sit with ye a wee," she told him after she showed up unexpectedly with a basket of apples for the men on the morning after he'd been moved here. Tasgall stood beyond her shoulder as she passed them out, then kept his distance when she approached Anders and handed him apples for him and Stellan. So, a guard presence was still required, but at least the guard was one of the few Sinclairs he counted as a friend. "Murdo may come down, too. Dinna he and Tomas make quite the pair? If they ever talk about anything other than fishing, it's sailing or sea currents or the weather. Ye'd think they never spent any time on dry land at all."

Both Anders and Tasgall chuckled at that. Stellan smiled

when Anders passed him one of the apples, but remained on his bench, alone with his thoughts.

The truth was that Murdo didn't have much to do since it wasn't safe to take Sinclair ships out to fish in their bay with Clan Rose patrolling the sea just beyond it. Talking fishing seemed to cheer them and others in the group as well.

Ailsa whispered, "How are ye? I'm so sorry Da insisted on moving ye here."

"Well enough," Anders told her. He didn't want to worry her. "'Tis good to be with family and friends. The more we talk, the more I remember."

"Ye'll remember best when ye can return home," she said, glancing around, then turned to meet his gaze with hers. "I want to help, I want ye out of here, and all yer men. Safely."

"I dinna want ye to take any risks," he said, frowning. "Yer father …"

"If 'tis done well, he will never ken who is responsible."

"'Tis too dangerous, lass. I canna let ye do anything that will jeopardize ye."

"Ye have nay choice, Anders. Ye will need help to get free of Sinclair."

"Aye, but no' ye. Someone else. Murdo, or even Tasgall, if ye think they can be trusted."

"I wouldna have brought them to meet ye if I dinna believe they could be."

Anders reached through the bars and lightly stroked her cheek. "If only ye wished …"

She leaned her head into his hand and wrapped hers around his. "What? If only I wished what?"

"Never mind, lass." Anders gestured with the apple still in his other hand. "Do ye need help with the harvest? I can think of more than a dozen here who would enjoy a day in the orchard."

"And out of the dungeon. Aye, they would. I'll speak to Cook and see if she can convince Raghnall to allow them to help."

"If a few of his men are there to ensure the work gets done, why no'?" Anders mused aloud.

How many guards would Raghnall insist on? And would Raghnall agree to devote men to guard them when he had to keep sufficient men posted to watch the force outside Sinclair walls?

A few men could be overpowered. Or he might instead tell Cook rather than having to stand guard while their prisoners did the work, his men could do it without the Sutherlands' help. But would they? Aye, if it meant fresh fruit for the table and sweets made from the rest of the late harvest to sustain the clan a while longer, they would.

"Have ye a story for us?" Anders finally asked, discouraged at the turn of his thoughts.

Ailsa let go of his hand and he watched her with sadness as he withdrew his inside the iron bars.

"I do."

She turned away from him, and he wondered how many more times she would do so before he was ransomed. Or before it became necessary to help him escape to save his life, and she watched him walk away from Sinclair before turning away from him forever.

He forced himself to set aside those thoughts and watch her.

"Are ye ready for a new tale?"

A chorus of *ayes* answered her.

"Verra well. Do ye ken the tale of the Dwarfie Stane on Hoy?"

"Nay, tell us," one of the men replied.

She smiled. "'Tis said 'twas the home of giants."

Anders soon lost the thread of the tale, but didn't care. He could hear her voice and see the magic she wove for his men. She had begun to regale the group with tales she'd learned during visits to Orkney, so each time she came, she told a new one.

Anders' heart swelled every time he watched the way she did what she could for his men. Food was being rationed, but she snuck down extras when she could, like apples as they ripened.

He knew her largesse couldn't go on for long, but it impressed him that she tried, and that she still cared enough about him and his men to see to their comfort when she could.

While the rest focused on Ailsa, Anders and Stellan talked quietly. "Ye have strong feelings for that lass. I can feel them. Our twin connection becomes more intense the longer we are together," Stellan told him.

"Proximity does seem to fortify it, but so does powerful emotion," Anders reminded him.

Stellan nodded. "Do ye remember finding me after Alber MacKay nearly killed me?"

Anders thought for a moment, picturing seeing his twin on the ground, bleeding. "Aye. Yer emotions were strong enough for both of us that day."

"If we are separated again, we'll at least have that connection for comfort."

"That is nay a comfort I want to need," Anders said.

Stellan studied Tasgall and the two other Sinclairs in the dungeon with him. "I've gotten friendly with a few Sinclair guards as well as Ailsa's friends. Despite the hardship of the siege, I see their sympathies growing for the Sutherlands in their care."

"They are good people," Anders agreed.

"But they are Sinclairs," Stellan had said quietly. "I am no' foolish enough to think they would betray their clan and help us escape."

Had Stellan heard what Ailsa offered? Did that make Anders a fool? He had pinned his hopes on that very thing.

"They have the same concern we have about starting a clan war. If we were no' here, there would be naught to fight over."

"Except perhaps one left-behind Sutherland *birlinn*," Stellan groused.

Anders grinned at that, glad to see that his humor relieved Stellan somewhat.

Tasgall approached them. "Ye might like to ken that along

with the MacKays already here, Clan Rose warriors have been spotted flanking the Sutherlands outside our walls."

Stellan nodded. "Does that concern ye?"

"Truthfully, I hope their presence brings a quicker end to the siege. I will deny saying this, but if it convinces the laird that he canna win and he will release ye, their presence is welcome." He nodded, then moved away to watch Ailsa tell the rest of her story.

Stellan and Anders exchanged a look. Their allies had arrived. Things were going to change. If only they knew how. "'Twould be good if Tasgall was right," Anders said. "And if his laird willna back down, he decided to help us."

Stellan nodded. "But we canna count on that. If Tasgall does as ye suggest, he could be executed as a traitor."

"Aye, but I worry how long the Sinclair will wait to start killing us, one by one, as he threatened, to hurry things along."

CHAPTER 16

At supper that night, Ailsa quietly ate her meal while her brother Boden prattled on about how Sutherland was spoiling Sinclair ground, and Sinclair ought to do something about it. Their father listened, but didn't engage until Boden, seeing he was making no headway, mentioned how often Ailsa was being seen crossing the bailey to visit the Sutherlands in Sinclair custody. And why were they still cosseting Sutherlands in the dungeon with good food and blankets and visits by the laird's daughter?

"If 'twere up to ye," she bristled, "they'd be dead by now, and we would be at war. I'm doing what I can to prevent that."

"Ach, ye? Stop a war between clans? Dinna make me laugh, Sister. If no' for ye, we wouldna have these men inside our keep and Sutherland wouldna be camped outside our walls."

"Where would they be if ye had been here?" Despite her better instincts, she challenged him. She knew picking a fight with Boden was dangerous, but she'd heard enough of his war lust and wondered why their da didn't interrupt him and tell him to cease.

"They'd be in the bay, where they'd never be seen again, and this problem would be over, Sister. 'Twould never have started.

This is all on ye, letting in the first one. Coddling them. 'Twas foolish. It still is."

"Being kind and showing hospitality is foolish?"

"To our enemies, aye."

"They werena enemies when we took them in. They were strangers. Anders was injured. What ye propose, Brother, would weaken any chance of alliances among the clans forever."

"Is that what ye are after, Sister? An alliance with Sutherland? Through what? Trading hostages? Or do ye have a betrothal in mind?"

"What if I did?"

Boden laughed and shoved away from the table. "Ye have lost yer mind."

"I willna agree to a match with that Sutherland," their father announced.

Ailsa's heart sank.

"We're under siege by his clan, Daughter. Whether ye thought them simple strangers or nay, ye now ken they are no'. They are members of a hostile clan. With enmity of long standing." He waved off Boden as his heir began to speak. "I still favor the Norse for many reasons. They are strong and important as a bridge between us and the rest of the far north. Sutherland has no similar standing."

Lady Sinclair chose that remark to enter the fray. "An alliance with Sutherland is better than all-out war or a never-ending siege, Husband. This is an opportunity. Dinna dismiss it out of hand."

Ailsa was glad her mother had spoken. Her father's expression had smoothed at her words. She could always make him reconsider. Make him think. Her brother was young enough to be all for the fight, but her father had years more experience and should know what Boden's tactics would cost. Sinclair lives.

❦

"Damn it!"

Ailsa jumped in surprise at her seat next to her father in the great hall the next morning. Someone had just handed him a missive of the sort he and the Sutherland had exchanged for days, most of which he tossed aside with a muttered oath. The negotiation was not going well. They'd spent the past week dithering about the force camped outside their walls. They'd sent messages back and forth that did nothing to end the siege or to satisfy her father's ransom demands. The Sutherland force grew by the hundreds as more of its Rose allies joined the siege on land as well as posting its ships off Sinclair's coastline.

Clearly, he liked what he read this time a good deal less than he liked earlier communications from Laird Sutherland. "Da?"

"The Sutherlands have captured the Sinclair hunters who didna make it back inside our walls before the invaders arrived. The Sutherland wishes to barter them and sends an offer of trade."

Ailsa leaned toward her da and read over his arm. Sutherland basically said *Ye'll get them back when we get all our men back—all of them.* Well, that would not make her da any happier about this whole situation. Worse, she knew what her brother's reaction would be when he heard about this. He'd be ready to start sacrificing the Sutherlands in his lust for battle. That idea appalled Ailsa, and she feared his influence on their father was growing. She still believed there were other ways to end this standoff than bloodshed. But as the siege dragged on, she knew her da was starting to wonder if she and her mother were wrong about using diplomacy, and that working toward an alliance was a waste of time.

"What are ye going to do about them?"

"Naught," he said and set the missive aside. "They'll be safe where they are for now."

"For how long? Until we or they do something to end this?"

"I ken what ye and yer mother advise, Daughter. Dinna lecture me."

"I dinna mean to, Da. I only wonder how this is going to be resolved."

"Likely nay in any way ye will approve." He shrugged, grabbed the missive, stood and left the table before Ailsa could say another word.

His response, or lack of one, worried her. His frustration was growing, Boden was spending more time with him, and she didn't know how much their mother was able to contradict or balance the laird's plans against what her son proposed. The only thing she was certain of was that Anders and the other Sutherlands in their custody were in greater peril every day.

THE NEXT DAY, Ailsa's expression when she arrived at Anders' cell door told him something was very wrong. "What *fashes* ye, lass?" he asked as he stood to greet her. He nodded to the strange guard who'd taken up a station near the stairs. He would hear if the guard moved closer. The guard would be able to hear their voices, but he hoped not what they said.

"I've learned something I fear to tell ye, but ye must ken and tell the others," she said softly. "Thanks to my brother, the Sinclair has begun to think more seriously that he has enough Sutherlands to sacrifice a few. He can not only use ye for yer worth, he can kill ye one by one to force Sutherland to yield, until perhaps not the heir, but the spare becomes be the final inducement."

Anders' belly hollowed at the news. He had been expecting this, but had also begun to think that Sinclair had tolerated the siege long enough he wouldn't take this final and devastating step. This news, along with the feelings he had for Ailsa convinced him it was time to reveal his thinking to her.

"He canna kill these men. He will incite the war that we have hoped to avoid. The war we have hoped by his patience he was wise enough to avoid. Sutherland will pull down Sinclair's walls. Ye say Sutherland has been joined by allies. How many men? Can ye guess?"

"A thousand wouldna be too many."

"More than Sinclair can defend against if they breach its walls. Many will die on both sides. And for what? Does yer da ken why we were in the area when the storm hit? Do ye?"

"Ye never told me."

"There's a lad at MacKay who needs a certain herb to help him breathe. MacKay's healer asked for help. She was nearly out of it, and next year's harvest is long away off. Sutherland had the herb in plenty. So, Stellan and I devised a race to see who could reach MacKay the fastest. Stellan did, and the lad will be well. Thanks to the storm, I ended up here. This was all done for good. To help another clan's bairn. Does that no' seem a better way for clans to live side by side than the way Sinclair and Sutherland are now aligned?"

Ailsa's eyes filled. For his misfortune or the ill lad's rescue?

"I'm so sorry it turned out this way," she said, "though I canna be sorry for meeting ye."

"Nor I for meeting ye, lass. But now that yer father will turn to killing my clansmen, I must do more."

"What can ye do? And how can I help?"

Anders was glad they'd kept their voices down. He heard footsteps in the hall above the stairs, and someone greeted the guard, who answered. That told him where the man stood. He was still far enough away not to overhear them as the footsteps went on their way.

"My men and I must escape. Can ye steal the key to the cells? Is there another?"

"I dinna ken, but Tasgall will. But even if I could, 'twillna be easy to escape the dungeon, especially with so many men. Perhaps if ye and Stellan could get out—"

"Unless we have help, lass, 'twillna work. We must all go. It does nay good for any to leave without all the others. Those men left behind would still be at risk. We must all escape together, or none of us will."

He could see the effort she was making to take it all in, to understand why he was so intent on taking action, and on how anything he might do would affect Sinclair. And affect her. "I want ye to come, too, Ailsa. We can be wed at Sutherland."

"Da willna accept that. He will come after me, and make war on yer clan and yer allies. Nay, 'tis better if ye go without me."

Anders suddenly knew how a heart shattered, and how breaking into pieces could slice the inside of the body to ribbons. His chest hurt. His gut, too. "Can we never be together?"

She shook her head, tears glimmering and threatening to spill over once again. "I dinna see how."

"We must find a way, Love. We will." Or he would die trying.

CHAPTER 17

*L*ater, Stellan and Anders held a quiet conversation while the others, including the Sinclair guards meant to watch them, shared hunting and fishing mishaps they had suffered, to roars of disbelief and hoots of laughter. The noise they made was the perfect cover for the twins to discuss their next move.

"Ye were right that I have strong feelings for Ailsa. Ye heard her say her father willna accept the idea of our wedding, but 'tis the best way to end this siege and let everyone go home. I believe Ailsa still hopes to convince her mother to change his mind. Somehow."

"'Tis worth a try."

"If Ailsa is right and Sutherland has more than one thousand men camped around Sinclair, her father must ken he canna win at this game he's playing."

"Nay, he canna. Sutherland would be in a stronger position, except for us being in here."

"And except for one very bad piece of news she gave me."

"How bad?"

Anders let his gaze rove over the Sutherlands occupying the other cells, all focused on making as much covering noise as they could. "The Sinclair has tired of the siege and has begun to listen to his son's counsel. If aught doesna change soon, he will begin to kill a Sutherland, one at a time, until the army outside his walls breaks camp and leaves. Ending with me, saving ye for a final inducement."

"Well, that's some comfort to me," Stellan quipped and Anders forced a laugh.

"If Sinclair is fool enough to start down that path, 'twill do him nay good," Stellan continued. "Da willna accept the deaths of our men. He will tear down this keep and kill every man in it."

"Aye, and he has enough men to do it." Anders shook his head. "I canna ken what Sinclair hopes to accomplish, save that their supplies are limited and so long as he has ye, he considers the rest of us expendable. The force outside his walls can hunt and fish, cut down his forests, do whatever they wish while he is locked up in here. Once food runs low and his people begin to starve, he'll start tossing the rest of us off his walls if by then he hasna already. All save ye. For the rest of us, dead or alive willna matter."

"Where are his allies? Has he sent word to the Norse king?"

"Ailsa hasna mentioned that. I dinna ken. But 'tis likely that Rose and Brodie ships guard the entrance to Sinclair Bay, so if he reached out before Sutherland arrived, they willna be able to reinforce Sinclair by sea, and ye can be sure Da has patrols out looking for trouble from the landward side. Ailsa hasna said yet whether Raghnall will allow any of us to help harvest the fruit trees in the orchard. It lies behind the kitchen garden, much closer to the forest outside its wall than anywhere else around the keep. But we can only get out that way if they are foolish enough to let all of us into the orchard together. A few at a time leaves the rest here to suffer for any who escape."

"Even if we canna get out that way, 'tis a good idea. These lads need some time out of this place," Stellan said and looked around with a frown. "I dinna ken what the season is outside but 'tis colder here, and at night, so dark I canna see my hand in front of my face. The only light is around the corner and down the hall for the guard. Little to none of it reaches these cells. During the day, they give us more light. What if they stop doing even that?"

"Ailsa would put a stop to all of this if she could."

"Aye, but she canna. We are Sutherlands. We will tolerate what we must and do what we can until this is over."

❧

AILSA HEARD her mother's voice as she entered the kitchen after her visit to the dungeon. Maesie would be waiting for her to help with the plant harvesting. They still had to keep a record of what was left and how soon it might be ready to use. Ailsa didn't see what was gained by doing this every day, but her mother insisted.

"I told him to leave the cats alone," her mother complained as she stalked out of the kitchen. Cook followed close on her heels.

Ailsa hurried to catch up. Her mother's angry tone was not something she often heard. That was bad enough, but Cook's worried expression chilled her. "What has happened?"

Lady Sinclair stopped, whirled to her daughter and pressed her lips together, her fury palpable in the sudden silence of the great hall. "Cook found rats in the granary," she snarled. "Rats that the cats wouldha killed, but the few that are left are hiding and no' doing their job. Yer brother decided they were more of a challenge to hunt than the rodents, and yer father said naught against him. What sort of son have we raised?"

She whirled, continued her stomp across the great hall to the solar, and flung open the door.

The solar was empty.

"Where are they? I'm going to flay them both!"

She hurried past both Cook and Ailsa and into the bailey,

barely letting the keep's heavy door open wide enough for her to squeeze through.

Outside, Ailsa spotted her mother's quarry. Her da stood talking to Boden and Raghnall near a set of stairs to the wall walk.

"Ye!" Lady Sinclair charged forward, nearly knocking down poor Raghnall in her haste.

"Wife, an offer has come to trade one of our hunters for Stellan Sutherland. Can ye believe the bollocks on Sutherland?"

"I'll take care of Sutherland's bollocks," Boden boasted, indignation reddening his skin.

Her father laughed off his son's bravado.

Ailsa's mother's temper only heated while he ignored her. "Husband!"

"Now Wife, what *fashes* ye?"

"Yer son, 'tis what. I warned ye about him harming the cats. Now we have rats in the grains. Ye," she huffed, "laughed when I told ye what he was doing. And ye," she snarled, turning on her son and stabbing a finger into his chest, "are going to find and remove every one of those rodents. Ye want to kill something? Have at *them*!"

Cook, when Ailsa's father turned to her for confirmation about the grain stores, could only nod. Ailsa remained mute.

Boden put a hand over his mouth, choking back laughter. "I have a better idea. Kill the Sutherlands one at a time to convince the invaders to leave. The grain stores willna matter."

His mother slapped him, shocking everyone around them into immobility. "Winter is coming, ye daft *eejit*. Even without an army at our feet, we must have that food for the clan. The next harvest is months away."

She turned back to her husband, ignoring the glowering rage on her son's face. "Keep him in line, and set him to catching rodents—*now*—or the first person tossed over the wall will be yer heir. He hasna the sense to be yer successor."

"'Tisna a fit occupation for the Sinclair heir," Boden objected, finally realizing his mother was serious.

"Any occupation I deem fit is what ye will do. For now, ye will do as yer mother directs," Sinclair ordered with a glance at his wife. She stood fuming and tapping her foot, while her glare burned at her son.

"I should be on the wall," Boden objected again.

Ailsa had to believe her father was smart enough not to fall for Boden's whining. Her brother didn't have the sense to know when to stop. She had never seen her mother so angry, nay, enraged.

"If I see ye on that wall before every rodent is expunged from this keep," Lady Sinclair snarled, "I'll make sure ye go over the side. Sutherland can deal with ye as he sees fit. *He* seems to ken how to raise responsible sons."

Ailsa swallowed a gasp. Surely her father would not let that cut pass. But he did, for the moment. The look he gave her mother promised they were not done with this incident.

"Boden, get to work," Sinclair growled. "And if ye touch another cat, I'll toss ye over the wall myself."

Now Ailsa wanted to cheer. It was rare for Boden to suffer consequences of any sort, and these were particularly humiliating, especially delivered at full volume in the middle of the bailey.

But she feared what he would do when her parents were not looking.

"He has a point," Sinclair said to his wife as Boden stalked away. "Fewer captives, fewer mouths to feed if food supplies run low. He counseled tossing one over the wall with a threat pinned to him to continue with one each day. I would bet before we got to the Sutherland's twins, any army out there would withdraw."

"Nay, Da, ye canna." The words slipped out before Ailsa remembered she was doing her best not to draw his attention while tempers flared.

Her mother gave her a warning glance.

"But I can stop coddling them," her father said, his tone milder than she expected. "If food is in short supply, their rations get cut first. Cook, dinna think to disobey me in this."

Cook nodded, but her expression said plainly that she didn't like his order.

This was one of the fears plaguing Ailsa. She couldn't believe the damage Boden had done. Good men might lose their lives because of his cruelty. Her mother was right. He was not fit to succeed her father. But when the time came, unless something drastic happened, he would. The thought saddened her.

In the meantime, the Sutherlands would suffer. Anders would suffer. And if her da came around to Boden's point of view, men she'd come to know and like would die. Men who should have been sent on their way immediately when they were found instead of brought inside the keep. And for what? Ransom? Gold and cattle that Sinclair did not deserve? None of it made sense to her.

*

AFTER AILSA FINISHED the latest count of viable plants in the kitchen garden with Maesie, she went to the orchard gate. In the orchard, six of the Sutherlands were helping several Sinclairs harvest ripe fruit from the trees.

Maighread's latest visit to the dungeon had turned the tide for the men to get out and help with the harvest. Some of the men were getting sick from being confined below, and Ailsa worried that if reports reached Sutherland of them being ill or dying, it would either spark the battle everyone feared or prolong the siege. Maighread had ruled that fresh air and sunshine, exercise and something to look at besides each other and stone walls would help them all.

Tomorrow, Raghnall would allow another six to continue the work, and so on until everything that could be picked had been, or until they were forced to await the ripening of the remainder of the fruit, or weather prevented the work. Then they would start again until everything was harvested. Even frost and freeze damaged fruit could be pared down and baked into pies or stewed, so little or nothing would go to waste.

Anders was not among the men outside today. Nor was his twin, Stellan. She saw Tomas on the ground taking fruit from another man's hands and placing it carefully in the baskets each pair had. They could have tossed around what they picked, bruising and damaging it. She was pleased to see them paying heed to what would feed them as well as the Sinclairs.

Her mother joined her at the gate and stood silent, watching the work progress. "They pay us respect I'm no' sure we deserve," she said after a few minutes. "Being so attentive with their work and our food. Others might have destroyed most of what they handled."

"They're good people, Mother. Hasna Anders shown ye that often enough?"

"Aye, well, 'tis no' me he must convince."

"I ken that. But we're running out of time, are we nay?"

"We are. I ken it. Yer brother has yer da's ear of late. I like it no' at all."

"Nor do I. These men dinna deserve what Boden proposes."

"Do ye deserve what ye propose? To be wed into Sutherland and leave us?"

"I'll leave eventually to be married somewhere. Anders suits me, and I him. 'Tis what we both want, and it gives Da an honorable way to end this," she added, sweeping a hand toward the orchard and the Sutherlands at work there alongside Sinclairs. "Why would he choose war over an alliance that could benefit both?"

Ailsa's mother straightened her back and lifted her chin. "Let's go ask him, shall we? He's listened to yer brother long enough."

Ailsa wanted to applaud. She knew that look and that posture. Mother was ready to fight to win. "Let's."

They entered through the kitchen and made their way from there through the great hall to the laird's solar.

"Husband, we need to talk," her mother said as she strode into the solar. Raghnall was standing before the laird's desk looking chastened, head down, while the laird frowned at him.

"Ye are excused," the laird told his head guard.

Raghnall turned. "Milady Sinclair, Ailsa," he said, acknowledging them as he passed and left them with the laird.

"What is it, Wife?"

"What was that about?" Ailsa's mother glanced toward the door Raghnall had just exited.

"I suppose the idea of using the Sutherlands to help pick the orchard was yer idea?" He turned a frown on Ailsa.

"Aye, and ye should go see them, Da. They're being most careful with their work. Ye would find naught to question or complain."

"Indeed?" He didn't look mollified.

"Yer daughter speaks the truth. I watched them myself for several long minutes. They take even more care than our Sinclair workers. Ye have misjudged those men, Husband. Ye canna listen to Boden and his warmongering. They dinna deserve what he proposes. Ye must continue to negotiate. Send a betrothal agreement between Ailsa and Anders to the Sutherland, and this siege will be over in hours."

"And the Norse king's offer?"

"He will find another bride for his son. Yer daughter loves Anders, and he loves her. This willna matter to Erik. Ye have the other agreements ye hammered out with him on our latest visit north. A wedding with a Norse prince doesna help us as much as ye think. An alliance with a powerful Scottish clan, one that already has many alliances of its own, will do us much more good. Let Ailsa and Anders wed and end this without bloodshed."

Ailsa held her breath, waiting for her father to respond. He held her mother's gaze for a moment, then shook his head. Ailsa's heart plummeted.

"'Twillna do," he said. "Ye women dinna understand what is at stake."

"We understand all too well, Husband. We are the ones who bind the wounds and sit with the fevered, and wash the dead for burial. Dinna try to tell me we have nay stake in this. We do, and ye'd be wise to listen to me."

"I can let the invaders sit until everything freezes. They'll be eager to leave Sinclair by then."

"Nay, Da. By then they will have built a village. And even if they dinna, letting men from every northern clan die of exposure willna help Sinclair now or in the future. Do ye ken why they came to be here on our land?"

Sinclair looked at her steadily for the first time since her mother had started this confrontation. "They never admitted their purpose in coming here. What could it be, save to spy on us? To cause trouble? They've certainly done that."

Ailsa shook her head. "Ye dinna ken the story." She explained about the mission of mercy to help a bairn at MacKay. The race, the storm, the search for Anders, all of it. "They were never here to cause trouble, Da. They truly sought our help. And look what we've done to them. Other than tending Anders' injuries, we've done naught that would make us worthy allies to a clan willing to go to such great efforts to help another clan, a recent ally, mind ye, to save a wee bairn."

"Anders was going to risk the Pentland Firth in a race with his twin to get to MacKay? What a daft idea."

"Perhaps, but their intentions were good. No one save Anders has been hurt, nay lives have been lost. Dinna make Sinclair the villain by listening to Boden. Better an alliance, even a weak one, with the powerful Sutherland clan and its allies. There is nay honor in letting people—good or bad—freeze to death, and these are good people."

"Nor is there honor in letting our people starve. Winter is coming, Husband," her mother said, speaking up at last. "I want this over and that army gone so our men can hunt and refill the larder before the snow comes. Before long, the summer garden will be exhausted and the cold weather crops willna be in yet. The damage the rats did to our store of grain is significant. We may need to appeal to allies—if we have any—before the next harvest comes in. And the men in the dungeon are getting ill. How do ye think Sutherland will feel about that when this standoff is over? This canna go on much longer."

He huffed out a breath, and she went in for the kill.

"Ye do recall the battle ye fought to win my hand, Husband, and what it cost. We owe our daughter the same chance at happiness, without what we went through."

Sinclair shook his head again. "Leave me."

"Da!" Ailsa couldn't help her cry, even knowing it would annoy him.

"Out," he said.

She traded a heartbroken glance with her mother, turned and left. Still in the hall, she heard her mother berate him.

"Ye are an old fool. Ye ken that, aye? Ye are willing to turn down the opportunity to make yer daughter happy and save yer clan the pain and bloodshed a clan war will bring them, and for what? Neither a siege nor a war would be happening if ye hadna demanded a ransom. All of this could have been avoided and an alliance made if ye had just sent the visitors on their way once they found their man. I've never been so disappointed in ye in my life."

"Out, woman!" Her father bellowed.

Ailsa slipped away from the door and down the hallway. What was she going to do now?

She felt reassured that the hunters captured by Sutherland

weren't killed outright. Their Sutherland captors recognized they had value to Sinclair that the laird would honor.

She hoped.

Though worried, she knew all she could do for now was to be vigilant, and to continue to honor whatever was growing between her and Anders. If they could get through this, perhaps she was right to be falling in love with him.

CHAPTER 18

$\mathcal{A}$nders took his turn picking apples early the next day. The weather was still fine and the fruit was ripening nicely. A few more days and they might finish. Then what? With tensions growing and Sinclair starting to take away the few small comforts the men in the dungeon had enjoyed thanks to Ailsa, Anders was forced to focus more and more on escape. Some were being put to work helping with the stables or cleaning up the accumulation of things in the bailey that were now harder to dispose of. They didn't seem to mind the work, and were grateful to be out of the dungeon, so Raghnall continued to be willing to assign men to guard them. Anders didn't expect that largesse to continue either. The longer the siege went on and the hungrier the people of Sinclair got, the less welcome their appearance out of the dungeon would be.

And with blankets having been taken from the men in the dungeon and cooler weather on the way, the dungeon would become a frigid death trap. Anders couldn't see any other option than to break out, but nor could he see a way to make an escape work for all the Sutherlands that Sinclair held. If only Raghnall had agreed to allow all the Sutherlands out at once, but he hadn't.

Of course. In his position, Anders would have done the same rather than risk more than a dozen men fighting for their freedom. They might die in the attempt, but it was better than dying slowly in a cold, dark dungeon. He glanced about and located the handful of Sutherlands out with him, tempted to signal them to make a run for it. But if having a few able to go over the wall meant leaving some of their men behind, Anders didn't think any of his would do it. Nor would it end the siege if Sinclair still held Sutherlands.

The idea of Ailsa marrying him would never be acceptable to Sinclair.

His gaze kept straying to the back wall and the gate he'd found within it. The temptation to rush to it and climb over was overwhelming, but he fought it down. He would never go alone or without all of his men getting over the wall and into the woods to meet Sutherland's forces before the Sinclair could be told what had happened.

And Anders would never see Ailsa again.

That thought made his heart hurt. He'd sworn to his twin on Stellan's wedding day that he would never settle, and would marry only when he found a lass whom he could love as Stellan loved Mariota. Anders believed he'd found that lass in Ailsa. How could he walk away from her?

Yet he and Stellan had sworn a vow to each other when they were but nine years old and facing fostering apart for the next seven years. They would return to Sutherland to rule it together when the time came.

And they would not marry any lass they could not bring home with them.

Stellan had found a solution to that problem in Mariota's willingness, even eagerness, to abdicate her inheritance as Laird MacKay to her friend Seamus. Stellan had found the love of his life. Anders couldn't bear to settle for anything less.

But if Ailsa's father wouldn't see past old clan rivalries to the opportunity an alliance with Sutherland would bring him, Anders would have to find a way to wed Ailsa with or without his permission. He had only the choice of risking clan war, or he would have to walk away from her.

He couldn't do that.

A shout, followed by a sickening crunch and a thud, pulled Anders from his musing. He turned toward the source of the sound and saw one of the Sinclairs on the ground, his leg splayed at an impossible angle and one shoulder crowding the man's ear.

Two other Sinclairs started to pick the man up, but Anders shouted for them to stop. "Go get Maighread. Run!" One of the men ran for the keep. The other stood over his fallen clansman, glaring at Anders. "Who are ye to tell us what to do?"

"If ye move him, ye might kill him," Anders said. "See that blood? That bone?" The injury was severe and sickening to look at. Anders suspected the two Sinclairs had avoided the sight of it. "The shattered bone will cut his leg, and Maighread may no' be able to stop the bleeding. Leave him be and let her decide what is best to do."

"We could take him to her."

"Nay, ye canna," Maighread's sharp tones startled the Sinclair into jumping back.

Anders hid a grin.

"Trust ye to be the only one here with the sense God gave one of these apples," she said and pitched aside one from the ground where she knelt by the injured man. "Help me. This man is a favorite of the laird's, the son of a friend of his from Orkney."

Anders dropped down beside her, heedless of the blood on the ground that soaked into his trews. The Sinclair man dropped onto her other side.

She studied the injured man's leg and shoulder, then nodded. "The shoulder must wait. I'm going to wrap his leg to stop the bleeding. Ye'll help me straighten it and get the bones back in line, or he'll never walk again and his da will never forgive the laird for keeping him here long enough past his fostering for this to happen."

"What do ye want me to do?" Anders asked. A glance aside told him the other Sinclair wouldn't be much help. He looked green and had started to sweat. He caught Maighread's gaze and nodded toward the man.

"Ye can go," she told him. "Now, before ye make things worse."

The man jumped to his feet and rushed away, one hand over his mouth and nose. "Weak in the belly," she muttered and turned back to her patient. "We're lucky the grass is thick here. Ye should be able to get yer hands under here," she said and pointed to his thigh, "and lift—just a wee—so I can tie a rope around it and stop the bleeding. Once that's done, I can decide what to do next." She sent one of the men after the things she needed.

Anders followed her instructions, vaguely aware they had gathered an audience while they waited as the other workers clustered around them to see how the healer worked to save their friend.

"Back up!" Maighread groused. "I canna see what I'm doing with all of ye blocking my light. Go fetch something sturdy so we can carry him inside when I'm done here. A tarpaulin or some sail cloth, no' a soft plaid."

The men obediently took a few steps back and two of them ran for the keep.

"Now, Anders, lift."

He did it slowly, no more than a thumb's width. It was enough for her to accomplish what she needed to do. She nodded and he let the upper leg back down, then pulled his hands from beneath it.

She tied off the rope, tied a thin branch atop it and twisted, tightening the binding around the leg. Anders was pleased to see blood stopped seeping from the break.

Only then did he glance up and see Ailsa among the crowd

that had gathered. She smiled and nodded, then turned her attention to Maighread, so Anders did, as well.

"I'm going to straighten his lower leg and will have to pull on it to line the bone up where it belongs. I need ye to kneel over him to keep the upper part of the leg from moving, and ye may need to help me by pushing from where ye are on the lower leg." She lifted it enough to get two ropes underneath, then said, "Ready?"

Anders nodded. "Aye."

The movement went amazingly smoothly. Maighread was an experienced healer, and it showed. She positioned the leg where she wanted it, tied two sturdy branches on either side to hold everything in place, sat back, and studied her work. "Very well, let me look at the shoulder before we try to move him."

Satisfied, she presided over rolling the man aside for the sailcloth someone brought to be laid at his back, then rolling him back onto it and carefully lifting him up. It took six men clustered around him so tightly, afterward Anders wasn't sure how they moved the man and didn't trip over each others' feet, but they got him into the herbal where Maighread could take care of him.

"Thank ye, Anders. Because of ye, this lad may yet keep his leg."

"I only did as ye asked, Healer," he objected, "but ye are most welcome."

She made that announcement in front of all the men who'd carried in the injured man, and when Anders turned, he realized not only was Ailsa still there, but her parents were, too.

"What happened?" The laird's voice cut through the sudden silence.

"He was climbing after some apples," one of the Sinclairs said, "slipped and fell. That Sutherland saved his life, no' just his leg. Two of us was about to pick him up."

"With a wound like that," Maighread said and pointed at the

leg, "he wouldha bled to death. Anders kept that from happening. This lad will live—and walk again—if he doesna take a fever."

Lady Sinclair laid a hand on her husband's arm.

The Sinclair cleared his throat. "Well done."

Anders thought it pained him to say so, but he'd take the praise over what else the laird might have done had Anders been found standing over an injured man without so many witnesses.

ANDERS' morning picking apples ended with the accident and caring for the injured man. Instead of escorting him back to the orchard, one of the guards returned him to the dungeon, where he filled everyone in on what had happened. "The other Sutherlands are still out there. Nothing has changed, so far as I ken. Since the Sinclairs told the laird what happened, he isna likely to confine us here. We've earned our time outside. If the siege continues, I hope that doesna change until the harvest is done. But we canna predict how long this will go on, or how scarce food will become. All we can do is endure until we get ourselves out of here, have help getting out of here, or the siege ends."

That started several discussions, the low rumble of male voices filling the dungeon while Anders and Stellan talked.

"That couldha gone very badly for ye had the Sinclairs no' spoken up," Stellan said.

"Aye, but they gave the laird nay chance to draw the wrong conclusion. I'm grateful for that."

"I, too."

Anders glanced up to see Ailsa coming down the stairs. Surprised, he must've stared at her a beat too long without speaking.

She tilted her head and gave him a hesitant smile. "Good day, Anders. Stellan. Am I disturbing ye?"

Anders backed up a step and swallowed a laugh. Disturb him?

Her presence was the high point of his day, and filled his dreams at night. The guards had placed the extra torches they provided during daytime hours, and the firelight lit her hair adding more red to the gold in it. He could stare at it for hours. "Nay, ye never could. What can I do for ye, Ailsa?" He gestured her to a seat one of the guards had left in the open space between the rows of cells.

"Ye made a good impression on my da today," she told them. "I hope that will make him reconsider some of the things he's been most stubborn about."

Anders could think of several. But beside the betrothal he wanted, little else mattered as much.

"I only did what was needful," he answered.

"Maighread made certain Da understood the danger of the injury and how yer actions saved the lad's life, especially when the Sinclairs nearby did little or naught to help."

"Maighread arrived almost immediately. There was naught for anyone to do save obey her. I did that. If my actions make yer da rethink anything that led to the siege or that is prolonging it, so much the better."

Ailsa nodded. "I want to talk to ye about the siege. How do ye and the other Sutherlands think it can be ended?"

Anders glanced aside at Stellan, who nodded for him to go ahead. "Why do ye ask?" It seemed a strange question for a lass.

"Something my mother and I discussed."

"Aye?"

"There are many options and just as many opinions. I thought it might help if ye had a say."

"So, ye will take my words to yer father? Ours?" He indicated Stellan.

"If I think they will help sway him, aye, I will."

Anders settled on the bench behind him so that she did not have to keep craning her neck to look up at him from her seated position. Looking at her, he could see the stairs out of the dungeon off to the side. The view gave him too many ideas, too many longings, for freedom and for her. He needed to pay her the respect of focusing on her questions and giving her a well-thought-out answer. "The first thing that comes to mind is trading Sutherlands for yer hunters I've heard were caught in the woods by one of our allies."

"How did ye hear about that?"

"We overheard the guards discussing it. 'Tis true Sutherland wants to trade all of us for a handful of Sinclairs?"

"'Tis what he wrote in a missive I saw. Da wasna pleased."

"Would that no' say to yer da that his men are worth more than two or three Sutherlands, each?"

"'Twould certainly appeal to my brother's vanity," Ailsa said after an unladylike snort. "But I dinna think Da would fall for it."

"He would still have our *birlinn*. 'Tis worth a great deal," Stellan said.

He'd been so quiet, Anders was surprised to hear him speak.

"I ken that is true, but Da asked for cattle and gold," Ailsa reminded him. "Ye dinna think the Sutherland would buy it back in the coin Da demanded?"

"I dinna ken," Anders said. His father would be more likely to find a way to steal it back, but Anders didn't want to plant that idea in her mind.

"Sinclair is well-supplied, but it canna withstand a siege forever," Stellan said quietly.

"Da thinks we must only wait until winter sets in, aye? Men in tents willna fare well against the weather once 'tis cold and dark."

"If the siege lasts that long, they will have built a village out of yer forest and have supplies put in to last till spring or longer," Stellan insisted.

"I told him so," Ailsa said and crossed her arms.

"And they can be resupplied by land and by sea. How long will Sinclair's supplies last when ye canna hunt nor fish?"

"'Tis a concern." Her gaze dropped to her hands. "But it should be a concern for ye, as well."

"It should be," Anders told her. "'Tis." He wanted to reach out and take her hand, but her gaze was on the floor and if he wasn't mistaken, her thoughts were on how hungry her clan would be by spring. "Yer da must be made to see that holding us is a fool's errand. Sutherland and its allies can outlast ye."

Suddenly, she looked up, tears in her eyes. "No' if he starts killing yer men to force Sutherland to relent. If our people are starving, he willna feed yers."

"Lass," Anders said and reached for her, a futile gesture given the space—and the bars—between them. He didn't know what to say to that. It had always been a possibility. Even a probability. No warrior wanted to die a prisoner, but rather honorably, on the field of battle, protecting his home and his loved ones.

"Besides yer other men, he holds ye and yer brother," she continued, fighting to speak as she stood and began to pace. "I canna bear to see any of ye killed for old men's pride."

Anders stayed seated, letting her walk off her frustrations, for he was certain that's what he was seeing. She had always cared for him, and now she had others of his clan she felt responsible for, too, and a situation that looked dire for all of them. He wished he had words of comfort to offer—and a solution to offer everyone. "'Tis more than that, and well ye ken it. On both sides. 'Tis blood. And history. And the future."

"There is another way," she said after a few calming breaths. She turned to face him and stepped up to the bars of the cell he shared with his twin.

"Marriage," Anders supplied quietly as he joined her at the bars. "Is that what ye want, Ailsa?" Hope was a bird, fluttering its wings in his chest, trying to beat its way out into the world.

"'Tis better than the alternatives. We like each other." She glanced aside at Stellan, who politely turned his gaze away. "We want each other," she added even more softly. "'Twould harm nay one, and would link our clans for that future ye mention."

"I will ask yer da for yer hand. 'Tis an alternative I like well."

"'Tis a fool's errand." She dropped her gaze. "He willna give his aye. He returned from Orkney with a betrothal offer from the Norse king for one of his sons."

"Is he *fashed* about an alliance with the Norse?"

"Nay, I dinna think so. But a betrothal ..."

"Aye, well, he would find Sutherland important, as well, if he stopped to consider it. Or look out over his walls at some of the number of allies we can call upon." He took her hand again. "We could handfast. Even through these bars, we could do that."

"We could, but how long do ye think he'd let ye live once he found out?" She pulled her hand away.

"Ye, my love, are worth the risk. Even the sacrifice." He could die a happy man after even one night with Ailsa. Nay, he couldn't. He would want more. All of their nights and all of their days, as long as they lived.

"Nay, I am no'," she insisted, brow furrowed. "It willna end the siege. And if ye are dead, what good was a hand fasting with a ghost? I willna allow ye to do something so foolish, even if 'tis brave, even if 'tis for both our clans. Da must agree to our marriage. So must yer da."

"Mine will, never fear. If he has any doubts, Stellan and I will convince him."

She eyed him. "'Twill be hard to do from in here."

"No' if I can get a missive out to him," Anders said and glanced around at Stellan, who nodded. "Who takes missives from yer da outside the walls?"

"I dinna ken."

"Could Tasgall?" Anders would ask him the next time he saw him.

"I'll ask him about it, but 'twould be dangerous if Da found out and thought ye were sharing Sinclair secrets with Sutherland."

"Let Tasgall read it. Give it to yer mother to read it first, if ye think she will support our betrothal." If Ailsa was right and she truly was an ally, she could make the difference. "I dinna want anyone ye care about harmed if yer da finds out."

"*When* he finds out. Surely he will. In fact, Mother might be the one to tell him, hoping 'twill be enough to convince him to accept our union to end all this, though she kens Da favors the Norse betrothal offer. She has tried without success, but if she keeps at him—perhaps he'll see reason. If he learns of this, I fear he will make certain we canna see each other. He'll forbid me visiting ye or any of yer men here." She cupped his cheek. "I dinna ken what to do, save that I will dream of ye tonight, Anders."

He took her hand and kissed her knuckles, holding his lips to her skin as if he could draw strength from her soul. "As I dream of ye every night, Love. I want ye more than anything. And if our marriage is the answer to ending the siege, even better. But we must find a way to make yer da accept it. Only then can it happen."

"GET DOWN THERE and get him out. Now!"

The moment Anders heard Boden Sinclair's voice, he knew trouble was coming. But for which Sutherland?

He and Stellan traded a look, then he stood and moved to the bars of the cell he shared with his twin. Stellan joined him. Their movement alerted the rest of their men. They stood, too.

It took only moments for four guards Anders had never seen to troop down the steps and shove Raghnall's man aside from his post at the bottom of the stairs. Boden followed them down, the smirk on his lips promising something more than an opportunity to taunt the Sutherlands.

"Anders Sutherland," he said, "I've come for ye."

"Really?" Anders slouched against the bars between him and Boden's men. They had to be Boden's and none of Raghnall's.

From the corner of his eye, he noticed that Raghnall's guard was gone. To fetch his guard chief and the laird, Anders hoped. "Is there aught ye wish to ask me?"

"Ask ye? Nay. I've other plans for ye. Ye think ye have earned the laird's good will after what ye did in the orchard? Ye'll soon find out 'twill change naught."

Anders glanced aside at Stellan and lifted his chin, his gaze making it clear he wanted his twin to move back out of range of whatever was about to happen. Their men couldn't help. It was up to him to protect the brother their father considered his heir from whatever Boden had planned.

Anders was certain he knew. Ailsa had mentioned several times that Boden was eager to start tossing Sutherland captives over Sinclair's walls. But she'd always thought if he managed to talk their father into the foolishly bloodthirsty scheme, they'd save the twins for last. So, what was Boden doing now, asking for him first? Did the Sinclair know he was down here?

One of Boden's men unlocked the cell door. Two more entered. Anders moved to block them from Stellan. They grabbed Anders by the arms and shoved him out into the space between the cells.

Stellan rushed forward, swearing, but the fourth guard slammed the cell door in his face.

The two with Anders yanked his hands behind his back and tried to bind them there.

Anders fought, twisted out of their grip and knocked one against the cell bars they'd pulled him from, then kicked the legs out from the other. He had no doubt his life was at stake. He could not lose, even though he'd lost strength and stamina. His injuries and time fighting a fever slowed him, and when the other two guards joined the fight, it was only a matter of time before all four subdued him. He didn't intend to make it easy.

Four against one was hardly fair. Clearly, Boden never intended for any fight Anders put up to be fair. Boden laughed at every blow one of his men landed. He also laughed at every blow Anders landed on his men. Anders did some damage, but not enough.

The Sutherlands did what they could to help, grabbing at the Sinclairs through the bars. Tomas got an arm across one guard's throat and yanked his head against the bars hard enough to draw blood. One of his fellows abandoned beating on Anders to rescue him from suffocating. He slammed both fists down on Tomas' arm to loosen his hold. The Sutherlands in the cell with Tomas pulled him back out of reach, cradling his arm.

In the end, despite the curses the Sutherlands rained down on Boden's men, they succeeded in binding Anders' hands behind his back. Then each of them landed another blow to his midsection, doubling him over.

"Where are ye going? What are ye going to do with my brother?" Stellan demanded as they forced Anders upright and turned him toward the stairs.

Anders shook his head, trying to clear it. It spun and his belly threatened to erupt. It would serve Boden right if he spewed all over him. Failing that, any of those four guards would make a good target.

"Naught to do with ye," Boden answered and jerked his chin upward. The guards with Anders shoved him toward the stairs. "I'm the only one with the cods to do what my da willna do himself."

Given what Boden had argued for with his father, Anders hated the sound of that threat. He fought to keep his feet under him. The beating had given him a new set of injuries and played havoc with his balance, especially with his hands bound behind him. But he refused to be dragged anywhere. He fought to get his battered body under control or he'd have no hope at all of protecting himself.

"Does the Sinclair ken ye are doing this?"

Boden rewarded Stellan's question with another laugh.

The other Sutherlands began beating on the bars holding them prisoner, tugging and shoving with their combined weight on the doors to their cells, and shouting invectives at Boden as he followed Anders and his men up the stairs.

Anders hurt everywhere. If he survived this, he'd be back in Maighread's herbal for another indefinite stay. He hoped Boden was so excited by the Sutherlands' reaction that he would fail to notice the missing guard. Anders' life might depend on whether the guard who'd disappeared had made it into the keep to raise the alarm. When they reached the top of the stairs and no more of Boden's men guarded the dungeon's entrance, Anders let himself hope.

The bailey was empty save for a lad headed from the stable toward the keep's main door. Boden grabbed him by the arm and dragged him with them.

So, Boden didn't want the lad to be able to report what he and his men were doing.

Where was everyone? The day was dim with clouds thick enough to obscure the sun and hide whether it was morning or midday or later. Midday would make sense if most of the clan went in for their meal, leaving none outside but the guards on the wall walk. Anders looked up. He could see three of them nearby, all with their attention on the ground outside the wall, not the men crossing the bailey with him.

"What do ye think ye're doing?" Anders raised his voice, hoping they would hear him. Even if they saw them, they wouldn't be able to get past Boden's group into the keep, but perhaps any guards further along the wall would be able to. And these three would at least delay whatever Boden had planned.

"Ye'll see," Boden said as they reached the stairs to the wall walk. "Climb."

"Or what?"

"Or I'll kill ye here and these lads will carry yer body up and toss it over."

Something in Boden's eyes told Anders he was eager to do it.

At the top of the stairs, Anders looked for a way out of this, but Boden's men followed on his heels and surrounded him. There was nowhere to run. Where were the three guards he'd seen on the wall? He spotted them headed for another set of stairs. One started down and the other two kept going. They were too few to fight Boden and his men, Anders hoped they were going after help.

Boden swaggered up to the wall without the stable lad and shouted for the Sutherland. "I've got one of yer *bastarts* here," he taunted. "Surely ye'd like to get a last look at him alive before I toss him down to ye."

Anders fought the men shoving him toward Boden and the wall, but they still outnumbered him. He fell forward over the crenellation, bent at the middle so that he hung halfway out of the wall. Before someone could finish pushing him over, he forced himself upright with a groan as his abused body protested.

His father came out of the trees, flanked by several men, including Seamus MacKay. "What do ye think ye are doing?" Sutherland's outraged tone didn't give Anders any hope that the conversation about to happen would calm whatever madness drove Boden to defy his father so openly.

"Ignore him," Anders shouted, wincing as his shout tore his split lip. "Go back to yer camp."

"I'm the Sinclair," Boden shouted. "Ye will hear me."

Every head on the wall twisted to stare at Boden, including Anders'. Had Boden killed his father? Was Sinclair truly in his hands now? If so, Anders would not survive this day, and the rest of the Sutherlands might not last much longer. *Think*, damn it! And stay alive.

Where was Raghnall? And Tasgall?

Where was Ailsa? Had Boden murdered his whole family? Anders' knees nearly failed him at that thought.

"In case ye had any doubts about who we hold, now ye ken,"

Boden shouted. "Pack up and leave Sinclair territory. No' with my men. I ken ye have a few. I'll be happy to give this one to ye in trade. 'Twill take only one wee push." He started poking at Anders, more like a small child tormenting a pet than a grown man threatening death to a captive.

Anders braced himself and held his ground, fighting not to reveal his pain. Boden's blows grew harder as his expression changed from boastful to enraged. Unable to budge Anders, he turned back to the Sutherland. "Leave or I'll send him out to ye. If ye are still there by sundown, ye can collect his body at the base of Sinclair's wall."

"The hell ye say!"

When Sinclair's voice rang out, Anders sagged against the cold stone at his side. So, Boden had lied. His father was still alive —and still laird.

Raghnall and several of his men mounted the stairs. The guards Anders had seen on the wall, plus a few men they'd gathered, ran back along the wall walk to join them. Anders had only a moment to look down at his father and nod to tell him despite the blood, he was all right, before Raghnall's men took charge of him.

"Return him to the dungeon and fetch Maighread to him," Sinclair ordered once he got a closer look at the damage Boden's men had done. "Put those four under guard in a stall in the stable," he ordered, his disgust plain in his grimace. "I dinna want them anywhere near the other Sutherlands. They'll answer to me when I'm done with that one," he added and gestured at his son. He shouted up at Boden. "Get down here. Now."

For a moment, Anders thought Boden would disobey, but he had nowhere to go except over the wall to the fate he'd promised Anders. After what he'd just put Anders and his father through, that would be too easy an end for the Sinclair heir. Anders paused long enough to see Boden start down the stairs, then turned toward the entrance to the dungeon. As his gaze swept the keep, his heart leaped. Ailsa!

She ran toward him from her place on the keep's steps, pushing through the gathering crowd, including men much bigger than her, to reach him. She stopped short and gasped. "What did they do to ye?"

"'Twas a friendly wee encounter with yer brother's men," he managed to say before she flung her arms around his neck.

"I dinna ken where ye are hurt, but Maighread will soon set ye to rights," she promised softly, laying her cool palm on his bruised cheek and staring into his eyes.

He dropped his head to her shoulder, suddenly wanting nothing but to be held in her arms. Forever. He took a deep breath, inhaling her sweet scent. Along with the smell of his own blood and sweat. Chagrined, he straightened. "Lass, yer da can see us."

"I dinna care."

"He does, and I dinna want any of his men to add to what Boden's already did."

She gasped and stepped back. "I'm so sorry, Anders. I wasna thinking. Go. I'll send Maighread to ye."

"I'm here," the healer said, as the crowd parted to let her through.

Anders hadn't noticed her arrival, but he'd been focused on Ailsa, and on the threat her father might pose. Maighread took a moment to look over his obvious injuries, then nodded to his guards and followed him. As they returned him to the dungeon, Anders' last glimpse of Ailsa was of her standing with her hands over her mouth, her eyes brimming with tears. For him.

CHAPTER 19

$\mathcal{A}$ilsa had watched with horror as Boden threatened Anders. Relief filled her when her father intervened until she saw the damage done to Anders' face and knew he likely bore more bruises or worse injuries on his body. Maighread was with him. If he needed more of her care, she'd ensure the guards moved him to the herbal.

Furious, she followed her father and Boden until they reached the solar. She knew better than to go in there with them, but she moved a few feet down the hallway, out of sight of the great hall and of the solar's doorway. Their voices carried, even though the door was closed.

"What were ye thinking? Ye had nay business taking one of the prisoners up to the wall. Did ye really think I wouldna do anything to ye if ye tossed him over to his da?"

"Ye wouldna touch me. Ye have done naught so far to yer hostages. Ye'll let this siege go on forever, and keep feeding those Sutherlands, too. I'm the only one with the cods to do what's needed."

"What I'm doing is better than the clan war ye wouldha started, ye *eejit*!"

Ailsa heard his fist slam into his table top.

"Ye are no' fit to be laird," the Sinclair raged. "Ye have nay sense. Risking one of the two most valuable prisoners? Daft. Worse than daft. Irresponsible."

"So, I should have tossed one of their sailors over the wall? I can still do that," Boden answered.

He sounded unbowed. He'd always had a cruel streak and a temper that flared at the slightest provocation. But this was worse, words delivered coolly, even rationally, but sounding as though they came from a place of total lunacy. Ailsa's belly clenched, her blood turning to ice in her veins. How would their father react to his son's daring?

"Nay, ye canna. No' without my order," her father said, his tone still enraged. It got quiet for a moment. More softly, he added, "If it comes to that, we will have lost. Everything."

Relief made Ailsa sag against the stone wall at her back. If he admitted that, he'd never do what Boden had attempted.

"Try anything like this again without my permission and ye will be the next one over the wall," her father added. "Those men are my prisoners, nay yers. My bargaining chips. 'Tis no' the time to start killing them, wasting them. No' yet."

At first, what Ailsa heard of her father's condemnation of Boden's actions had reassured her. And his admission that killing the prisoners would destroy Sinclair, as well. But the turn their conversation now took frightened her. Despite acknowledging the stakes, he was not dismissing the idea of sacrificing a few Sutherlands. *'Tis no' the time to start killing them, wasting them.* When would he decide it was time for the killing to start? His statement was more than she could excuse or accept. She suspected even her mother's influence on her da would not be sufficient to stop the waste of lives her brother—and now even her father—contemplated.

It was time to get the men out of the dungeon and out of Sinclair before her father acquiesced to Boden's bloodthirsty demands. Without waiting to hear any more, she hurried silently away. As soon as she was out of earshot, she ran to find the one person in a position to help her. Tasgall.

❧

"WHAT ARE YE DOING HERE?" Anders kept his voice low, but he couldn't have been more shocked if Ailsa had run him through with his own sword. It was the middle of the night and she had called his name, waking him, but softly enough that he wasn't sure he'd heard anything at all. Until she called again. He'd rolled to sitting, and groaned at the pain in his torso the movement caused, though Maighread had assured him there was no damage that would not heal on its own. He stared at Ailsa, disbelieving.

She stood outside the cell, holding a torch that cast flickering light and shadows on the cell walls around them. Men had started to awaken to the light and the sound of their voices.

Ailsa's gaze raked him from head to feet and back again. She spoke, low and urgently as she twisted the key in the cell door's lock until it clicked. She pulled the door open. "God, yer beautiful, battered face. Damn Boden! Can ye walk? Run if need be? Grab anything ye want to take with ye. Plaids. Water skins. Tasgall is keeping watch above. We're going to take all of ye out of the keep by the orchard postern. Now."

"What? How?" He shook Stellan awake. "Tell me what's going on."

"Tasgall is helping me. Helping ye. I got nowhere with Da, and with Boden still in favor of violence, after what he did today, the only thing left to do is to make certain ye all escape. Together."

Anders didn't know whether to believe her or not. "Ye must come with me. We can be married at Sutherland."

"Nay, I canna. I told ye why," she added as she pulled open the door. "If I am missing, Da will assume ye took me against my will. He will start the war we fear. I must stay behind. I will make

211

my presence obvious in the great hall where everyone can see me. That will give ye plenty of time to join yer clansmen and head south." She handed Stellan the key to the other cell doors and he squeezed her hand before he passed by her.

"I canna leave ye, Love," Anders protested. "What will yer da do to ye when he finds out who freed us?"

"I dinna care." She lifted a hand and gently stroked his battered face. "I willna allow any of ye to be killed. If ye can convince him, tell Sutherland to send a betrothal agreement that ends this standoff," she said. "Mother and I will talk Da into accepting it and I'll walk out of the gates to ye as yer betrothed."

Anders feared he would never see her again. "Ye have said yer da will never agree. I'll stay with ye in the hope that he will eventually relent. Stellan will tell Da I chose to stay behind."

"He willna agree to such as that, and neither will yer brother," Ailsa hissed as Stellan moved around, unlocking the other cells and freeing their men.

"Ye are right, I willna," Stellan said. "We all go. It does nay good to leave anyone behind."

Anders knew that, but the reminder hurt as much as the blows Boden's guards had landed on his belly.

"Ye must go," Ailsa insisted. "My da willna have yer men any longer, but he will still have an army camped outside our gates. He deserves to *fash* over that." She gave him a quick grin. "Even Mother wants ye gone, and she can be very persuasive with Da when she wants to. Now gather what ye have. The longer ye try to talk me into coming with ye, the more ye risk yerself and yer men being caught."

Anders did as she bade while she went about checking on the other men. Satisfied they were all able to move, she led everyone quietly out of the dungeon. Tasgall took charge at the top of the stairs and hurried Stellan and the other Sutherlands in deep silence around the keep's wall to the kitchen garden's gate that led out to the orchard.

Ailsa paced at the rear with Anders, her hand gripping his as if she, too, knew this might be the last of their time together. She didn't speak, and Anders found he couldn't. Silence had helped them move like wraiths around the bailey. The guards on the walls were focused on the forces outside and either never noticed the furtive movement inside Sinclair, or dismissed it.

At the postern gate in the outer orchard wall, Tasgall stood with Stellan. "The others have gone out already," Stellan told Anders quietly. "Tasgall and Ailsa risk much to free us. We must go now."

"If he hurts ye, either of ye," Anders said, glancing at Tasgall, "I'll see he regrets it."

"Kiss her," Stellan ordered. "We must go now or we may never be free of here."

Ailsa stepped up to Anders and gently took his face into her hands. "Send for me."

"I will. Today." He dropped his head to hers and claimed her lips.

"Who's there?"

A voice reached them from the other side of the orchard.

Tasgall faded into the trees.

Ailsa gasped and pushed Anders toward Stellan. "'Tis the guard! He'll come this way soon. Go!" She hissed. "Send for me. After this, Da will happily be rid of me."

"Ye are mine, Love. Mine," he repeated softly as Stellan grabbed his arm. "Hide, Ailsa. The guard will see us leaving. He canna see ye or this is all for naught."

"I am yers," she whispered and touched her fingers to her lips. "Be safe." Then she did as he suggested and disappeared behind nearby trees as the guard arrived.

Anders turned back to show himself, then ran to join Stellan, crossed the last of the verge and disappeared into the nearby forest. There, he paused to make sure Ailsa had gotten away.

"Damn it," the guard muttered. "The laird will lash the skin from me for this."

Tasgall appeared behind him and hit him over the head with the hilt of his dirk. The guard dropped like a stone.

Anders stepped into view and waved.

Tasgall waved back, left the guard on the ground, and closed the gate.

Relief flooded Anders. The guard saw only him and Stellan. When he woke up, he would assume one of the Sutherlands hit him. Ailsa and Tasgall would be safe.

Anders followed his twin into the woods, knowing he might be disappearing from Ailsa's life forever. The knowledge tore at his gut and he almost turned back, but the gate was closed and the orchard silent. He'd heard no outcry, so took comfort that Ailsa and Tasgall had probably gotten back into the keep without attracting any attention. Anders shuddered to think what would have happened if the postern guard had come upon them unannounced.

He paced just behind Stellan, fighting for calm. He was going home. But it would take a miracle for Ailsa to go with him. He would never have what Stellan and Mariota had. He had just walked away from the only happiness he would have been granted in life.

"I KEN WHAT YE ARE THINKING," Stellan said once Anders caught up to him. They were deep in the woods, following the soft sounds of the other Sutherland former captives ahead of them, and nearing the expected ring of guards Sutherland would have assigned to keep watch over the woods and the siege camp against any surprise incursion by Sinclair or its allies. "Ye canna go back into Sinclair to get Ailsa. Besides the fact that Tasgall likely locked the gate to confuse the guard into wondering what he saw, Ailsa is right. Her father would come after her, and that would force a fight we dinna want. Ye must trust that she is as eager for the betrothal as ye are. If she is, she will make it happen. If no', 'twas never meant to be, and she is no' yer Mariota."

"Her da wants to strengthen his alliance with the Norse. Her mother and the healer and Cook are on Ailsa's side, but the decision is his."

"Those are important voices in the clan. If her father is as wise as we hope, he kens to listen to them."

"He also listens to Boden. Look where that got us. Especially me." He shrugged and winced as the movement aggravated his new injuries. "I hope ye are right, Brother. I wouldna want to live in Sinclair under Boden's rule. I dinna want that for Ailsa, either." He took a breath. "My head kens the truth of what ye say. The rest of me, nay."

"Then remember that we swore to rule Sutherland together. Ye canna do that from up here."

"There was a time when ye were willing to have me do it from MacKay, wed to Mariota. Ye kenned Da wouldna let ye wed her and remain at MacKay and ye thought the two of us could somehow join Sutherland and MacKay together."

"Mariota gave us a better solution when she turned MacKay over to Seamus and came to Dunrobin to wed me. Mine was a temporary madness, and I got over it, didna I? Ye will, too, and ye will have the lass of yer dreams if 'tis truly her dream as well. Patience, Brother. Patience."

CHAPTER 20

By the time Anders and Stellan reached the central Sutherland camp, the joyful, though quiet, reunion was already well underway. The Sutherland and the lairds of their allies welcomed the men, but voices stayed low to keep from alerting the Sinclair keep that something was going on in the siege camp. Firelight revealed the worry still in their father's eyes. It lasted until he spotted his twins coming out of the darkness between the trees. In that moment, Anders would have sworn tears filled his eyes.

Stellan and he went straight to their father.

"Ye are here!" He exclaimed as he grabbed them together in a bear hug and pounded their backs.

Anders hissed and clenched his teeth against the pain of his father's grateful embrace. "Easy, Da," he said. "Ye may recall I had a wee run-in with some guards earlier today."

Sutherland let go of Stellan and held Anders at arm's length. "I saw ye on the wall, but didna see all of this. What did they do to ye? God's teeth, I'll tear them apart."

"The Sinclair has likely already done so," Anders assured him. "After his son took it upon himself to threaten ye—and me—he was no' pleased. Nor with the four guards it took to subdue me and get me up there, where ye saw me."

"Aye, and now, when ye didna lead the others into camp, I feared ye had been caught. Or worse."

"Nay, Da," Stellan reassured him. "Anders delayed to have a few words with Ailsa, the Sinclair's daughter, before we could get away. We are here, safe and whole."

"Ye are?" Sutherland peered intently at Anders.

He had to know about the memory loss by now. "Aye, and whole. Mostly. The other men must have told ye?"

"Aye, they did that, but there's been nay time for aught else."

"My memory is recovered, Da. I ken who ye are, and all these others. This walking mirror-image beside me does surprise me now and again, though."

"What?" Stellan's visage paled for a moment in the firelight, then reddened. "That was a jest, I think," Stellan told their father. "Anders, now is nay the time for them."

"Aye, I ken it. Sorry, Da."

"I'll forgive ye much, Son, save for yer inability to stay aboard a perfectly good Sutherland *birlinn*."

Despite his injuries, Anders had to laugh at that, but it took effort. Stellan had said much the same. The events of that night and the days that followed were too fresh, and still stung.

"While ye get something to eat and drink, I will send for Seamus MacKay and the Rose leader to meet with us, and ye can tell us how ye managed to escape."

"We can talk while we eat and drink, Da," Anders said. "The sooner ye ken, the sooner we can plan what to do about the Sinclair response to our escape."

Sutherland nodded. "Very well. Get what ye want and bring it to my tent. I'll round up Seamus and Drake Rose."

Once everyone was settled, Seamus gave them some good news. "Did ye ken several of the crates from yer *birlinn* have washed up on nearby beaches since the storm? Among them, we found one with the herbs ye meant to deliver to MacKay. Still dry and useable. Our healer will be pleased."

"'Tis the best news I've heard so far," Anders said. "Our ill-fated trip wasna wasted."

"Tell us what happened," his father demanded.

Anders launched into the story of what had happened to him, and how he had been treated while he recovered. And after, when the *birlinn*'s crew had been found. How their efforts to protect him and his to protect himself and them, kept them from meeting until after Stellan and his men arrived. "Ailsa and I became close. With her mother's help, she tried to talk her da into a betrothal between us, but he wouldna hear of it. Her brother the heir was all for a fight, and her da began to be swayed to his way of thinking, even to the point of contemplating killing us off, one by one, until ye lot left Sinclair land."

"'Tis barbaric," Seamus muttered.

"Among her friends, Ailsa counts a guard named Tasgall. When she became convinced her da was seriously considering his heir's plan, she knew the only way to save our lives and prevent a clan war was for us to escape. They led everyone from the dungeon—"

"Dungeon!" Seamus shook his head in disgust.

Stellan spoke up. "We were well cared for, again, thanks to Ailsa, with food and drink and blankets. Only in the last week when Sinclair began to think harsher methods were required did they take away most of the blankets. With the season turning, the dungeon was cold, but we managed with the help of some sympathetic guards and Ailsa."

"There was no other way for us to leave," Anders added. "There were too many of us. Tasgall silenced the dungeon guard. We left by a postern gate on the outside of their orchard. It lies closer to the woods than anywhere else around the keep. From there, we crossed a narrow bit of glen and disappeared into the trees."

"What of Tasgall and Ailsa?" Seamus asked. "They could be in danger."

"I saw Tasgall hit the postern guard from behind," Anders said. "They werena seen by either the dungeon or the postern guard, so likely our absence willna be noted until one of those two wakes up and raises the alarm. They'll think we managed to break out ourselves, though they'll be puzzled as to how we did it."

"I still have the key to the cells," Stellan said, holding it up. "They may assume one of us lifted it from one of the guards, but they will be unable to discover who."

"Well done!" Sutherland exclaimed.

"Lads, I'm overjoyed ye are well, and sorry that yer errand of mercy on my clan's behalf went so wrong," Seamus said. "I'm proud to stand with Sutherland to get ye back."

"Rose, as well," Drake said.

"We are grateful our allied clans supported us," Stellan said. "Yer numbers kept Sinclair from acting foolishly."

Seamus snorted "I shouldha kenned ye wouldna need our help, but would manage yerselves to find a way to escape."

"And left another broken heart behind," Stellan teased Anders. The others laughed until they noticed that Anders was not laughing.

Anders took a breath. "I wanted Ailsa to leave with us, but she was insistent her da would come out fighting to find her. She asked that the Sutherland send in a betrothal agreement. She and her mother would convince her da to accept, and she would walk out to join me."

"I am nay keen on the idea of a betrothal, either, after all this, Son," Sutherland said. "What Sinclair did—"

"Was to allow his people to take care of us," Anders said with the clarity that came from being outside Sinclair's walls. "He couldna see a way out of this stalemate, either, since he held a betrothal agreement from the Norse king."

"That is still a problem," Stellan interjected, "but 'twas Boden causing the most trouble, nay Sinclair."

"Ailsa is to me what Mariota is to Stellan," Anders declared. "I must do everything I can to have her with me. If ye willna approve a betrothal, if I must, I will go back to Sinclair." He knew his father would never allow that, but he had to say it.

Sutherland ignored the challenge. "Even if I send one in, he may reject it."

"Ailsa will have to decide whether to obey her da or listen to her heart and leave the same way we did," Stellan said. "Write the agreement. Have MacKay and Rose witness it. Brodie, too, if one of theirs is here on land and no' all out at sea, blocking Sinclair Bay. Send it to Sinclair."

"Then I must wait," Anders added.

"So shall we all, Anders," his father agreed.

"So shall we all," Stellan and the others echoed.

AILSA SAT in the great hall the next morning, waiting for her father to find out how the Sutherlands got out of Sinclair and punish her. The voice they heard in the garden last night calling out *who's there* had been the guard assigned to the postern returning to his post. Why had he left it? A call of nature? Or had Tasgall somehow diverted him before collecting the Sutherlands? Thank the saints Tasgall had been able to hit him from behind and knock him out. Now that the Sutherlands' absence had been noticed, if the guard had seen her or worse, Tasgall, word would have gotten back to her father in no time.

She could hear everything going on in his solar. Her mother was in there with him, trying to calm him, but Sinclair was furious.

"How did they get out? How did they overpower the dungeon guard? Where was the postern guard? Damn it, giving that

Anders Sutherland access to the keep was foolish. He showed them the way out," he ranted. "This is Ailsa's fault. And why are they still camped out there? They've gotten what they want. They should be leaving."

Ailsa listened with bees buzzing in her bloodstream. She expected to be called into the solar at any moment to suffer her father's wrath. Even if he couldn't prove she'd had a part in the escape, he blamed her. And she would hear about it.

A messenger came into the great hall and headed for the solar, a rolled up vellum in his hand. Her heart skipped a beat, then resumed, beating even faster. Please, let that be the betrothal agreement from Sutherland, she thought. And let Da sign it!

She heard her father break the seal and swear as the messenger quit the solar and passed through the great hall on his way out.

"Do no' dare to destroy that!" Her mother's voice sliced the air, as sharp as the blade stabbing Ailsa's heart at the realization that her father was about to tear up the betrothal agreement. She'd been foolish to hope he would ever sign it.

"Ailsa wants this, and ye need the alliance to heal the wounds ye have caused," her mother continued in a more reasonable tone. "Do the right thing and sign the betrothal. Make yer daughter happy."

"Her happiness is no' a factor, Wife, as ye ken fine. 'Tis the matter of the betrothal agreement with the Norse king. 'Twould be dishonorable to break that agreement."

"And where is that Norse king now? Do ye see his ships on our bay, or his men driving away the siege force around us? What value is his strength to us?"

Ailsa wished she could see her father's face. He must be red with fury. Her mother's attempt to force him to see reason could make him even more resistant.

"And do ye remember the prince's reaction to the negotiation?" Her mother's tone softened. "I was there, and I do. I watched him when his father broke the news. He was no' in favor. Likely he has his eye on another lass his father kens naught about. He will be as happy as yer daughter to see ye annul the betrothal."

"Ye dinna ken that."

He didn't shout, as Ailsa expected. But he didn't sound ready to agree, either.

"As well as ye do, Love. The prince was surprised, then angry. Ye'd recall it if ye thought about it for a moment or two. I imagine he and his father had words after we left the chamber. Perhaps by now, the prince has made his father so miserable, he'll be relieved to hear yer daughter willna accept his son. He willna be dismayed at a quick response. 'Tis done all the time."

"No' by Sinclair."

The solar got very quiet. Ailsa held her breath. What other arguments could her mother marshal?

"Ye say yer daughter's happiness is no' a factor. Perhaps that is true, though as her father, ye must feel something for the lass ye have raised from a wee bairn. Ye loved carrying her about, hearing her laugh, teaching her to ride, to swim. I believe deep down ye still care, even though that wee lass is grown. Ye have always said she is bonnie and bright. She deserves the respect required to make her own choices. And in this case, her choice will benefit Sinclair and bring to us a host of alliances within Scotland that we sorely need."

His sigh was so heavy, Ailsa heard it.

"Ye speak wisely, Wife, as ye always have. I should never have begun to listen to Boden when I have ye by my side."

Ailsa wondered where her brother was. Locked in one of the cells in the dungeon, she hoped.

"For all our lives, Husband. I swore that to ye on the day we wed. Hear me now. Make yer daughter happy, and make me happy. Ye ken how much ye like the ways I reward ye when ye do."

Ailsa had to summon a smile. Her mother's tone had softened even further, cajoling and promising things best left unspoken.

"Damn it, Wife."

Ailsa heard the capitulation in his tone and wanted to jump up, run to her mother and hug her. But not until she was certain his signature was firmly affixed to that document.

"Here," he said. "I've signed it. Both copies. She can marry that Sutherland. Anders. If she had aught to do with their escape, 'tis better she leave Sinclair, anyway, and soon, before someone betrays her and I am forced to punish her."

Ailsa's breath left her in a long sigh of relief. In the next moment, she wanted to run out of the gate to Anders and tell him the news. But she dared not anger her father any further.

"Write yer letter to the king," her mother said, her tone still softly cajoling. "I'll find Ailsa and give her the good news."

Ailsa stood, fairly vibrating with excitement as her mother came out and found her. In her hand she held the rolled up betrothal agreement. "Ye heard all that?"

"I did. Thank ye, Mother." Ailsa reached for her and hugged her tightly.

"Yer da doesna need to see ye. Best if ye stay out of his sight for the rest of the day. We have a wedding to plan. Send Tasgall to the Sutherland with this," she said and proffered the rolled up betrothal agreement.

"I want to take it."

"Nay, Daughter. Ye may no'. Now is the time to demand the respect from Anders' clan due to his betrothed. They sent two copies, so yer da has one for Sinclair's records. Once they receive this signed copy, they can begin to take part in the preparations. I will arrange them with the Sutherland's man, whomever he sends. They can hunt and fish to stock our larder for a wedding feast. And call in their allies from our bay. While I do that, ye and Anders can have some quiet time together. No' before then."

"I canna wait, Mother."

"Ye can, and ye will. Ye have waited yer whole life for the right man to find ye, or for ye to find him. A few more hours willna matter. Go to yer friends and give them the good news, or I'll send ye to the kitchen to help Cook. That will keep ye occupied."

Ailsa laughed. "I hear ye. I'll find Siobhan. She'll need to start on a suitable dress for the wedding."

"Good thinking. Go on with ye." She leaned in and kissed Ailsa on the cheek. "I love ye, my bonnie daughter. I pray ye will be very happy in yer new life."

Ailsa fought tears, knowing her mother was already looking ahead to the day when she would leave Sinclair. "Thank ye, Mother. I will visit as often as I can."

"And bring my grandbairns, too."

That brought a chuckle out of Ailsa, making a tear leak from her eye. "I love ye, too, Mother. Thank ye for making Da see sense."

"I've lots of practice at that. Now, off ye go to Siobhan. Ye'll need that new dress."

ANDERS SURVEYED the revelry in the great hall, a gathering so large it spilled out into the bailey. "Ye and yer mother ken fine how to celebrate a wedding," he told Ailsa, who sat next to him at the head table dressed in silk the color of heather that bloomed on the hills in the summer. It made her luminous skin glow, putting him in mind of tales he'd read in her book of fairies and sprites, fae of the kinder and happier variety. She was so beautiful, it almost hurt to look upon her, but he couldn't take his gaze from her.

"'Tis a miracle it came together at all. I feared Da would still object, but Mother has always had a way with him."

"I realized once I was outside the gate that yer da *allowed* all of this to happen. He could have done much more to prevent it, to harm us, to discover who helped us, but he's done naught. If that is due to yer mother, I'm grateful for her support. And the way she has with him," he added and grinned at his bride. "Do ye think to have such a way with me?"

"Aye, of course," Ailsa told him with an answering grin. Then she sobered. "I hope she and Da can unite in bringing Boden around. Else when it comes time for him to become laird, Sinclair could be at war with everyone."

"I havena seen him since …"

"Da confined him to his chamber." She frowned, then an evil grin lit her face. "I wouldha locked him in the dungeon. 'Tis the best place for him."

"Would yer da punish him that way?"

"He should. Boden should be embarrassed about what he tried to do to ye. And fear what yer da might do to him."

"Perhaps he'll grow out of it, aye? He's short-tempered and impetuous, but age and experience have been known to mitigate both of those traits." Anders knew he was giving Boden much more grace than he deserved, especially after he'd threatened to toss Anders over the wall, but he'd said it more for Ailsa's sake than her brother's.

"I pray ye are right. Anyway, I dinna want to talk about my family. I want to talk about yers. And yer allies. They supplied most of the food for this feast. 'Twas enough to restock the Sinclair kitchen with fresh meat and fresh-caught fish. They deserve our thanks, despite the fact that the Sinclair stores were so low because of the siege." She quirked her mouth to the side, a gesture Anders found endearing. "But they have redeemed themselves this day."

"I'm certain they had that in mind, Love."

Suddenly, Ailsa straightened. "Ach, they're starting the lasses' dance."

"Go, have fun." He gave her a quick kiss and a smile, then stood and helped her from her chair. Anders enjoyed watching her join her friends and take part in their celebration of her marriage.

Soon enough, Stellan slid into her seat. "How are ye, Brother?"

"Well enough for both of us, I think," Anders told him, and lifted a mug of ale, still full. At Stellan's knowing grin, he boasted, "I ken better than to drink too much."

"As do I. I wish Mariota could be here for this. She deserves some of the credit, and should have some of the fun, too."

"She willna *fash*. Enjoy this a wee longer."

"I will. But I owe ye and Ailsa the same courtesy ye gave Mariota and me. I will be long gone before ye take yer bride to bed."

Anders knew what he intended. Stellan would give Anders the same privacy to make Ailsa his wife that he'd granted Stellan and Mariota by his absence—and distance—from Sutherland on their wedding night.

"Thank ye, Brother."

"Nay thanks needed. Our bond is a blessing and a curse. At times like these, 'tis good to share the happiness, but nay more than that. Once we are home, since it has strengthened while we were here, we will work on building a barrier we both can use when we need it." Stellan turned his head to watch Ailsa and the other lasses dancing hand-in-hand, their circle moving briskly, smiles and laughter on all their faces. "I am happy for ye, Brother. Ye have found a love that will last yer lifetime." He turned back to Anders. "Enjoy it, safeguard it, and teach yer bairns to find the same thing when their time comes."

"The same to ye," Anders said and took a sip from his mug, letting his gaze return to his bride, Stellan's words making him dream of the life ahead of them.

Stellan did the same, lifted his mug in salute, and stood. True to his word, he returned to his five escorts and ate well, but drank little. Before long, Anders walked them outside where they got on their horses. "Give my love to Mariota. Ye'll be with her tomorrow eve," Anders told his twin.

"I will," Stellan vowed, signaled to his men, and taking advantage of what daylight remained, left Sinclair.

With a full heart, Anders watched Stellan ride away until he disappeared into the trees. Their twin connection would weaken with every mile he put between them. Anders turned for the keep and his new bride with an eager smile.

CHAPTER 21

*A*ilsa waited in her chamber for her husband to arrive. Siobhan and Maesie had helped her prepare, taking down her hip-length hair from the braids and pins they'd put in it for the wedding and brushing it out until it shone and rippled like silk. Siobhan had gifted her with a beautiful gown of lavender silk that she'd embroidered in green leaves and deep purple flowers. Ailsa had wanted to cry over it but Siobhan warned her not to redden her eyes. So, she'd hugged them both and sent them on their way.

Anders had gone outside some time ago to see his brother off. She wasn't clear on why Stellan was determined to leave so early, but Anders' explanation that he was eager to return to his wife and son rang true, if incomplete. She expected to learn more about the twins' relationship and about their family when Anders took her home to Sutherland. In two days! She couldn't believe her life was about to make such a drastic change. And so quickly. Drastic but welcome. No more being ignored by her father in favor of her brother. No more fears about being bartered away to a Norse prince and living far to the north, unable to visit her friends, and they to visit her. No more risk of her da being forced to punish her for releasing the captive Sutherlands.

Sutherland wasn't all that close, but it was an easy sail down the coast—in good weather. She expected their marriage to strengthen ties between the clans and to help keep her brother from ruining relations with every clan around Sinclair.

Anders thought they would do exactly that. She hoped he was right.

In the meantime, sitting in her bed, dressed in the lovely gown Siobhan created for her and her new husband to enjoy on their wedding night, she was becoming impatient. She wasn't nervous. Both her mother and Maighread had long ago taught her what would happen and what she needed to know. She wanted to get on with it. With Anders. She had never expected to be an eager bride, but she found herself avidly awaiting his arrival.

Finally, she heard male voices and laughter along with heavy footsteps coming up the stairs. Anders must have been waylaid by his clansmen and hers. No doubt they expected to bring him to bed.

The door opened and Anders backed in, shoving at the men outside. "Go on with ye. I dinna need yer help." Raucous laughter greeted his comment as he slammed the door on them, turned the lock, and clearly not trusting that to be enough, wedged the claymore he had slung over his back through the brackets meant to hold a thick wooden bar.

"Where did ye get the sword?" Ailsa asked, amazed that he could have entered the keep with it.

"The lads out there thought it made a good jest. One I'd rather no' explain. They'll no' be getting it back, so the jest is on them."

Ailsa clapped and snickered. "Well played, Husband."

He stood with his back to the door, his gaze fixed on her. "Ye are the most beautiful lass I've ever seen," he told her.

"So, still having memory problems, are ye?" Ailsa didn't mean to sound prickly, but she always had something smart to say when she was nervous, and right now, her belly was full of birds flitting from side to side and top to bottom, and they flew faster the more Anders stared at her. Maighread had tended his cuts and bruises, so his face did not appear quite as battered as when Boden's men finished with him. His eyes had gone dark enough to get lost in. His breathing sounded deep and rhythmical, as though he was preparing for a battle to begin.

"Nary a one," he answered, ignoring her jibe. "But looking at ye, I can attest that I've happily forgotten every other lass I've ever met. Are ye certain ye are no' of the seelie, lass, like the fae I read about in yer book? Beautiful and kind, they are, like ye."

His adoring smile heated her blood, but she suddenly regretted her jest. The weeks of not knowing himself were not something to laugh about. "I dreamed ye might be a selkie. Strong and handsome as a seal as ye are as a man. Ye came to me from the sea. Perhaps ye left yer seal skin somewhere in the woods below the castle, intending to explore the land or visit us and leave again. But something happened, and ye were touched by the fae, robbing ye of yer memory."

"Perhaps, lass, we both read too much of yer book," Anders said and grinned. "I'm nay more a selkie than ye are a seelie. We are man and wife. I wouldna change that for anything."

She threw the covers aside and quit the bed. As she stood, Anders sucked in even more air. His chest expanded and his shoulders, already impossibly broad, seemed to grow broader, stronger, and more alluring. She marched up to him, eager to put her hands on them. "Have ye never—?"

"Of course I have. I'm admiring my wife, and looking forward to making ye my bride in truth." He pulled her to him and wrapped his strong, loving arms around her. "This will be different than any … encounter … I've yet had."

"Nay wives before me?" She looked up at him and grinned, breaking her own vow not to jest about his unreliable memory of his past, but at the serious set to his mouth, she lost any nuance of humor in the subject.

"Nor after, Love. There will only be ye, with me, for as long as we both live. The life we make together is all I want. And after us our bairns to carry on with Sutherland and Sinclair blood in their veins, stronger for the melding we create with our love."

"Anders ..." She found herself transfixed by the future he painted with his words. "I want that, too, Husband. With ye. Only ye."

"Ye shall have what ye desire, Wife," he told her. With gentle care, he picked her up and carried her to their bed. When she reached for him, he held up a hand. "I have waited and searched my entire life for ye. I willna rush this moment. 'Tis too important for both of us."

She nodded, her emotions making it impossible to speak, and pulled him down beside her. The feelings he aroused in her were new and unfamiliar, but sweet. So sweet. Her heart seemed too large for her chest. She couldn't wait any longer to touch him, so she gripped his upper arm, marveling at the tightly leashed strength she found there. He would never hurt her. "Ye make me love ye more every moment, Anders. Ye have been naught but kind and honorable. Now, ye may be loving. That is what I desire in this moment and for all the moments we shall have."

He traced the pad of his thumb across her lower lip. "So beautiful ye are. I canna believe ye are mine." His gaze traveled over her face, then settled on her eyes. "And that ye love me."

"I do love ye, Husband. Now, make love to me."

"With pleasure, my lady wife. With pleasure." He traced his fingertips from her brow down her cheek to her jaw, leaving a trail of tingles that spread down her throat, then he bent to take her lips with his.

She opened to him on a moan that came from depths she'd never known she had within her.

He plundered her mouth and drew a trail of fire to the mounds of her breasts with his fingertips, tightening her nipples.

Ailsa arched into his hand, lost in the way he touched her. Strong, yet gentle, determined to please her. "More, Anders, more."

"Patience, my love," he murmured. "Ye will have all of me when ye are ready, and nay before then."

He followed the trail of his fingers with his mouth, pulling aside the embroidered bodice of her gown to reveal the hard peaks of her nipples. He brushed his thumb lightly over one while he teased the other with his tongue. Then he lifted his head. "Ye must let me undress ye, Love, or I will have to tear yer gown."

"Ye first," she replied with a challenging lift to her lips. "I wish to see all of ye."

"Ye have. When I was ill."

"No' quite all. And 'tis no' the same. Ye were ill and weak. Now ye are healthy and strong. Stand, Husband. I will help ye."

She didn't have to ask him twice. He grinned and sat up, kicked off his boots and stood, awaiting her pleasure.

Ailsa stood, too, undid the pin at his shoulder, set it aside, and unbuckled his belt. She held it in place for a moment while she gazed up at him. "Are ye ready?"

"More than ready, my love."

She dropped the belt and pulled the wool from his shoulder, letting his great kilt unravel and fall from his body to pool around his feet and over hers. She looked him up and down, grasped the hem of his léine and lifted it. He took it from her and pulled it over his head to drop on the floor behind him. Now he stood before her naked and rampant.

"Ye can see how hungry for ye I am," he told her.

She wondered for a moment how they could ever make this work. He'd once told her he was a big man everywhere. She saw the truth of that. After a nervous swallow, she looked up at him, reassured by the smile he gave her. "I ken ye willna hurt me," she said, partly for him but mostly for herself. But the bruises on his body told her his determination to protect her might cause him pain. "Ye must take care of yerself as well."

"Dinna fash about me," he told her. "Now, 'tis my turn," he added softly as he looked at her, his gaze roving from her bright hair to her feet and back, lingering on the swell of her hips and breasts. He grasped the silky fabric of her gown and pulled it slowly over her head, as though determined to draw out the moment, and to give her time to object. Once the garment cleared her head, he slid it down the length of her hair before letting it fall to the floor, leaving her standing proudly bare before him.

She smiled. "Look yer fill, my love. All that I am is yers."

"And all that I am is yers." He shook his head, admiration in his eyes. "I havena the words to describe how beautiful ye are to me," he told her, unable to take his gaze from her. "When I first saw ye, yer hair fascinated me." He brushed an errant lock off her cheek. "'Tis like the dawn, gold with a touch of blush to warm it. But now, seeing all of ye … I could never have imagined the beauty that awaited me."

She stepped closer to him, lifted her arms and wrapped her hands around his neck. The sensation of his body pressed against her sent waves of heat rolling through hers. He picked her up, and she wrapped her legs around his hips. His manhood teased her yearning center. But he reined in his desire, though from the way his jaw clenched and sweat beaded his forehead, it took all the strength he had.

A heady sense of power roared through her. He was bigger and stronger, but she could drive him to his knees.

Instead he walked to the bed and laid her on it, then knelt with her legs over his shoulders and kissed his way up her thighs.

"Anders …"

The plea in her voice encouraged him to taste and suckle her until she arched up and cried out his name. While her body danced in joyful spasms, he used his finger to stretch her and extend her peak. When she stilled, he stood and slid her more fully onto the bed, knelt over her and paused. "'Tis time, Love. If ye are ready?"

"I am, Husband," she answered with an eager smile as she opened her eyes to his handsome face. How she wanted him! Her body cried out for his touch, for him to fill the emptiness within her. "Make me yers."

&

ANDERS GAZED at his bride with love and amazement. She was far from his first, but she was different from all the others. She reached into his soul and made him feel things he'd thought himself incapable of feeling. The bond between them was deeper than any he'd experienced before her, and after this night, it would be unbreakable. He'd once despaired of ever finding a love like his twin shared with his bride, but in Ailsa, Anders had everything he had hoped for, and more. She had cared for him when he didn't even know himself. She had fought for him against her father and laird. And she had saved him and his men. His was a bride worthy of Sutherland. Worthy to be the wife of a laird. Worthy to give him bairns and a future he had only dreamt of.

He could barely breathe with wanting her. Her skin under his fingertips was softer and smoother than the finest French velvet. Her breath warmed his skin and her scent made him crave her taste all the more. He needed to touch her, to press her body against his and take her mouth. The thought was sweet torture. His pulse pounded in his throat like the slap of oars on deep water. He wanted more, but he didn't dare move too fast. "I will take care with ye, Love, and never hurt ye, save this once. Do ye ken?"

"I do. All of it. And I ken ye will always take care of me, Anders."

"As ye have taken care of me, Love. I owe my life to ye several times over."

"I will happily spend mine with ye," she said.

His member prodded at her entrance and she slipped her legs apart in invitation. He pushed inside, slowly, gently, until he met a barrier. "Now, Love," he breathed to warn her. At her nod, he pushed all the way in, breaching her maidenhead. Even though she said she expected it, her gasp made him regret the harm he'd done.

After a moment, she assured him, "I'm well, Anders. 'Twas a surprise the way it felt, 'tis all."

"Take as long as ye need, lass, to accustom yerself to me. I ken 'tis strange."

"Aye, 'tis. And wonderful. We are joined as one. I am truly yers now, and ye are mine. 'Tis time, Husband. I want more."

"Ye shall have more." He pulled most of the way out, then slid gently back in, letting her set his pace by her reactions, how she moved, how she gripped him with her sheath. When she lifted her hips to take him deeper, he answered her demand, increasing his pace until she cried out his name and shuddered with the pleasure he gave her. Then, he surrendered to the desire he'd fought for weeks. She was his! His climax took him under, rolling him as though he was caught in a heated undertow, until he broke the surface and saw stars—bright, beautiful stars. All while his seed filled her and she cried out his name yet again. "I love ye, Ailsa," he told her when he could speak again. "I always will."

IT TOOK ALL of two days to prepare Ailsa's belongings for the move to Sutherland. Her mother wisely made an event of what could have been a sad chore, letting her friends Siobhan and

Maesie and others help her pack her belongings and choose mementos of Sinclair to take with her, many of which were gifts from her friends and admirers. She had not expected so many, or such expressions of sorrow at her impending departure, but she accepted them with grace, grateful to realize she had more friends in Sinclair than had ever made their feelings known.

The wedding gift from her parents, a heavy gold chain from which hung a rare bright blue topaz gemstone framed in more gold, she wore under her clothes.

She thought she was nearing the end of her packing when Siobhan knocked on her door. "I just finished these," Siobhan told her, arms full of dresses as she entered the chamber.

"What have ye done?" Ailsa hugged her and after Siobhan put down her burdens on the bed, smoothed and admired them. Siobhan had made her wedding dress and nightgown, but now also gave her three new dresses. "Yer parents asked for these, for ye to wear at Sutherland. I also made several nightgowns yer parents ken naught about."

"When did ye have time?" Ailsa asked, amazed at her friend's skill as she admired the dresses. Two were everyday, serviceable woolen kirtles, and the last was meant for special occasions, made of a pale, clear green that would complement her coloring, embroidered in the same shade along the neckline. "I will make Anders proud, wearing these," she said. "Thank ye. They are beautiful." She set them aside and admired the three nightgowns Siobhan made for her. One was made of ivory silk, another in a blue that nearly matched the stone in the necklace her parents gave her, another in a warm, pale peach. "These are exquisite. The silks. The needlework!" The more she studied them, the more excited she became. "Siobhan, how can I ever thank ye. They're wonderful. I love them. Anders will, too," she added and grinned, then pulled her friend into a hug.

"I was only going to make one, but I worried that he might tear it in his … enthusiasm. So, I made two more."

Ailsa laughed as she held one up to herself and twirled around. "He'd best no' damage them if he kens what's good for him." She looked forward to Anders' expression when he saw her in them.

Then she sobered. "I will miss ye, my friend."

"I'll miss ye, too. But ye will visit. And bring yer bairns."

"Ye must visit Sutherland, as well. We've yet to find ye a husband, and there may be several good men for ye to meet there."

"Mayhap I should travel with ye," Siobhan quipped, grinned, and left her to her packing.

As Ailsa finished, Maesie, Cook and Maighread arrived with their gift. "We collaborated on a notebook about plants, their care, and harvesting instructions, along with packets of seeds," Maighread explained, "in case Sutherland lacked anything ye were accustomed to having, from food and herbs to flowers."

Ailsa's mouth dropped open. "I dinna ken what to say. This is true wealth," she told them, so grateful she could barely speak. Her eyes glimmered with unshed tears. "Thank ye all for yer thoughtfulness, for all ye have taught me, and for all ye did to help Anders. I love ye all."

"We'll miss ye, lass, and that big, handsome husband of yers, too," Cook told her.

"But ye will visit," Maesie insisted, "or we'll go to Sutherland and find ye."

"I understand," Ailsa said, her heart in her throat. "I have even more friends here than I kenned. I'll miss ye all."

Anders returned in time for the evening meal. He had little to pack, but he had been busy with his father and his men from the *birlinn*, who were making preparations of their own and tearing down the siege camp.

"Will Sinclair keep the *birlinn*?" Ailsa asked that evening once they returned to their chamber. She couldn't believe Sutherland would agree to leaving it behind, but perhaps in the interest of the improved relations between the clans, he counted its sacrifice to be worthwhile.

"My father and yers have inspected it," he told her. "Because of damage it might have taken in that storm, Sinclair declared it should not be trusted to be seaworthy without a more thorough inspection and repairs, which his men will do. After the animosity of the siege, 'tis a generous gesture. Even my da appreciates it."

"We willna sail south?" She wasn't sure how she felt about traveling for several days with so many men. And a cart full of her belongings, including two trunks of clothes and all the gifts bestowed on her and Anders. She'd assumed everything would be loaded onto the *birlinn* for a swifter trip to Anders' home.

"We must ride. Sutherland and our allies brought sufficient horses for everyone. Ye will be in nay danger. I will be by yer side the entire time. We have tonight here," he reminded her, "and if all goes well, only tomorrow night on the way. We'll spend the rest of our lives together when we return to Sutherland."

"I can do that, easily," Ailsa promised, hoping she was speaking the truth. She'd never traveled overland so far from home. But Anders would be with her, and they would have an army of Sutherlands and allies around them.

Anders cupped her cheek and kissed her. "If ye tire of riding, I will hold ye in my arms, or ye can rest in the cart. I ken this is a time of joy, but also of sorrow and uncertainty, my love. I promise ye, all will be well."

Ailsa knew he was right, but her worries still plagued her. Would she be happy at Sutherland? Would the people there accept her as Anders' bride? Would she find any friends or have to depend on her husband and Stellan for everything? She would know the answers to those questions in a very few days.

"I would like ye to practice a wee before we make the trip," Ailsa told him.

"Practice?"

"Aye, holding me in yer arms," she answered and gave him her best wide-eyed, entreating look.

"I can do that," Anders said with a smile and pulled her to him, lifted her into his arms and sank onto a chair by their hearth. "Any time ye wish, milady, I'll be happy to hold ye."

She snuggled into his warmth, content for a moment. "And kiss me?"

"Aye," he said and did so until she was breathless. "Anything else?"

Ailsa smiled up at him. She treasured the many ways Anders showed his love for her. "Keep doing what ye are doing, my love, and ye'll find out."

CHAPTER 22

"How do ye do that?" Ailsa watched Mariota fire arrow after arrow in quick succession and hit the center of each of several targets set up in a row against Dunrobin's outer wall.

"Practice," Mariota told her and grinned. "Even with this wee bairn in the way," she said and patted her protruding belly, "I can usually hit my target. But 'twill be easier once I deliver this one. He or she tends to kick at the most inopportune times and spoils my aim. Best we no' have any invaders below the walls before this bairn arrives, aye little one?" She patted her belly again.

"I want to learn," Ailsa told her. "And how ye handle Valkyrie, as well. Nan said ye raised her from an egg. Ye must tell me the whole story."

"We've plenty of time for stories," Mariota said with a smile. "And training. Of course I'll teach ye. Nan and Brighde can help, too. They've learned so much since I got here that they help me train the lasses, and even some of the lads. The more we lasses are prepared to defend the walls with our arrows, the more our men can use their strength elsewhere."

Anders and Stellan came around the corner and hailed them.

"What have ye learned?" Anders asked after he pulled Ailsa into a hug and gave her a kiss.

"That I have much to learn. But ye ken how I enjoy that."

"Ye will have the best of teachers in Mariota, Brighde, and Nan."

"Did I hear my name?" Brighde came around the corner carrying her bow and a sheaf of arrows.

"Anders just said ye were one of the best teachers I could have," Ailsa told her.

"What? He paid me a complement? Anders, did ye forget all about me while ye were at Sinclair?"

Anders rolled his eyes. "If only I still could."

Ailsa elbowed him, and he made a show of doubling over.

"Enough," Stellan said, laughing at their antics. "I'm glad to see everyone in such fine spirits after our little adventure to Sinclair, but 'tis time for the midday meal and I, for one, am ready to eat."

"Still haven't caught up on the meals ye missed?" Brighde asked.

"Dinna let him fool ye," Anders told her. "He didna miss any. Ailsa saw to the care of the Sutherlands while we were there."

"And we owe ye much," Stellan told her.

"Nay, ye dinna. Ye gave me yer twin. He's the best gift a lass could ever receive."

"I might have a different opinion on that," Mariota chimed in, laughing.

"Aye, ye might," Anders said, "but ye'd be wrong."

ANDERS STOOD with his father and brother at Dunrobin's gate while Ailsa and Mariota waited at the door to the keep. Though it had been only a fortnight since they returned to Dunrobin, Sutherland had received a missive from Sinclair two days ago, warning of an impending visit. From the walls, two *birlinns* had been spotted approaching earlier in the day. They were beached now, and the men on board were climbing the bluff to Dunrobin's seaside gate.

"That's Sinclair," Anders said. "I dinna believe my eyes. He has already brought back our *birlinn*. I wasna certain when we left it behind that we would ever see it again. The other one is large enough for him and all his men to return home together."

"Well, this is a good sign," was the Sutherland's comment.

Anders' father expected Sinclair's visit was intended to firm up ties between the clans.

Anders harbored a kernel of fear that at best he'd come to make sure his daughter was being treated well. Or would he try to steal Ailsa back?

At worst, both Stellan and Anders were suspicious of his motives. Stellan had put the Sutherland guard on high alert, determined to keep the peace while their father wined and dined their new ally. Their father had not seen the Sinclair heir in action. Had Ailsa's mother been able to temper Boden's influence on her husband? Or was this visit a way to get into Dunrobin with enough men to attack the laird or take over the keep?

When the visitors approached the gate, they paused several paces outside and the Sinclair strode forward. "Sutherland, I hope this visit isna unwelcome. As ye can see, I'm returning yer *birlinn*."

"'Tis most welcome any time an ally visits, even without the return of our property, though I appreciate it, and the work yer craftsmen did to make it seaworthy," Sutherland answered. "Be welcome in Dunrobin, Sinclair. Come visit with yer daughter." Sutherland stepped to one side of the gate while Stellan and Anders stepped to the other, opening the way for the Sinclair laird.

His men followed as he approached, but he signaled for them

to stop outside the gate. "My men will camp outside yer walls," Sinclair offered.

He'd come with fewer than Anders expected. Raghnall stood at the head of a dozen men, all well-armed. Tasgall was in the group behind him. Anders was relieved to see he was still alive. He'd feared once the wedding was over and the Sutherlands and their allies left, Sinclair would find out who'd aided the Sutherlands' escape and punish Tasgall.

"Thank ye," Sutherland told him, but added, "Yer chief guard is welcome."

"As is Ailsa's friend Tasgall," Anders added.

His father glanced his way and nodded, then turned back to the Sinclair. "Yer men will be welcome inside for meals so long as their weapons remain in their camp."

Anders glanced around to see Mariota nod and step through the door into the keep. She'd likely gone to find a chamber for the two guards. One had already been prepared for the Sinclair.

Sinclair nodded his agreement. No doubt he'd expected those conditions.

Ailsa approached and greeted her father. "'Tis good to see ye, Da. Is Mother well?"

"Aye, lass," he told her, giving her a hug, "and unhappy that she couldna make this trip, but I insisted a *birlinn* was nay place for her. And she can keep yer brother out of trouble while I'm gone."

Ailsa nodded, doubting that anyone, even their indomitable mother, could accomplish that miracle. She walked with him, arm-in-arm, into the Sutherland keep.

That afternoon, while Sutherland and Sinclair conferred, with Stellan and Raghnall in attendance, Anders and Ailsa had a chance to talk to Tasgall.

"I canna believe he hasna insisted on finding out who released the Sutherlands," Ailsa said after Tasgall gave them a brief update of what had happened after the wedding.

"My guess is he thinks ye did it by yerself or with Anders'

help," Tasgall told her. "He isna happy about it, but I think he also respects the initiative it took to carry it off."

Ailsa smiled at that. "So long as it doesna come back on ye or any of the other men, I'm satisfied," she told him. "Does Raghnall suspect?"

"Ach, aye, he kens. He willna say anything, though. He was glad to have ye lot off his hands," he added, grinning at Anders. "He was no happier about Boden's notion of killing ye than ye were."

"What is Da doing about Boden?" Ailsa asked with a frown.

"There have been some conversations in the laird's solar," Tasgall said soberly. "Or shouting matches. Call them what ye will. Boden is angry, but we hope he'll grow out of his desire for a fight. Probably after he's been through one or two."

Anders nodded. "If he survives them. There's nay better lesson that bloodshed is no' usually the best answer than to watch yer men being injured and killed. Or yerself."

"If he doesna grow up," Tasgall added, "ye have cousins, one or two of whom I could easily support."

"So, why this visit now?" Anders wondered about the timing, so soon after the wedding.

"I think 'tis Da's way of apologizing to Sutherland for holding his men," Ailsa interjected before Tasgall could say anything. "I told my parents the story of why ye were on Sinclair land. It may have changed his perception of ye, though not in time to prevent the escape. And before the wedding, Mother shamed Da for not taking better care of ye, and for threatening ye. He's had time to cool off and think through everything that happened—and could have happened."

"Better allies than enemies," Anders said. "Thanks to ye, my lovely wife. Had ye and Maighread no' cared for me, had ye no' insisted the men in the dungeon receive good care, we could be in a very different place today."

"I ken it. And I'm glad I had friends willing to help," she said and smiled at Tasgall. "We can be proud of what we did, even if we went against what the laird thought he wanted at the time."

That evening, Sutherland provided a feast to welcome Sinclair and his men. Later, Anders and Stellan remained behind in the laird's solar after meeting with their father and Sinclair, who shared a whisky, then went to his chamber. Anders repeated the conversation with Tasgall and Ailsa for Stellan and their father.

"I dinna recommend letting down our guard," Stellan advised, "but we can make it less obvious."

"Aye," Sutherland agreed. "If Sinclair is truly here to extend an olive branch, and to ensure Ailsa is happy, we reciprocate. Keep the guards on duty, but only half as many on the walls, the others posted around the bailey and its lesser buildings. The smithy, the stable, hell, even the weaver's shed, out of sight or with weapons hidden so they are not obviously on duty but helping the craftspeople or just spending time in conversation. As long as they keep their eyes and ears open, that should suffice during the day when his men come in for meals. Sinclair has only two men inside with him at night, quartered across the hall from him. Easier to control, if need be."

"How long does he intend to stay?" Stellan asked.

"No more than a sennight, I'd wager," Anders said. "That's what Ailsa thinks. Likely even less if he thinks he's accomplished his mission. Part of which may be to become as familiar with Dunrobin as I was able to at Sinclair."

"'Twillna do him any good," Stellan remarked.

"At least he didna bring Boden," Anders said. "Had he done so, I wouldha expected trouble."

"The heir made an impression on ye, did he?" their father quipped.

"Aye," Anders and Stellan agreed in unison.

"Ye could say that," Stellan answered grimly. "Unless he learns sense before he becomes laird, or the clan elders get behind someone else, he'll be trouble in the future."

&

"WERE ye sad to see yer da leave today?" Anders asked Ailsa three days later. Alone in their chamber after supper, he could finally ask the question that had been on his mind since they watched Sinclair and his men board their large *birlinn* and sail north.

"Aye, a little. But he and Mother are no' so far away. A day's sail up the coast could be quite pleasant."

Anders shuddered. "I'll no' be doing that for a while, ye ken," he said, making her laugh.

She clasped his hand between hers. "I would no' expect to have to swim to shore as ye did."

"Aye, I learned my lesson. Next time, I'll listen to Tomas when he says 'tis time to put in and wait out a storm. Still, I have to be glad for what did happen. Sutherland and Sinclair are now allies, which also means better relations for Sutherland with the Norse king. We have proven to all that we can count on our other allies in case of trouble, and best of all, I found ye."

"Aye, ye did, though barely. I feared I'd killed ye when ye passed out at our door. I hated myself for days, fearing ye would still die, even after Maighread and I began caring for ye."

"I'm tougher than ye kenned, Love."

"Ach, I ken that now. But then? Ye scared me. Ye looked so sad, so defeated, when I told ye to go away. I'll never forget yer face in that moment, and I'll regret putting that despair in yer eyes to my dying day."

"Forget it, lass. It all worked out well in the end. I have ye to love. I canna imagine anything better."

"Thank ye, my love. But I willna get over it any faster than ye get over yer aversion to sailing. Perhaps helping each other, we will get beyond both our fears."

"I ken just how to begin," Anders said and pulled her to him. He kissed her softly at first, but as she responded, he firmed his kiss and deepened it when her lips parted on a sigh. "I want ye, my love. I always will. But right now, I want ye in my bed, making love with me."

"There's naught I'd rather do," she answered with a smile, her gaze shining with love as she met his. "Now and for the rest of our lives."

EPILOGUE

MIDWINTER, 1413

"'Tis a bonnie lass, like her mother!" Stellan exclaimed from the top of the stairs above the great hall as he held up his new daughter. Swaddled in soft linen and a Sutherland plaid, she was meant for the clan to see, but Anders was disappointed.

"The healer has overdone the wrappings," he leaned over to Ailsa and told her under the din of shouts and cheers for the heir's second bairn. "I canna see the wean. Can ye?"

"Nay, and up there, where the heat rises from the hearth, 'tis warm enough no' to need so much. Then again, the world must be a cold place to a newborn, aye?"

"I suppose so." Anders shrugged and hoisted his cup of ale, a salute to his brother. "Should we go up?"

"Aye! I want to see how Mariota is."

"Stellan wouldna be out here if she had any problems," he assured her.

"'Tis no' the point. She needs to ken family is nearby, and I want to see my new niece."

Anders grinned and set his cup aside. "Ah, the truth comes out. Lasses and bairns." He stood and offered his arm. "Shall we?"

Ailsa leapt to her feet and allowed him to open a path through the crowd in the great hall. News of Mariota's labor had drawn in most of the clan once the sun went down, both for supper and to await the new Sutherland.

At the top of the stairs, Stellan stood speaking to one of the healer's helpers who was trying to take his daughter from his arms. "Lady Sutherland is demanding ye bring back her daughter, Stellan. She must be fed."

"Ach, let me hold her," Ailsa demanded of Stellan, then winked at the helper.

Stellan proffered his daughter. "I ken what ye are doing, Ailsa Sinclair Sutherland. But go ahead. Take her to her mother and ye lasses can have a fine *blether* for as long as Mariota can keep her eyes open. The healer is still with her."

"A moment, Wife," Anders said, stopping her. "I wanted to see my niece, too, remember?" Ailsa suffered Anders' touching the wean long enough to pull the plaid from around her face and get a look at her. Her eyes were open and blue, her lips plump and rosy pink. If she had any hair, he couldn't see it for the swaddling over her head.

"She's a beauty, Brother," he said, nodding for Ailsa to take her to Mariota. "Do ye have a name for her yet?"

"Nay. We both like Elana, and we've thought of a few others, but we'll wait a wee and see what suits her personality."

"Stoic like ye and stubborn like her mother would be my guess." Anders grinned.

Stellan snorted. "Or the opposite of both. Beathan isna an exact match to either of us, so no doubt his sister will be her own person, too."

"Of course she will. I'm glad she has an older brother. If she takes after the two of ye in looks, ye'll have to beat the suitors off with a stick, and ye'll need his help."

Stellan held up a hand. "That's years away."

"'Twill go faster than ye think."

"And ye ken this how?"

Stellan's incredulity led Anders to be truthful. "We're trying for our own, but it has only been a few months since our wedding. Beathan didna come right away. I doubt ours will, either."

"Enjoy the time ye have before the bairns come. Afterward, ye'll have little time to yerselves."

"So, I've heard," Anders said drily. Stellan had complained about that very thing many times since his son and heir had arrived. But, they had found the time and privacy to make Elana, or whatever her name would be.

Ailsa appeared without the new bairn. "Mariota wants to see us. Both of ye," she told them.

Anders exchanged a glance with his twin.

"Very well," Stellan said.

They followed her into the chamber. Mariota sat up, a mound of pillows at her back, as she nursed her new daughter, a sheet over the bairn covering them both to Mariota's shoulders.

"Our daughter needs guardians," Mariota announced.

Anders knew what that meant. He was already named guardian for Beathan, so that if anything happened to Stellan, Anders would be responsible to see the lad raised to become the next Sutherland laird once both twins were gone. But for a lass?

"I see what ye are thinking, Anders," Mariota said, then yawned. "I want to say this before I fall asleep. I want Ailsa to be my daughter's guardian."

Anders smiled at his bride. "Are ye willing, Ailsa? To help raise her as yer own should something befall her mother, or God forbid, both her parents?"

"'Tis a great responsibility, but one I will bear gladly, Mariota. Yer daughter will be safe and well cared for with me. But I hope never to have to take that joy from ye."

"I ken it," Mariota said, then yawned again. "I'm at my limit, I think."

"Very well," the healer spoke up. "All of ye, out. I'll take charge of the wean for now. Her mother needs to rest."

Anders had forgotten the woman was in the room, but her word was law. "We'll go. Sleep well, Mariota. Ye gave us a wonderful gift today."

She smiled and closed her eyes.

"Stellan, ye, too. Go. Ye can come back later." The healer bent to take the infant from Mariota's unprotesting arms. She was already asleep.

"Just one more look," he said and took his daughter from the healer, where the wean, too, had dozed off. He cradled her for a moment, then reluctantly handed her back to the healer. "Call for me if there's any need."

"They're both well and strong," the healer told him. "There will be nay need. Go to yer rest."

Stellan closed the door behind him and took a breath.

Ailsa gave him a hug. "Ye look as knackered as yer wife, Brother. The healer is right. Ye should rest, too."

"I will, as soon as I speak to Da. He'll have heard the cheering." He headed down the stairs.

Anders took Ailsa's hand. "I think we should go to our rest as well."

"I ken that look in yer eye," Ailsa said with a grin. "Ye want to make a bairn of yer own."

"Ye dinna?"

"I do, Husband. I dinna care how long it takes."

"Nor do I, Ailsa. Making love to ye makes me a happy man. Loving ye? 'Tis a joy I will never forget."

Waiting for a Forever Love

Other Novels

Highland Seasons

Highland Beginnings

ABOUT THE AUTHOR

Willa Blair is an award-winning Amazon and Barnes and Noble #1 bestselling author of Scottish historical, light paranormal, and contemporary romance filled with men in kilts, psi talents, and plenty of spice. Her books have won numerous accolades, including the Marlene, Merritt, National Readers' Choice Award Finalist, Booksellers' Best Award Finalist, National Excellence of Romance Fiction Awards Finalist, National Excellence in Story Telling Award Finalist, Romance Through the Ages Contest Finalist, Reader's Crown finalist, InD'Tale Magazine's RONE Award Honorable Mention, and NightOwl Reviews Top Picks. She loves reading and writing novels set in the past, present, and future, as well as scouting new settings for books. She has visited six continents and can get by in several languages. She thinks being an author is the best job she's ever had.

Willa loves hearing from readers!
Contact her:
www.willablair.com
authorwillablair@gmail.com

Sign up for my Newsletter
Find links to the rest of my books

www.ingramcontent.com/pod-product-compliance
Lightning Source LLC
Chambersburg PA
CBHW020416110726
47899CB00006B/2006